PRAISE FOR TH

"Myriad *is a clever time-travel premise wrapped up in a very human story of surviving trauma. An action-packed sci-fi thriller told with depth and heart, this book will grab you and not let go.*"
– Cadwell Turnbull, bestselling author of *No Gods, No Monsters*

"*Joshua David Bellin is a master craftsman. In* Myriad, *he's reached an all-time high for plot twists that rock your understanding of what has come before... and after. Enjoy the fast-paced action that will leave you dazzled.*"
– Diane Turnshek, Carnegie Mellon University astronomer and science fiction author

"*Joshua Bellin's protagonist is traumatized by her past, and because of her job as a time cop, can't avoid reliving it.* Myriad *is a dark and clever exploration into the horror of getting answers to all your questions and, worse maybe, getting a second chance to make things right.*"
– R.W.W. Greene, author of *The Light Years*

"*Joshua David Bellin's* Myriad *blends the time-travel genre with a compelling cast to tell the story of Agent Miriam Randle, a woman caught up in the Gordian knot of her brother's untimely death... Bellin masterfully weaves suspense with non-stop action to create a heroine and a story that will be impossible to forget.*"
– Ginger Smith, author of *The Rush's Edge*

"*Exciting and thought-provoking,* Myriad *posits a truly original twist on time-travel. Joshua Bellin's first adult novel hits all the right notes from its conflicted main character trying to undo a tragic, life-changing past event to multiple twists, turns, and surprises the reader won't see coming.*"
– Larry Ivkovich, author of *The Sixth Precept*

Joshua David Bellin

MYRIAD

ANGRY
ROBOT

ANGRY ROBOT
An imprint of Watkins Media Ltd

Unit 11, Shepperton House
89 Shepperton Road
London N1 3DF
UK

angryrobotbooks.com
twitter.com/angryrobotbooks
Time has a way of changing things

An Angry Robot paperback original, 2023

Cover by Francesca Corsini
Edited by Robin Triggs and Alice Abrams
Set in Meridien

ISBN 978 1 91520 246 8
Ebook ISBN 978 1 91520 249 9

Printed and bound in the United Kingdom by TJ Books Ltd.

9 8 7 6 5 4 3 2 1

MIX
Paper from
responsible sources
FSC
www.fsc.org   FSC® C013056

For Roger

But how is it
That this lives in thy mind? What seest thou else
In the dark backward and abysm of time?
If thou remember'st aught ere thou camest here,
How thou camest here thou mayst.

–William Shakespeare, *The Tempest*

Thursday, August 31, 2017

I hear the sound of fireworks, *crack crack crack*.

Except it's not the Fourth of July, I know because Daddy took me and Jeremy to the parade in Lancaster the month before we moved to our new house in Pittsburgh.

Is this the way they do it in this place? Is this how they celebrate the start of school?

My teacher moves quickly to the classroom door, pulls the black blind and turns the lock. She opens the side drawer of her big wooden desk, scrambles through it as if she's trying to find something, then closes it and edges the desk in front of the door. When she shuts off the lights, there are shrieks of surprise. She spins toward us, her face twisted in fear.

"Children." Her voice is a band pulled tight. "Remember what we learned. Be as quiet as can be."

I can't remember what we learned. It's my first day in a new school, and I can't even remember anyone's name, including hers. The only name I know is Crystal, the pink fish in the tank under the windows.

The other children rise from their desks and march to the back of the room, all of them sitting cross-legged on the floor in front of the cubbies. No one is laughing anymore. Some are crying quietly, some not so quietly. All are holding something sharp, or as sharp as they could find inside their desks. A pencil, a ruler, a pair of purple safety scissors.

The teacher walks from child to child, counting off with her fingers, laying a hand on the shoulders of the crying ones before moving to the next. When she's done, she turns to see me sitting at my desk.

"Miriam," she whispers. "Do as I said."

I slip out of my chair and stand there for a second, my fingers nervously rubbing the smooth metal and plastic. Some of the children have curled into balls, their heads tucked between their elbows or in their laps. Some are rocking back and forth, some holding so still it's as if they're playing hide-and-seek.

The fireworks erupt in the hall again.

Children scream and cry. The teacher spins, a finger to her lips, and the moment her back is to me, I run to the door. The desk blocking my way is huge, but hot fear gives me strength to shove it aside and free the lock.

"Miriam!" the teacher whisper-yells, but I can see in her eyes she's too scared to come after me.

Another second later I'm outside the room, where the flash of fireworks lights the dim corridor and the explosions hurt my ears. I glance over my shoulder and see my teacher standing at the classroom door. Then the fireworks explode again, and she shrinks into herself like Chicken Little waiting for the sky to fall.

"Miriam," she calls out weakly. "You must stay here…"

I don't listen to her.

"Jeremy!" I cry, and run to where I left him.

PART ONE
No Exit

CHAPTER 1

I step through the doorway five minutes before the man kills his wife.

The penumbra crackles like a thunderstorm played in reverse. Nausea folds me in two. I fang my lip to make the pain my own. There's a taste of blood on my tongue, but the world grows sharp, reality replacing the memory I relive every time I travel.

I'm standing in a guest room in the Sleep Rite Motor Lodge, just off the interstate in Monroeville. Low cost and proximity to the highway make it a favorite spot for a midday frolic. It's the tail end of another sweltering Pittsburgh summer, the blinds closed against a hot, bright sky. The room has that baked-in smoky smell universal to such places, adding insult to injury since I haven't had a cigarette all day – no stimulants allowed on the job.

In the dimness, I scan the unexceptional décor. Ersatz wood paneling, faux-bronze floor lamp, rustic paint-by-number scene above a nickel-plated headboard. The rattletrap air conditioner competes with a daytime soap, *Days of Our Lives* or something, while the shower hisses and spits behind the door to my left. More like the Last Rites Motor Lodge if you ask me, but the clientele this place caters to aren't choosy.

A specimen of that clientele stands by the rumpled bed, waiting for the other occupants of the room to emerge.

He's in his forties, badly overweight, sweaty in his brown business suit. Graying, unshaved. Whiskey on his breath. So nervous his hands shake. I know what he's going through, and I feel for him. He doesn't want to be here any more than I do. But the gun he's holding doesn't leave either of us an option.

I train my eyepiece on his trembling hand until the AI returns a match.

Smith & Wesson M&P 380.

An older model, the kind the trade shows used to pitch as a safe bet for newbies. Even if I didn't know that, even if I didn't know every salient detail of this man's recent history, the tentative way he handles the weapon would tell me he's never fired a handgun before, possibly never touched one until today.

He looks amazed to see me. They always do.

His story's the oldest one in the book. Businessman gets a funny feeling, decides to turn detective. Tracks receipts and bank transactions, pockets the pistol his wife bought for home protection when the kids were babies and follows her to the Sleep Rite, where she's been humping his business partner on her lunch break. This shouldn't come as a surprise, since the husband's a neglectful lover at best and the twentysomething year-old partner has the time – and stamina – to give the wife what he can't.

But the hubby's not thinking clearly, what with the booze and betrayal. He confronts them in the act, shouts, threatens legal action. Only means to scare them, but gets so worked up when his wife taunts him, he squeezes the trigger like he's letting out an accidental fart. After a single, stunned moment to eyeball what he's done, he turns the gun on himself in a spasm of guilt and despair.

The result: two dead bodies, lots of brains and blood, a pair of orphans. A tragedy any way you look at it.

That's where we come in.

The blinds rustle as Vax arrives a second later. Thunderclap played backwards, face fighting the urge to vomit. He holds his trusty Glock out straight, left hand cupping the grip to steady it over the nausea.

The husband's eyes flick from me to my partner. Obviously terrified. Absolutely no idea what's going on.

Vax briefly takes his left hand from the gun to flash his badge. "LifeTime Law Enforcement. Place your weapon on the floor and raise your hands above your head."

The man stares, chews the end of his mustache as he nervously processes what must look like two glowing aliens who've unaccountably crash-landed in the motel room. Will he feign bravado, misunderstanding, innocence? Or will he be a good boy and do as my partner says?

None of the above. He blinks, stares, but holds on.

"Sir," I say, trying for a steady, soothing tone. "We're going to have to ask you again to place your weapon on the floor and raise your hands above your head. You're under arrest."

"What for?" A primal wail.

"Attempted murder."

"I didn't kill anybody."

"Not yet."

He sucks in a breath, looks us over again. His eyes are teary from the strain or the hooch or both.

I've often thought we could save ourselves a lot of trouble if, instead of confronting imminent murderers at emotionally fragile moments like this, we nabbed them well before the act. But the law's the law. You can't arrest someone for a crime they haven't committed, even if they've already committed it, until you have what the government calls "reasonable inference" that they're about to commit it again. Booking the husband in the motel room passes the test as, say, collaring him while he's downing his last shot of Jack Daniel's at the neighborhood pub doesn't. We've debated among ourselves whether anyone could actually make a violation of the timecode stick, but in the end, we've opted for playing it safe.

"Sir," I say. "Make this easy on yourself."

He wavers. I see it in his eyes. Like most people, he's naturally timid, doesn't want to hurt anyone. If we can get the gun off him, set him up with a cup of black coffee and a long talk with the court-appointed shrink, he'll be all right. At least he won't have to carry around the burden of knowing that, the first time around, he did exactly what he never dreamed he was capable of doing.

He's edging toward me, the gun held gingerly like a bag of dog doo he's about to drop in someone else's trash can, when the bathroom door bursts open.

All eyes shift as the two emerge from the steam. They're naked, beaded with water, the wife's legs wrapped around her lover's waist, his face buried in her long black hair. Both of them so focused on the moment they seem unaware that their exclusive party has become something of a social hour. She moans as he carries her to the bed, arranging her in what must be one of their tried-and-true positions.

The husband takes a step back, his fleshy face turned scarlet. I see the change come over him, and I know what he's about to do.

"Now, sir!" I say. "Drop your weapon!"

The wife screams. Untangles herself from the business partner, who drops to the floor, shouting something incoherent. The husband bellows right back as he stumbles toward the bed. I've got him lined up for a shot that should hobble him, not kill him, when he slips in the pool his wife and former partner left. His hands flail to catch himself against the headboard.

Deafening explosion. Blood smears the sheets. After a moment of silence, the word "Babe!" comes from his mouth.

Vax leaps for him.

You'd think the newly minted murderer would be too paralyzed by the sight of his wife's head pumping blood to react, but no. He dodges, shrugs off my partner's charge. Vax goes for him again, but now that the man knows what he's capable of, he eludes his much fitter adversary and wields the gun with newfound purpose. Vax should be over the wobbles by now, but he seems more sluggish than usual, and the husband has weight and desolation on his side. He throws Vax against the lamp. The bulb shatters, plunging the room into deeper dark.

"Vax!" I cry.

He's rising woozily. I can't see if he has his Glock. The husband is a lot closer than I am, and he takes aim like a sharpshooter. He even smiles, his teeth gleaming in the TV's ghostly glow.

I fire two rounds from my Beretta. The first hits the husband in the chest, spinning him against the wall. The second reddens the paneling behind his head, and he slumps to the floor.

Blood. Brains. Bodies. The only one left alive of the original three is the cowering, whimpering business partner, who's curled into the fetal position beside the puddle his bladder left on the shag rug.

Vax stands, feels the couple for a pulse. A mere formality. He shakes his head.

"You OK?" he asks.

I nod.

"I had to do it," I say.

He looks me in the eye. "I know."

My hands fumble as I holster my gun. My partner peels the sole survivor off the floor while I make the call.

CHAPTER 2

Later, I'm working my way through a pack of cigarettes outside the station when Vax shows up to put in his report.

"You want to talk about it?"

"Not particularly."

He stands beside the bench while I blow smoke into the muggy twilight. LifeTime Travel bought the old Amtrak station on Liberty when the maglev complex opened across the river, which means Vax and I work out of possibly the most beautiful historic building in the whole downtown area. Rose-colored stone, high vaulted lobby with ornate fixtures, wooden balustrade curving sensually to the boss's office on the second floor. Infinitely nicer than the regular cop stations, and don't we let them know it.

Old-timers gaze around in shock when they wander into our headquarters by accident, but that's because they're carrying around the newsreel from a half-century ago. Pittsburgh as a decaying mill town, deserted train station full of cobwebs and memories, cue the string section. In reality, the city came back from the brink earlier than most, spurring a nationwide renaissance. If the Steel City is a time capsule of the nation's fall and rise, it makes sense that it's also the nexus of actual time travel.

Of course, everyone thinks we book flights to Disneyland, so there's that too.

Vax puts a hand on my shoulder. I brush it off, readjust myself as far away as the bench will allow. He digs in his pocket

and holds out something that looks like a miniature accordion
with a penny whistle stuck out of one end.

"Personal grooming device?" I ask.

"Vintage nicotine delivery system. Guaranteed cancer free."

"I'll stick with the devil I know, if it's all the same to you."

"Come on, Miriam."

"Myriad."

"Miriam," he says firmly. "I fucked up too. You saved my ass
back there."

"By nailing his."

"The guy was going to die anyway. *Did* die before we
arrived."

"He didn't have to die again. That one's on me."

He stands there a minute, then stashes the vaping gizmo
and sits on the bench beside me. I slide even farther away until
my left butt cheek is hanging off the edge. Vax is his usual
rocklike self. No reaction at all. Which is either the best thing
or the most infuriating thing about him, depending.

"It never went that way before," I say, my words smoky
avatars on the leaden air.

"There was that kid over on Carson."

"A clerical error."

The year I joined the force, LifeTime dispatched the two of
us to the South Side to stop a drug deal turned gangland-style
execution. Trouble was, forensics must have reconstructed the
wrong case or the guy who operates the chamber must have
sent us to faulty coordinates, because we walked smack into
the middle of a suicide. Talk therapy not being my forte, it
didn't end well. I can still see the girl's body departing from the
Birmingham Bridge, somersaulting twice, colliding with the
Monongahela.

"The husband was in the room," Vax offers. "Maybe he
was…"

"One of us?" I shake my head. "You read the report. He was
part-owner of the Sleep Rite. She was having an affair with

his buddy in his own hotel. I guess to make him feel bad for missing their anniversary."

I try to laugh. Vax's hand settles on my shoulder, and this time, I let it be.

"Do you think it was a knot?" he asks.

"Highly unlikely."

"What, then?"

"A gratuitous slap in the face. The gods of time having a laugh at us mere mortals."

"I don't believe that. There's no fate–"

"–*but what we make*. I've seen the movies too, Vax. Not exactly where I go for answers to life's existential dilemmas."

"Great special effects, though."

"For the late twentieth century, maybe."

I turn away. Vax's hand doesn't budge.

It's like this. When you travel, even for the measly week the agency takes to reconstruct a murder before sending us back to stop it, you learn things. Your body and mind return to the scene of the crime, then proceed forward along whatever altered trajectory you've precipitated. So far as anyone can tell, the reality you create becomes *the* reality, with each part of the sentence rearranged in its new syntax. People, places, things. Verbs too. When it works out according to plan, you're the good guy – no ticker-tape parades or keys to the city, but at least the shock to your system was worth it. Conversely, when things go the way they went today, *that* becomes your reality. The new *you* you have to live with from here on out.

Either way, it raises a question I've wrestled with since I joined the force. What happens to the *other* you that would have lived its life if you hadn't doubled back? For that matter, what happens to all the other lives that would have played out differently if not for you? The lives that *did* play out differently – yours included – between the original occurrence of the event and your return to alter it? Do those lives cease to exist? Or are they hanging out somewhere else – in another place, another time?

Maybe the genius who designed the system knows. I sure don't. A strong body and receptive mind were in the job description, not an advanced degree in quantum physics.

Still, it seems to me I can sometimes feel the ones I left behind. The strays. All of the other possible Miriams that might have been, each of them trapped in her own personal limbo.

Hence my alias.

Myriad.

We all use them on the job. Vax told me the story behind his the day we became partners. Back in the academy, some semiliterate trainer mispronounced the double "c's" in his last name, so it came out "Martin Vaxaro." He tried for years to shake it, but it stuck.

"Miriam," he says.

"*Si, Signor Vaccaro?*"

"I have to submit my report. What are you doing later?"

"Killing myself slowly, as usual."

"Try not to finish before I get back, OK?"

He lets his hand slide off my shoulder as he climbs to his feet. Electricity tingles in me. Just before he enters the station, he half-turns and flashes a smile.

He'll be in there for hours. Quality Control brings us in one at a time to reduce the possibility of partners concocting an alibi. I've already been through the wringer. Weapons check, review of my body cam footage and AI interface, lie detector test. Endless questions about what I did and didn't do, infinitesimal dissection of events that have already played out twice, with subtle and not so subtle variations.

It's a painful but necessary process. Changing time erases the reports that were written, the memories that were made. Why write them, why make them, if the event never happened? The only record of what used to be is lodged in the minds of the travelers, and QC needs us to tell them whether we succeeded in what we were assigned to do.

Or, in my case, failed.

Legal was called in. I've been demoted to desk service pending a full investigation. When your job is to prevent a murder and you end up committing one instead, they want to know what went wrong. I do too, but at the present moment, what I want even more is *not* to know.

I call Chloe, the cheerful middle-aged woman from Angel Care who watches my mom three days a week, plus weekends when I'm working. The scheduling gets complicated when I travel, but I've managed to figure it out so far. I tell her I'm tied up with my partner, which isn't entirely untrue, or at least it won't be. She tells me sure, no problem, take my time. See me when I get back.

Conscience cleared, I put my phone away and watch drones skim through the darkening sky like high-tech bats. With me and Vax, a day on the job can go any number of ways. Good, bad, ugly. But it almost always ends up in bed.

CHAPTER 3

Most nights, it's his bed.

Vax's condo looks nothing like your stereotypical bachelor's paradise. It's oppressively neat, with books aligned on shelves, dishes scrubbed and gleaming in the drainer. Pillows plumped, sheets tucked. I suspect he actually dusts and vacuums, and not just for special occasions like this.

"Are you still Myriad?" he asks. "Or Miriam?"

"Who do you want me to be?"

"I prefer Miriam."

"Ta-da!" I say. "Like it?"

"Very much."

"Show me."

He does, with expert lips and fingers. Once I get my breath back, I sigh deeply, then reach out and touch his face.

"I wish we could travel," I say.

"You've told me that before."

"So is there a law? Against telling you again?"

He's quiet.

"You wish we could travel," he says as I climb on top of him.

"When we make love."

"When we make love."

"Because then, we could go back."

"To the moment just before."

"To the moment just before. And that way…"

"That way, it wouldn't have to end."

That's what Vax thinks. No matter how many times I tell

him, he thinks it's the sex I wish could last for all eternity. Don't get me wrong, the sex is something else. What he doesn't understand is that it's not the *during* I'm trying to hold onto. It's the *before*.

As always, it slips away. I roll off, flop on my back. He breathes hard, satisfied. Oblivious.

"Did you ever kill anybody?" I ask.

He doesn't answer right away, and I brace myself for a post-coital pun.

"No," he says.

"Me neither."

"They say it sticks with you."

"It wouldn't be so bad. Except..."

"Except?"

"Today's the day."

He turns to face me. "*Today?*"

"Last of August. Twenty years."

"Jesus, Miriam, I'm sorry. I–"

"Forgot. I know."

"Why did you come in? Dispatch would have understood. They could have given it to someone else."

"We worked on the case for a solid week. I didn't want to bag out on you."

"But you knew when you took it that it was the day. You had to know."

I think it over. Did I choose to travel back to today of all days, even though I knew it was today of all days? Am I that determined to put myself through hell, or am I just a really bad planner?

"I must have thought it would help," I say, the excuse sounding farfetched even to me. "You know, to keep my mind off of it."

"Did it?"

"Not really." I clear my throat, look at him. He's looking right back. "Not at all, actually."

And then the tears come.

I press my face into his shoulder. It doesn't help. Before I know it, I'm shaking with sobs, and the only thing that keeps me anchored to the present is the steady thrum of his heart beneath my ear.

"It was like a part of me was gone," I say in a voice that sounds nothing like my own. "Like with Myriad, only worse. Because I *know* what got left behind. I *saw* it."

To his credit, Vax says nothing. Just puts an arm around me and pulls me close.

"I'm such a mess," I say.

"You're upset."

"Do you think that's why I nailed that guy today? Because I was thinking about what happened to Jeremy?"

"You did it because he gave you no choice. End of story."

"I wish." I lift myself on an elbow, trace patterns in his chest hair with a finger. "Did I tell you we had different birthdays?"

"Twins can have different birthdays?"

"We do. Did." I swallow. "It was one of those deals where I was born six minutes before midnight, and he was born one minute after. I remember Mom telling me when I was little that she held him in her belly extra long to make sure we had our own special days. She knew how hard it is for twins to individuate. And then, afterward, she said…"

"What did she say?"

"That she wished she'd held on forever and never let him go."

That's it for me. Vax doesn't budge while I water his shoulder. When I'm done, he leans down to kiss the top of my head.

"You should move in with me," he murmurs in my ear.

"Because that would work out so brilliantly."

"I'm serious, Miriam."

"Where is this coming from?"

"My heart."

"Might want to clear it with your head. I'm a rule breaker, remember? I don't clean up after myself."

"We could compromise."

"Plus there's my little habit."

"I was thinking you'd quit?"

He flourishes the vaping doodad. I'd swear he had it in his pocket the whole time if I wasn't in a pretty good position to know he's not wearing pants.

"I can't leave my mom," I say. "Speaking of which…"

He pulls me back down. "You said you have till midnight."

"Mom gets funny. I should be there."

"She could move in with us."

"Now I know you're not serious."

"I've never been more."

"Vax."

"I don't want to lose you, Mir."

"Vax. Bad time, OK?"

"Can't help how I feel. Is that so terrible?"

I pull away from him, sit up in bed with the covers bunched over my knees. Vax looks at me, dark eyes shining beneath thick lashes.

"Don't," I say. "Not now. Not today. Not ever."

"Miriam. Twenty years is a long time."

"Not for me."

"You have to live your life."

"I am living my life."

"Reliving's not the same as living."

I'm about to say something I'll regret, but I hold my tongue. This has been a lovely evening, all things considered, and I don't want to ruin it. Instead, I reach for the handy excuse resting beside my phone on the nightstand. "Be right back."

He watches as I slip from bed, but doesn't try to stop me.

On the balcony, dressed in Vax's discarded uniform top, I stretch my legs out on his lounge chair and light a Marlboro Red, feeling the tension drain from my body. The city aura is dimmed for nighttime, but its glow stays strong enough to smother the stars.

I moved to Pittsburgh at the age of six. Vax's family has been here forever, multiple generations living and dying in the Bloomfield neighborhood where his ultra-high-rise stands. Little Italy, they used to call it. When I joined LifeTime and he found out I was originally from across the state, he took me on a tour of neighborhoods I'd never heard of, enclaves tucked out of sight like pockets in an infinite pool table. We ricocheted from corner to corner, grabbed a beer here and there, never staying in one place long. And then, that night, we ended up for the first time where we remain two and a half years later. In his bed, him showing me ever newer and better surprises, me no closer to resolution than I was back then.

This must be why I'm thinking about urban design, because I can't think about what he wants me to think about.

Move in with Vax? Not so fast. He's a good partner – work partner, sex partner, hold me together when I'm falling into a million pieces partner. But when a man pushing thirty-five starts reading lines like *I don't want to lose you*, there's only one place that script can go. To him, the next step might seem like a cakewalk. To me, it feels like a headfirst dive into a penumbra that'll hurl me sixty years into the future and hold me there as I gasp out my final breath. Which is even more unnerving than it sounds, because agents can *only* travel to the past, not the future.

I could stay out here all night. I would, too, if I thought it would make any difference. If I thought Vax might roll out of bed in the morning and open the balcony door to find me dissipating into the blue like mist off the distant river.

"If only," I say to myself.

I stand, stretch, try to muster the courage to go inside. Half of me hopes he's fallen asleep so I can sneak out unimpeded, the other half hopes he'll find me so irresistibly sexy slinking into his bedroom that we can pick up where we left off. All of me knows that, whether he's asleep or awake, there's only time for me to give him a quick kiss before throwing my clothes on and heading back to my place.

Ready or not, I say, not quite out loud, *here I come*.

That's when I feel the old familiar tickle, hair rising on my forearms accompanied by the nonsound of interrupted spacetime.

I wonder what Vax thinks he's doing. At the end of a day's travel, your core holds enough charge to let you skip back a few hours. But you'd have to have something *really* important to skip back to in order to put up with the side effects of a second ride.

"It won't work," I call out as I step into the living room. "I'll say *no*, no matter how many times you ask."

I'm closing the balcony door behind me when I hear the shot.

CHAPTER 4

Mom stirs dry ingredients in a stainless-steel bowl.

The wooden spoon clacks noisily. This is one of those mornings when she woke up with a threadbare memory of baking a cake, but she's been at it for the past half hour and hasn't turned the oven on. (Doesn't know how.) In another few minutes she'll forget what she's doing, lose interest, set the project aside. Leave it for me to toss in the garbage, since I don't bake.

I haven't said anything to her about Vax. Why waste breath?

He's stable, though that's nothing short of a miracle. I raced into his room last night to find him where I left him, blood gushing from a stomach wound. No assailant was visible, but the weapon was. Vax's own Glock, plucked from his nightstand and left on the floor after firing its single round. I stared at it as I leaned hard to stop the blood. The horrifying thought flitted through my mind that this was my fault. That my hot-blooded Romeo had tried to end it all in a fit of spurned-lover pique.

But that thought lasted only a second. I know Vax too well, plus a traveler's wake lingered in the air like glowing streamers. The shooter must have entered the room through a penumbra, fired the round, then used the energy from the first jump to initiate a second. I've never heard of anyone making a double jump that fast, but if your purpose was to escape detection, I suppose there's no technical reason you couldn't do it. The fact that they didn't stick around to kill me makes it seem they were eager to leave a witness to their handiwork.

25

Either way, it's why I pinged the paramedics instead of HQ. A risky move, because if the robosurge were to discover Vax's core while poking around in his stomach, that might blow LifeTime's cover. I took the risk for one simple reason: if the shooter traveled to Vax's room by way of penumbra, they had to be someone with access to the company's proprietary technology. One of us, in other words.

It sickened me to think that a member of our own team or any of the other regional offices would do this, but I wasn't taking chances. As soon as Vax got out of surgery, I arranged for him to be transferred to a private room and paid for it out of pocket, which will deplete my crypto in no time at the rates they charge. But he and I are both off the clock at the moment – I don't need to report for desk duty until tomorrow, since agents get a day off to recover from the trauma of traveling – and I felt guilty enough about my part in all this to take the gamble.

The cops grilled me at the hospital, of course. The regular cops. They're the only ones outside of select government officials who know the truth about LifeTime, and that's only because we need to work with them now and then. They tolerate us as a necessary evil, though there's no love lost on either side. In previous contacts, I've picked up hints of jealousy and distrust. After the Sleep Rite fiasco, I picked up a lot more than that. But though last night's circumstances were enough to arouse suspicion, they didn't have the goods to hold me. No prints on the attempted murder weapon. No witnesses. Motive? Well, maybe in the lovers' quarrel sense, but they couldn't lock me up for that. So I was free to go, but I fully expect to be called back in after Vax wakes up and they're able to question him. My only consolation is that they dislike the LifeTime higher-ups even more than they dislike me, so they won't be in any rush to share the results of their investigation with HQ.

In the meantime, I putter around the apartment, cleaning

up after Mom, debating whether to ping the detective in charge to see what he's found out. I'm dying for a smoke, but I must be subjecting myself to some twisted form of penance for what happened to Vax, because I've fought off the cravings all morning. That's made me even buggier than usual around Mom, not that she notices. I can hardly wait for Loretta to show up for her shift, which will give me a chance to escape these four walls for a time, if not to liberate myself from the combination funhouse and prison cell I call my brain.

My own part in this quagmire aside, the question that's driving me battiest is this: assuming forensics reconstructs the crime and a team goes back to stop the shooter – and, unless last night was an inside job, that would be the logical move – what happens next?

If the team succeeds, will life magically rearrange itself around me, the way a dream on the cusp of waking yields to reality? Will that dream slip away as most dreams do, leaving me with the miasma of last night's spat but not the miracle of Vax's resurrection? Or will I find myself right back in his bedroom, our lovemaking on pause, our differences unresolved? Having always been the change agent, never the one whose spilled soup someone else was trying to mop up, I have no idea what to expect.

What if my pet theory is right? What if the team barges in at the critical moment, thwarts the would-be killer, and walks out with him in cuffs, but their actions affect only the *me* who inhabits their version of events, not the *me* who's already lived through mine? The me who's cooped up right here, with Vax under heavy sedation and no one I can confess my misdeeds to except–

"Mom!"

I lunge for the bowl she's balanced on the edge of the counter, but I'm not fast enough to catch it before it topples, spilling sugar and cocoa across the linoleum.

By the time I've swept it up, she's moved to the living room, where she stands with her face striped by the Venetian blinds. As always, her gray eyes are vacant, passive. A friend of hers, a fellow faculty member from the CMU psych department, called when she heard the news. She told me how brilliant Deborah Sayre used to be, what a stimulating teacher and colleague. I wouldn't know. I wasn't quite seven when she disappeared from our home, and I can't remember either her fierce, restless intellect or the warning signs that it was slipping away for good. All I know is that by the time she came back, the damage had progressed to the point where she couldn't remember anything at all.

That's what I tell myself. A daughter's bitter wish for the mom she never knew.

Her lips twitch, the vestige of a smile. The docs diagnosed early-onset Alzheimer's, though there's no family history and the genetic screen came back inconclusive. For seventeen years, from just before my seventh birthday to just after my twenty-fourth, she simply winked out of my life, left no note, sent no pings, not even to let me know she was all right. She became nothing but a distant memory that blurred a little more with each passing day, until I could no longer be sure if it was true memory or something I made up in place of her.

And then, after all that time, when my dad was gone too – into the dirt, which was more than he deserved – and I'd started working my brand new big-girl job, the cops called to tell me she'd turned up on the streets of the city she'd abandoned nearly two decades before. Homeless, tattered, mute. DNA tests confirmed her identity. Which was a good thing, since she bore no resemblance to the woman I loosely remembered.

I think about her now pretty much the way I think about my own past selves: there but not there, or there *because* not there. A ghost who haunts me with her absence, not her presence. Another Myriad strewn along the way, different only in the sense that in her case, I have no idea where she's been most of my life.

"Hi, Mom," I say softly.

She turns at the sound of my voice, looks through me as usual. As if I'm her ghost as much as she's mine.

I'm trying to think of some other project to distract her when Loretta pings and I buzz her up. She seems to be only a few years younger than Mom, but the distance between them couldn't be greater – Mom a drifting wraith, Loretta businesslike and efficient in her robin's-egg blue uniform with the wings-and-halo decal of Angel Care over her left breast. She's not friendly like Chloe, who held down the fort last night when I pinged her from the hospital, but she gets the job done. Today she looks tired, probably working a double shift. She seems less than thrilled when I tell her it's baking day, since Mom sometimes resumes her abortive experiments once I'm gone.

I run through the list of what I've already done and what needs doing. The latter includes lunch, laundry, a sponge bath if she can coax Mom near the stall. That was too much of a struggle for me today, so I dressed her without worrying about the way she smells. It's never too bad unless she has an accident. Most days her skin exudes a dry, stale odor, like books left too long in an airless room.

"I'll be back by four," I say, and Loretta nods professionally. She's already started redding up the warzone that passes for my living space. Mom watches with her head cocked to the side in an uncanny likeness of a baby bird's. I give her a peck on the cheek as I do every day. I'm pretty sure it's more for Loretta's benefit than hers or mine.

Out in the hallway, I take a deep breath and lean against the door. Guilt boxes me in at leaving Mom with a stranger, though I know I'm as much of a stranger to her as anyone. I can barely afford what Angel Care charges, but I definitely can't pay for a private facility, and I can't bring myself to put her in a government-sponsored group home. Most of all, I can't stand the thought of her disappearing from my life a second time.

Strange I should feel this way. You'd think of all people, I would know that you can't get the time back. You can steal a week to fix someone else's mess – or foul it up even worse – but you can never recover what you've lost.

Which calls me back to the present. I contacted Angel Care so I could visit Vax. Or I'm visiting Vax to give me an excuse to leave Mom on a day I could have stayed home. Either way, the door's closed now, and I'm not about to open it back up.

CHAPTER 5

As soon as I step out of the elevator and onto the street, I fish in my pack for my last cigarette. Passersby look askance at me for violating the public smoking ban, but they haven't had the kind of twenty-four hours (times two) that I have.

It's another steamy day in the 'Burgh, as the weatherbots like to say. Pedestrians swim through town in sweat-stained blouses and business suits. Many have on surgical masks. A few are rigged up in hazmat suits with respirators, which strikes me as a bit ostentatious. There's a trickle of traffic at lunch hour, mostly self-driving cabs and delivery trucks, plus the usual complement of wheeling, swooping drones. The vehicle fleet's gone electric in the past fifteen years, which is why the sky's so blue, the streets so quiet. Too late to turn down the thermostat, though. If I could do that, I would in a heartbeat.

But I can't.

As a safeguard against LifeTime agents tampering with the remote past, the agency is prohibited from authorizing trips longer than a week – the maximum the forensics lab takes to reconstruct a crime. To make sure none of us tries to break the law, our transponders are calibrated to debit as much lifetime as we travel. Up to seven days at a jump, ripped off like some kind of satanic Brazilian wax job. More pieces of yourself lying in the cosmic gutter to remind you you're not whole. You could try to prevent the Kennedy assassination or the dawn of the Industrial Revolution, but you'd arrive at your destination either very decrepit or very dead.

I ping one of the robocabs and climb in, scan my phone. There's a nervous moment when the screen hiccups, but the green light comes on immediately afterward: approved. I'm not broke yet, but I will be soon if I can't figure out a better arrangement with Mom.

I don't want to think about that now, so I turn my thoughts to my reunion with Vax. Riding smoothly through town, the cab purring and an almost cool breeze blowing through the half-open window, it's easy to picture him awake and alert, arms open to receive me. I imagine teasing him, giving him a hard time for not dodging faster, no offense meant or taken.

It's only when the cab pulls up in front of the medical center that the rosy vision wilts. Assuming Vax is awake, do I really want to see him? More to the point, does he really want to see me? Last thing he remembers, I was fleeing his proposal, abandoning him to the whims of fate. For all I know, he thinks I'm the one who shot him. That would certainly be the ultimate Dear John letter, but it's a bit of a stretch even for me.

Plucking up my courage, I take a deep breath and walk through the sliding glass doors into the front lobby.

My phone buzzes on the way in. I check it, expecting Loretta. Instead, it's from LifeTime, with instructions for me to report to the boss's office at thirteen hundred hours.

I freeze, unwilling to believe that despite my efforts, they already know about Vax. Or could it be they've found out something about the Sleep Rite? Either way, I can't face this right now. I delete the ping and plunk the phone in the basket at the metal detector. It buzzes again when I put it in my back pocket, but I tell Sibyl, its resident AI, to pay the ping no mind.

I wander through the hospital's familiar-unfamiliar geography. Every corridor looks the same, every doorway seeming like one I entered yesterday. The color-coded stripes on the floor are supposed to help, but I can't remember which color I followed last night, much less the name of the unit I had Vax transferred to.

I've circled aimlessly for fifteen minutes when a set of purple elevator doors sparks my memory. A masked orderly – human, not robotic – pushes an old man on a gurney into the elevator beside me. He reaches for the same floor I'm going to, presses the button for me. The old man is out cold, head back and shallow breath forming beads inside his oxygen mask. Fleecy hair, fig face. Timer ticking down.

My heart gives a little leap to match the elevator's jolt. It's like I'm looking at Vax fifty years from now, a stranger in a bed who never got the answer he was looking for.

The illusion evaporates when we reach the floor and the doors open. Just an old man in a hospital, dying on schedule. I wonder if he has family, or if he's taking his final ride all on his own. I look the other way while the orderly pushes the bed down the hall, its wheels squeaking against the shiny-clean floor.

The robomed at the desk asks my name, then waves me ahead once it sees I'm the one paying. Outside Vax's room, I give myself a moment to breathe.

Hopefully he'll be asleep and I can sit beside him for an hour in peace, just looking at him. If I'm feeling more than normally bold, I might hold his hand, tell him things I can't tell him when he's awake.

Or I might walk in to find his bed empty, the wound having reopened or the area around the stent having gotten infected and him being rushed to emergency surgery, where he'll die on the table without me getting a chance to tell him anything at all.

It's that thought that pushes the door open and makes me peek inside.

The room's darkened and quiet, except for the soft beep of a monitor. The curtain around the bed is pulled back, showing me the evidence: Vax lying peacefully for all I can tell, unless that means he's dead. The glow of the monitor outlines his face in stark relief, his features whittled down like a corpse at a viewing.

Then his head turns and his eyes open, shining with the monitor's amber tint. He smiles, which gives me enough reassurance to enter the rest of the way.

"Hey, partner," I say.

"Miriam." A hand reaches out, IV line trailing. "I'm so sorry."

He's apologizing to *me*. I cross the distance in two quick, jittery steps and take his hand. It feels cold, but I think that's just the room.

"How are you feeling?" I ask.

"Beat. But there's some good news."

"They caught the guy?"

He frowns in momentary confusion. "The doc was just in. Told me they were able to use a new procedure so I won't need the ileostomy bag."

My heart soars. "Did they give you any idea how long before you get out?"

"Days, probably. Then some rehab. You're going to have to find a new partner, at least for the short term."

My throat tightens. "Any hidden cameras in here?"

"Not that I know of."

"Hot nurses?"

"They're bots, but sure."

"Scooch over."

As carefully as I can with all the wires and tubes, I crawl into bed beside him. He winces when I accidentally jiggle something, then relaxes. I hold onto him.

"I was so scared," I say.

"They tell me you were as cool as if you'd done it a hundred times. That if it hadn't been for you…"

I put a finger to his lips. "If it hadn't been for me, I could have shot the son of a bitch and saved you a world of hurt."

"You saved my life. Twice."

"You're just saying that because you're on pain meds." I touch the concavity of his cheek. "So you didn't see anything?"

"You were out there a long time. Guess I must have fallen

asleep. Next thing I knew, I had a bullet in my gut and you were shouting at me to hold on."

"It was a traveler," I say.

His eyebrows lift. "You sure?"

"I saw the penumbra. Couldn't see the guy. He'd already jumped out by the time I got there."

"Hm."

He's silent, his eyes searching away from mine. As if he's trying to figure out which of his coworkers would want him dead. Or as if he already knows. Something he never told me, some trouble he's in... Maybe I'm not the only one who isn't talking.

"They pinged me earlier," I say. "LifeTime."

"Cassidy?"

I nod against his shoulder. "He must want to talk about last night."

"Oh?"

"I don't know how they found out so fast. I tried to keep this quiet, because I thought they might be, you know, involved somehow."

"That's not why he called."

I raise myself on an elbow to look at him. "It's not?"

"It's because of my report."

"Which report?"

"The one I gave yesterday. After the Sleep Rite."

Instant heart-freeze. "What did you tell them?"

He looks away again. He's silent for so long I think he's fallen asleep on me. Then he turns his head and says, "I told them about you."

"Told them what about me?"

"That you're..."

"Losing it?" I sit up in bed. "Is that what you told them?"

He sighs.

"I told them you were struggling," he says. "That the job has taken more of a toll on you than they know, and that you found the guy's death at the Sleep Rite particularly hard to handle. They were looking for an excuse to terminate you," he says before I can respond. "I had to tell them something to get you off the hook."

"And you thought that would do the trick? Telling them I'm mentally unstable was going to make them decide to send me out onto the streets carrying a loaded gun I already killed somebody with?"

"Of course not," he says. "I thought they might give you some time off. This job, the work we do... It's killing you, Miriam. You need time away. Time to heal."

"What I need is a steady paycheck, not another trip to the funny farm."

"That's not what I meant."

"How am I going to pay for my mom?" I ask. "How am I going to live? If you're so worried about me, shouldn't you have thought that through? Or" – the truth strikes me as the words are leaving my mouth – "did you think I'd agree to move in with you if I had nowhere else to go?"

"I–"

"You can't extort my love, Vax," I say. "It's mine to give when I choose to. Or choose not to."

He tilts his head and looks at me. His face is wan, thin, nothing like the Vax from last night. The Vax from the past two and a half years. His expression is curiously detached, as if I'm a science project he's been trying to figure out all that time.

"I can't do this anymore," he says at last.

"You're blaming *me* for last night?"

"Not that. *Us*." He lets out a breath. "I'd take a bullet for you any day. But it would never be enough."

"You forgot the anniversary," I say, my throat clenching around the words. "The most important day of my life. If you want to talk about *enough*, how about you start with that?"

"I didn't forget. I just thought, after twenty years, maybe you could choose a new most important day. *Our* anniversary, for example. The birth of our child."

"Don't talk to me about children when I–"

"Not children, then. But something that would help you move beyond it."

"You think I can *move beyond* watching my brother get killed?"

"I think you have to. For your own sake."

I'm trembling, unable to form a coherent thought. "You said you were… you said you didn't want to lose me. Did you forget that too?"

"Getting shot clarifies things." He reaches for my hand, but I shrink from him. "I've been holding you back, Miriam. All this time, I thought that if I gave you everything I had to give, showed you a new way, you could start living again. Now I see that I've just been another excuse for you to run and hide. And that I can never be more than that until you come out and face what happened on your own."

"I *can't!*" I say. "We were this close, don't you understand? I was six years old. I was…"

"This is what I'm talking about," he says quietly.

"I was *there!*" I scream. "His blood was in my mouth, my eyes. All I could see was red. When they took me to the hospital, they had to clean away bits of bone and… oh, my *God*…"

I curl into myself and moan. Vax doesn't try to touch me, doesn't say a word.

It wouldn't matter if he did. My body is right beside his in the narrow bed, but my mind is a billion miles away, back in that hallway, that lifetime, just like it's been since the moment my future was stolen from me by the same bullet that stole Jeremy's. My grief is a penumbra hanging in the slim space between us, crackling with enough energy to consume us both and take the room with it for good measure.

But that doesn't happen, because a robomed enters right at that moment for a vitals check. It shoves me aside like the random obstruction I am, switches out Vax's IV, lifts the dressing to inspect his wound. Its face-screen flashes numbers, which

I assume to be in the normal range since it's not emitting an alarm or bursting into flames. I retreat to the corner, hugging myself, until the machine's satisfied and rolls smoothly into the hallway to check on its next trauma case.

I look at Vax. He shows no more expression than the bot.

I back toward the door, reaching behind me to grip the knob. It's only then that he breaks into a small, sad smile, and I could run to him or kill him, whichever comes first.

"Goodbye, Miriam," he says. "Get better, OK? Get help."

"Go to hell," I say, and walk unsteadily out the door, down the hall to where the elevator waits to gather me in.

No sooner does it deposit me on the streets than Sibyl dumps a flood of insistent requests on me. My hands shake as I ping my reply.

CHAPTER 6

I'm in no condition to show up at LifeTime, but I have no choice.

Vax's betrayal is an abscess in my heart, bleeding pus. I've never sat down for a one-on-one with the boss before – I've barely seen him, since he stays in his second-floor office while the rest of us minions scurry around below – but I can't believe he's the kind of man I can convince to change his mind. With my core depleted, I can't travel out of this either, can't go back to yesterday and nip in the bud whatever Vax told LifeTime. All I can do is move forward, like an inmate being led to the death chamber.

The archway before the main entrance has a crazy intricate skylight that looks like a giant kaleidoscope or God's eye. Most days I don't even look at it. Now I do, and the afternoon sun shining through the multicolored glass reminds me of the visions I see when I travel. The cement beneath my feet is stippled with rainbow light. When I look at my hands, I find the pattern dancing across them too.

I went to church only once in my life, when I was six years old. If I knew how to pray, I might try it now.

I push open the revolving door with its old-fashioned brass handles. The hardwood floors gleam in the light from tall side windows. The receptionist, Therese, stands behind the desk in the middle of the space, the only piece of furniture in the whole airy atrium. The company motto is written in raised gold letters across the front. I read the words I've read a thousand times as if they're the lines of an opaque chiromancy.

LifeTime. Commitment.

Other offices are hidden in the way back, with the forensics lab and locker rooms, firing range and travel chamber tucked out of sight downstairs. I try to walk softly, but the echoes make Therese look up.

She's tall, slim, pretty in a robotic way. Her headset heightens the impression that she's not quite human. I've always wondered why they don't use an actual robosec like everyone else to save money.

"Dr Cassidy will see you now," is all she says before she goes back to her computer. I try to say *thank you*, but my throat's too dry.

Marble stairs lead a curving path upward. I hold onto the polished balustrade as if it's a lifeline.

I exit into the open loft Cassidy calls his office. It's as spartan in its furnishings as Therese's lower-level fiefdom. There are the same sun-kissed hardwood floors, along with an even larger wooden desk. Maple, I think. A huge lunette window behind the desk looks out over what used to be the train yard. Though we're not that high up, I experience a spell of lightheadedness. This is what it must have been like for the ancient Greeks to be summoned to Mount Olympus.

My one possible connection to Cassidy is that he used to work at CMU like my mom. Not in the same department. Cybernetics. I've never had the guts or the invitation to ask if he knew her.

He's turned away from me in his swivel chair, facing the yard. His body forms a slim silhouette against the midday brightness. There are easily thirty feet of hardwood between the top of the stairs and the desk, and I'm not sure if I'm supposed to approach or wait for him to beckon. I try clearing my throat, but that produces a sound too minor for my own ears to hear.

He swivels nonetheless. I can't make out his face, and he says nothing. I feel like a fool standing there, so I cross the space to the chair in front of his desk and sit.

My eyes adjust. He's a good fifteen years older than my mom. Tall, lean, clean-shaven. An immaculate dresser, with a full head of dark hair. Considering his age, I doubt much of the coif is real. The height of his chair would give him an edge over me even if he weren't six feet plus to my five-four.

"Agent Randle," he says. "We have a problem."

So much for the pleasantries.

He taps the surface of the desk, bringing up a virtual screen. The standard agency contract appears, the one I signed when I joined LifeTime. Small comfort: at least I won't have to watch him tear a physical document to pieces.

"There are a number of conditions to which you agreed when you were offered employment as a LifeTime travel agent," he says. "Please note the highlighted portion."

The screen zooms to a bullet point. My electronic initials are clearly visible beside the text. My heart skips a beat when I scan the particular item he's called up. I wonder if he expects me to read it out loud.

"Agents are prohibited from entering into extra-operational relationships with fellow agents," he spares me the trouble. "You agreed to this stipulation when you signed your contract, Agent Randle?"

I nod. Agreed to it, and then, a few weeks into the job, broke it. I can't remember if Vax and I discussed the risk we were taking, but I can't pretend we didn't know.

I clear my throat until I find something that sounds like my voice. "I never understood the purpose of that one."

"And yet you initialed it nonetheless."

"Could you explain it to me again?"

"Liaisons between agents are messy, Agent Randle. As well as contrary to the company's interest."

Messy is Vax's guts spilling from his stomach, the emergency AI calmly feeding me instructions by speakerphone, bright red gore to my elbows. *Messy* is the big boss showing me the door an hour after my ex-partner, ex-lover shoos me out of

his life. Not exactly your run of the mill office romance type
of messy.

"I," I say, then correct myself, "*we* made a mistake. It won't
happen again." If he knew how I know that, would it matter
to him?

Apparently not.

"The damage has already been done," he says. "Damage that
LifeTime will be obligated to devote considerable resources to
undoing."

"But Vax is all right. I saw him, and he's–"

He holds up a hand to silence me.

"You know the extremely sensitive nature of our work,"
he says. "The importance of shielding the company from the
potential fallout of travel assignments. Yet you and Agent
Vaccaro have flagrantly violated the terms of your contract,
putting us in the position of having to authorize nonessential
travel to address this past night's events."

"Has a team already gone back?" The thought of agents
storming our love nest and seeing just how flagrantly Vax and
I have violated company policy makes me sick to my stomach.
"Have they found anything?"

He shakes his head, his expression almost believably
regretful. "We cannot make an exception to protocol in this
case. A forensics team has begun the work of reconstructing
the events of last night, and, if warranted, agents will return to
the crime scene at the conclusion of their investigation."

My immediate reaction is relief, but that doesn't last long.
Mortifying as it is to picture coworkers nosing around in my
bedroom business, there's a chance they'd be able to stop the
shooter. If they did, there's a chance Vax and I wouldn't have
to go through our farewell scene. Either way, there's also a
chance I'd never know. Would I rather have Vax healthy and
whole in some other Miriam's life than weak and wounded
and lost to me forever in my own?

"In light of the serious nature of these infractions," Cassidy's voice comes to me, "I'm afraid we have no choice but to dismiss you from the agency. Effective immediately."

"What about Vax?"

"Agent Vaccaro's case will be reviewed in due course."

He makes it sound as if they're going to cut Vax a break, because... why? Seniority? Some wrinkle in his contract? Or because this is what men do when one of their own bends the rules?

"There's a rogue travel agent on the loose," I say. "I'm the sole witness. You might want to keep me around."

"If the forensics team finds evidence of any such renegade, you can rest assured we'll deal with them appropriately," he says. "At present, our investigation is focused on another person of interest. Someone, shall we say, closer to the victim."

I'm stunned, unable to respond. They think *I* shot Vax – and before I had any reason to want to.

"I had nothing to do with it," I manage to say.

He waves a hand. "It would be highly inappropriate for me to discuss this matter with you. You may expect a visit from our investigators later today. In the meantime, please report to HR to turn in your badge and schedule the deactivation of your LifeTime transponder. And, so you know: should you seek to publicize any of what has passed between us today, I must remind you that you signed an NDA when you joined LifeTime, and that our legal team prosecutes quite vigorously those who seek to drag the company's name through the mud." He swivels in his chair, dismissing me. "Good day, Ms Randle."

Ms Randle. Just like that.

I get up from the chair. Feeling numb. Thinking about me under criminal investigation and my mom in a state-run dementia ward.

I turn to go, but stop when I'm halfway to the stairs. There's one last thing I need to say to this self-righteous bastard, even if it's to his back.

"You're going to have a hard time keeping me quiet if you

charge me with a crime," I say. "My NDA doesn't invalidate my right to defend myself."

His chair budges an increment, but he doesn't bother to answer. Why should he? Once they go back and tidy up the mess from last night, none of what I say to the press or the pols will make a bit of difference, because none of it will have happened. For that matter, I probably won't remember any of it. Conversely, if they fail to nab the perpetrator and the present remains as is, who'll listen to some wild story from the primary suspect in an attempted homicide investigation? My face burns as I realize how stuck I am: stuck in this moment, stuck in my life, stuck in all the lousy decisions I've made or haven't made these past twenty years.

Vertigo buffets me as I try to find my way to the stairs. My first thought is that it's a natural response to the fix I'm in.

Then a wave of intense nausea buckles my knees, forcing me to the floor with my head hanging and my breath coming in gasps. My ears pop from a sudden, inexplicable change in pressure. It's a minute before I can fill my lungs with enough oxygen to steady myself and clear my swimming vision. I lurch to my feet and face the man who just fired me, wondering what he must think of my latest performance.

But he's not thinking anything anymore, because a shot rings out and he falls back in a spray of blood.

That's when I realize I'm sick because the last traces of a penumbra shimmer in the air before me. And because the gun that just blew away my ex-boss's brain is clutched in my nerveless hand.

CHAPTER 7

My hand. Not some other hypothetical Miriam's. *Mine.*

I'm tingling with the penumbra's energy, so I can only conclude that I skipped back a few minutes and then – I can't imagine how – made a second jump to return to the present.

But this time, armed.

And not with my own Beretta, which, like a good girl, I handed over to QC when I showed up at the office yesterday. The gun I'm holding is unfamiliar for a second, then it clicks.

Smith & Wesson. M&P 380.

The same model the husband was waving around in the Sleep Rite. The same type of gun he used to kill his wife.

Alarms scream in my head. This couldn't be *the* gun, could it? That one was downstairs in the crime lab along with mine. Did I travel to an earlier point in the day, swipe the gun, then return to the boss's office to shoot him? Or did I go back even farther, to yesterday's debacle in the Sleep Rite, and take the gun from there?

But Vax – yesterday's Vax – would have stopped me if I'd showed up from his future and tried to remove a murder weapon from a crime scene.

Wouldn't he?

I try to think it through. Assuming I snookered or overpowered him and made off with the gun, we never would have ended up in bed last night, which means – maybe – he wouldn't have gotten shot. Or if he did, he would have died. But if that were the case, we wouldn't have been busted for sleeping together, and I wouldn't be here kowtowing to the Almighty in the first place.

How much did I change when I got my hands on this gun?

And then there's the larger question: unless I'm losing my mind as much as Vax thinks I am, how could I have snuck into the travel chamber for a boost to my depleted core, taken a trip to the past, armed myself, then impossibly jumped *forward* to kill a somewhat innocent man in cold blood – all without willing or even knowing it?

I'm sweating, choking back vomit. The reception area is just beneath the open loft, and Therese must have heard the gunshot.

I have to get out of here.

The lunette window behind the slumped corpse is bolted shut. There's a double-hung window to the side that opens onto a fire escape, the kind that adorns old-time elementary schools and apartment buildings. It was restored and the rusted-out parts replaced when the building was refurbished, so it should hold my weight.

The only problem, I see when I open the window and lean out, is that it stops more than ten feet short of the pavement. Maybe if I run downstairs and duck out the emergency door…

Heels click on the staircase. The fire escape it is.

I push the window the rest of the way open and climb out. I'm still clutching the gun, which means I'm going to look guilty as sin to Therese. But that ship sailed the moment the shot was fired. If I'm going to run, I'm not about to do so without a means of defending myself.

I catch sight of her as I'm closing the window. To my surprise, she's armed, supporting her pistol with both hands and sidestepping the way an experienced agent would. She shouts and fires simultaneously. Glass shatters, but I'm not hit.

Now I know why they hired a real secretary. Apparently, LifeTime is even more keen on protecting its assets than the ex-boss let on.

I scramble down the fire escape. Glass rains from above as Therese clears fragments. She lets off four rounds, but the bullets glance harmlessly off metal.

At the bottom of the fire escape, I take a deep breath and drop. I land with enough impact to send a scary freezing sensation up my back, but nothing's broken, at least not that I can tell through the adrenaline making me flushed and wobbly.

People on the street have dived for cover. Some are staring at me from behind stopped robocabs and the corners of buildings.

I look around for the best escape route, but realize I'm going to have to expose myself one way or another. I can only hope Therese isn't a very good shot and the gun is just for awkward moments like this.

I take off, turning briefly to shoot upward as I clear the fire escape. It's a wild shot that I'm sure goes nowhere near her, but it has its intended effect. She doesn't fire again until I'm across the street and well shielded behind a dumpster. She's a far better markswoman than I expected, her bullet striking metal.

A long pause ensues while she reloads or thinks it over. I tell myself she wouldn't dare take another shot, not with the possibility of pedestrians between me and her.

Or would she? She went after me like a trained assassin, not even pausing to check the boss or call for help. What kind of organization have I gotten myself mixed up with, anyway?

I sprint down the alley, dodging trash cans. It's not until I've put a palisade of skyscrapers between me and my assailant that I slow my pace and tuck the gun inside my belt with my shirt covering it. I'm breathing hard and my heart is hammering, but the adrenaline rush is wearing off enough for me to be reasonably sure I'm not injured from the fall or from any of Therese's bullets. My knees ache, that's all.

I walk fast, but not too fast, toward the river. Why putting water between me and LifeTime seems like a good idea I don't know, but I have to walk in some direction, and that's the one my legs select. If I can lose myself on the North Side, that'll give me breathing space to come up with something resembling a plan.

I cross the Clemente Bridge, then circle the luxury hotel where the stadium used to stand before the Pirates moved to Nashville. All that's left to mark the hundred-plus years they played ball in this town are the bronze statues that stand on their pedestals like ghosts of doormen past.

My brain has started functioning by this point, but the extent of my plan remains, *Jesus Christ, I'm totally fucked.*

The tiny bit of good news: I've come to the conclusion that I didn't travel after all – not to the past, and certainly not to the future. I'm crazy, but not *that* crazy. Seconds were creeping along at their normal pesky pace right up to the moment when some invisible assassin splashed Cassidy's blood all over the lunette window, and there's no gap in my awareness the entire time. Come to think of it, the little jostle in Cassidy's chair when I offered my parting riposte should have tipped me off. I've seen that kind of random displacement when Vax trails me on a job, and it happens just before his penumbra forces its way into the room.

The supersize helping of bad news: the killer had to be an incredibly adept traveler if they were able to jump into Cassidy's office, put the gun in my hand a split-second after they fired the shot, then jump out a split-second later. That would explain why I felt the effects of their penumbra, because they couldn't have gotten close to me without some of the energy from their core bleeding into my own. Though I didn't catch sight of them, there's no doubt in my mind it was the traveler from last night, since it strains belief that there are two people running around who can make a back-to-back jump so fast and with such pinpoint accuracy. They must have planned this for some time, which means they either wanted Cassidy dead, me framed, or both.

I can imagine ex-agents who might want revenge on the

creep who terminated them. Or crooks LifeTime busted who might have it out for the head honcho. But I can't begin to think of anyone who would want me to go down with his ship. The wife of the man I killed is gone, his kids not past their preteens. A sibling of his? A drinking buddy? The advantage to not having friends is that I don't have enemies either. At least, none I knew of until they started coming out of the woodwork today.

But none of this matters from LifeTime's perspective. If I'd stuck around after the shooting, there'd have been an investigation, and it's possible they'd have found the one who did the killing. For that matter, if I'd been thinking clearly, I could have tried to nab the shooter myself before he jumped out.

Now I've got nothing but prints all over the murder weapon and multiple witnesses to me fleeing the scene of the crime. Thanks to Vax's report, LifeTime already believes I've come unglued. They probably think I shot my lover in a psychotic rage when I found out he'd betrayed me, then killed the boss when he told me I'm under investigation. They won't look for another suspect, because I've given them all the suspects they need.

I've got to run. That's the only option left.

But running from time travelers is easier said than done.

Anywhere I go is risky, because a team from the future could have reconstructed my flight path and be waiting for me. Some routes I might take, though, are much more perilous than others.

Home, for starters. That's the first place I think of, which means it's the last place I should go. What would be the point? To say goodbye to Mom? To take her with me? If I leave, she's not even a ghost anymore. She's out of my life entirely, abandoned to the slender mercies of the state when they discover I'm gone.

She's the one who abandoned me, the thought enters my mind.

The one who walked out of my life when I needed her most and left me with dear old Dad, whose idea of positive parenting was to drive me to trauma therapy when Jeremy's murder first happened and then, years later, to my recovery groups, where he'd mosey off to the nearest watering hole and leave me under the care of whatever semi-adult was encouraging us to bare our souls. The same paternal role model who finally had the decency – and, let's give credit where it's due, dexterity – to wrap his self-driving vehicle around a telephone pole, but only after I'd endured ten years of hell and gotten a reputation in high school as the spooky bitch who cut herself and would cut you too if you came close.

All of that, one way or another, was my mom's doing. And now I'm worried about leaving her to bake a nonexistent cake and dirty up an apartment she doesn't have the mental wherewithal to burn down for good?

I ping Loretta anyway.

It's the worst move I could make, leaving a location where LifeTime can track me. I justify my action on the grounds that it doesn't matter, that if agents from the future are fated to find me, they'll jump back to five minutes from now and arrest me when I turn the next corner. I tell Loretta I'm running late, would she mind staying a few more hours, at overtime? She sounds wiped, but agrees.

For the rest of today, my conscience is assuaged. As a bonus, maybe this'll buy me a few extra hours before Loretta reports me as MIA.

I pitch the phone in the river the first opportunity I have. There's no time to erase the data, but there shouldn't be much to lead them to me – only old pings exchanged with Vax, full of raunchy talk and lewd emojis. My ex-lover is the first one they'll go to once they figure out I'm not hiding under Mom's bed, and I can only hope that dumping me earlier today doesn't mean he'd also sell me out for an encore.

That leads to a thought I can't bear.

Maybe Vax is behind what happened today.

Getting back at me for refusing his proposal? Manipulating me from his hospital bed-slash-evil-lair? But that's ridiculous. All I did was turn him down. He's the one who ended it for good, so we should be even when it comes to romantic payback.

My heart rate and breathing have returned to normal, but my core is swirling with leftover energy. The device was surgically implanted beneath my upper abdominals, which is why I feel like I'm about to lose the contents of my stomach every time it's activated. It itched like the devil for a month after it was inserted, but the only time I feel it anymore is when it's charged, and that happens only when I'm in the presence of a penumbra, my own or someone else's. Its insistent pulsing is doing a number on me now, but there's no way to clear it unless…

My heart starts its drumbeat again.

With my core charged from the other traveler's double jump, I should have enough juice to make a jump of my own. It won't be anywhere near as precise as the ones we make from the chamber, which can get us within nanoseconds of our target. But if I concentrate hard enough, picture the spot, tell myself where and when I want to go, I should be able to make it back an hour or two. Before I showed up at Cassidy's office, before I was framed for his murder, before his agents had a reason to search for me.

I glance around suspiciously, as if anyone – everyone – knows that the dark-haired girl out for a lunchtime stroll is about to vanish in a burst of light as she hurls herself across spacetime. Traveling is chancier than anything I've thought of yet, because if LifeTime is monitoring the grid and realizes I'm self-activating my transponder, they might be able to take control of the signal and divert me to the spatiotemporal coordinates *they* choose – as in, the boss's office twenty-five minutes ago with a circle of armed agents penning me in.

But it's the only thing that might work. My best chance,

if I'm quick and a lot luckier than recent history suggests, of slipping past their guard.

I duck through a hole in the chain-link fence near the exit ramp to Heinz Field. Just beyond, there's an underpass no one uses except when there's a Steelers game. It's dark and musty and smells like a porta potty, plus the ground is littered with needles from your friendly neighborhood junkies. I keep an eye out for the sailing bird shapes of drones that deliver packages and/or monitor for suspicious activity. LifeTime uses them to reconstruct crimes, including some that I've stopped. One could have been hovering outside Cassidy's window, in which case I really do have a big red bullseye painted on my back.

I reach the underpass without apparent incident, stop in the dark to catch my breath and gather my thoughts.

I'll need a few moments to visualize my destination, a few more to activate my core. I'm alone and can't hear any sounds of foot traffic. I take out the gun just in case. If they descend on me while I'm in the act, I'll have little time to shoot, much less aim. If all else fails, I hope my hands are steady enough to turn the gun around and squeeze the trigger.

I close my eyes, breathe deeply, chase the bad thoughts away. Once I've found a rhythm, I center on my core, feel it pulsing within me like a second and slightly lower heartbeat, its energy connecting me to the moment I just left, then the moment before then, then the moment before the moment before then. A whole train of lost moments, each about to be lost all over again as I take myself back to before they ever were.

I call to mind the place I want to go, the time. No one needs to tell me it's one of the most colossally stupid targets I could choose. As has become more and more evident with each passing second, colossally stupid is what I do best.

This could work, I tell myself to regain my equilibrium. *It will work. So long, Miriam. Welcome, Myriad.*

It starts with a tingling in my inner ear, early warning of the nausea to come. Each second is no longer passing but retreating. I see the images parade before me, reminders of the Miriam I was. The Miriam I'll never be again, not exactly.

The final vision is the same as ever.

It's the one I most want to change, the one I'm least able to. The one that set all the others in motion. There's no penumbra in the world strong enough to send me back that far. I can leave the world as it is and step into the world as it was, but I can never escape the memory of that day, which clings to me like the smell of sulfur or the scars my teenage self traced on her wrists.

Sickness clutches me. The pull in my gut is as strong as an undertow. I fall, but not to the needle-strewn pavement. That would provide a soft landing compared to where I'm headed: the gaping abyss of time.

Thursday, August 31, 2017

It seems like I run forever.

Daddy told us on the long drive that our new school would be much bigger than our old one. He said Pittsburgh was much bigger than Lancaster, and the new house we were going to live in with him and Mommy was much bigger than our old house. Plus our other school was only for babies.

This one is for big kids, which is why they put me and Jeremy in different classes.

Mommy and Daddy told us why when they dropped us off. They kneeled in the shiny hallway and put their hands on our shoulders and told us wouldn't it be fun to be in a classroom with other children we didn't know so we could make new friends? When I told them I didn't want any friends except Jeremy, Mommy kissed my head and told me I'd always be best friends with Jeremy, so making new friends would be like getting an extra book at bedtime.

They walked both of us to his classroom door to show me where he would be, and they said I would see him at the end of the day. I hugged him and cried, and he hugged me back until Mommy and Daddy pulled us apart and took me to my room, all the way at the other end of the hall.

So I know where his room is. I remember what the number is above the door. I memorized it in case Jeremy needed me before the school day was over.

And he needs me now. I know it. I can feel it.

I run as fast as I can while the hallway flashes and rumbles like a rainstorm. There are no other sounds except the slap of my patent leather shoes – a first day of school present from Mommy – as I race across the tiles. No other people either, teachers or children. Just me, with my shadow sliding across the black-screened classroom doors.

All the way down the hallway, second door from the end on the left.

When I get close enough to see the door, I find that it's closed like the others, and I worry it might be locked. That's something I never thought about. I'm almost there when it opens and a small figure slips out.

"Jeremy!"

He puts a finger to his lips as he runs toward me.

We collide, throwing our arms around each other. His hair feels scratchy against my cheek from getting it cut the day before, but his smell and his touch are the same.

"How did you get out?" I ask into his hair.

He shushes me again, then takes my hand. "Come on."

We run.

Not back down the hallway. Through the heavy door at this end of the building and up the stairs with the wooden banister and the leaded glass window at the landing. The sound of explosions grows softer when the downstairs door shuts, softer still when we climb the second set of stairs and push the metal bar that opens the door to the second-floor hallway. When that door closes, I can barely hear the sounds at all, though I can feel the floor shaking beneath us.

"This way," Jeremy says, and I let him lead me, because he's holding my hand and I never want him to let go.

The second-floor hallway is lined with paintings and drawings. All of the classroom doors are closed on this floor too, black blinds pulled down in their single windows. There are no noises coming from the hallway, no whispers from the rooms on either side. It feels as if Jeremy and I are the only two people in the whole school.

At the end of the hallway, there's a covered bridge that leads over the parking lot to another building I didn't know was there. A sign says "Middle School" with an arrow.

Jeremy pulls me onto the bridge without slowing down. There are glass portholes embedded in the floor, and as we hopscotch from one to the next, it's like we're walking on air or even flying.

Jeremy glances at me and raises his eyebrows. I giggle. I know it's not a game, but with him it feels like one.

We reach the end of the bridge, where there's a set of double doors with a single window in each. There are no black blinds covering the windows, and when I look through the one on the left, I can see the hallway of the other building. I let go of Jeremy's hand and pull the door handle, but it won't open. I try the other door with the same result.

Jeremy gets a puzzled look on his face, and I laugh because he looks so silly. He turns to me, and I stop laughing when I see the confusion in his eyes.

"Jeremy–"

"This is supposed to be the way out."

"How do you know that?"

"My teacher told me."

"Which teacher?"

"Eddie."

I laugh again, I can't help myself. It's such an un-teacher sounding name. "Eddie?"

"Yeah." He looks around us, but there's nothing to see: only the doors, the bridge, the trees and houses through the bridge windows. "He told me where to go. He said we'd be safe here."

More firecrackers explode, their sound muffled by distance. Jeremy says something, but I can't hear his words over the sound of the firecrackers. I take his hand and try to make him smile.

"We are safe," I say. "We're together."

I'm surprised when he pulls his hand away. His eyes are

angry, not like my brother's eyes at all. "I'm not a baby, Miriam. I can take care of myself."

He's never said anything like that to me, and it makes me angry too. "Go ahead," I say. "See if I care."

"I will."

He takes a step toward the doors, as if he expects them to open by magic. I cross my arms and wait for him to be disappointed.

Then the door on the left does open and a man walks through.

A tall man, as tall as Daddy. His hair is long, just like his body and face. His skin is pale, his eyes shadows beneath his eyebrows. At first I think he's one of the teachers or even the principal, but then I realize he's not dressed in a suit and tie like Daddy wears to work. He's wearing blue jeans and a white T-shirt, untucked. His pale arms are long and thin in a way that makes me think of spiders.

He smiles at us, but I don't smile back.

"Eddie!" Jeremy says. "I came here like you told me to."

"Good boy," the man says in a deep voice. Something about his voice or his eyes makes me scared, and I tug at my brother's hand.

"Run, Jeremy!" I say.

I pull at him, but he doesn't run. He stands as if he's frozen in place, staring at the man. No matter how hard I tug, he won't move.

The man's long arm reaches out toward us, and there's something in his hand, something ugly and black, and I know what it is but can't say the word, not even in my head. I pull Jeremy's hand and scream in his ear.

"Run, Jeremy! Run!"

But he doesn't run.

I feel his pulse through the place where our hands meet, and I know he won't run, can't run, as long as the black thing is pointing at him, so I let go of Jeremy's hand and jump at the

man called Eddie. He's looking straight at my brother, and he
seems surprised when I try to grab the black thing from his
hand. But he's much stronger than me, and he jerks his hand
away and points the black thing at Jeremy, whose eyes open
wide for just a second.

"Miriam?" Jeremy says. "What are you doing?"

Feet pound across the bridge toward us. I see a flash of red.

Then there's a noise so loud it makes my head hurt, and
everything falls apart.

PART TWO
Shooter

CHAPTER 8

From Vax's perspective, I just walked out the door of his hospital room, and here I am walking right back in.

That could explain why he looks even more ghastly than he did an hour ago.

On second thought, maybe *I'm* the one who looks ghastly from taking a jump so soon after being exposed to the other traveler's penumbra. My legs are gumbands, and the conversation that's about to ensue is going to have to wait.

"Miriam," he says, as if it's a question.

I hold up a hand and walk into the bathroom. When I'm done and have rinsed my mouth with cold water, I come out with all the dignity I can muster.

"Shut up," I say. "I have to talk to you."

"I said everything I needed to say."

"That's what you think. But there's more. Just listen."

He opens his mouth as if he's about to object, but I give him a look and he stays quiet.

"First things first," I say. "I don't forgive you."

"I never asked you to."

"Good, because I don't. You might have thought it was incredibly noble to dump me at this particular juncture in my life, but I'm here to tell you: it wasn't."

"I can't keep apologizing for–"

I show him the hand. "Vax, please. Just *listen*."

He closes his mouth, nods.

"Second: I'm in trouble. Or I will be. Might be."

He takes that piece of bizarreness in stride. Admirable, since to my ears it sounds like I just told him I missed my period. "What kind of trouble?"

"Like, world imploding around me kind."

"Could you be more specific?"

I try. For the two or three minutes it takes to fill him in on my latest mishap, the thought is in my mind that the whole thing must have been a setup. That it was LifeTime that shot Vax last night, LifeTime that planted the gun on me that killed the boss, LifeTime that's been pulling the strings since... when? Since forever. There is no *when*, there is no *now*. They could be standing in the hallway even as I speak, waiting for me to finish my confession so I can deliver myself into their grasp.

Vax eyes me the whole time, pokerfaced.

When I'm done, he does nothing but stare. And stare. It's as if the man never heard the expression, *Time is money*. Or, *Holy crap, your ex-girlfriend's life is a five-alarm dumpster fire!*

"*Say* something," I beg.

"You're in trouble," he says. "Or will be."

"I didn't do it, Vax. I mean, technically, I haven't done it yet, but I didn't do it before, either. You have to believe me."

"I'm trying to, Miriam. But here's the part I keep getting stuck on: Cassidy handed you your walking papers, and then someone shot him? As a favor?"

"I know it sounds bad. But I'm not a killer."

"That we know of."

"Vax, *please*. It was – I don't know how this is possible, but it's the only way – it was a traveler, someone who jumped in, put the gun in my hand, pulled the trigger, then jumped back out so fast I didn't see them or even *feel* them. Or maybe they're the one who fired the shot, then put the gun in my hand. I swear it. It had to be someone else."

"Any suspects?"

"A few."

"The guy who shot me last night?"

"He's a strong candidate."

"Or Myriad?"

"It's not out of the realm of possibility," I admit, because that thought has been in my mind as well. "But not *me*."

He shakes his head. "I don't know, Miriam. Someone from another time, maybe even *you* from another time, conveniently shows up right when you feel like killing the boss, to do the deed *pro bono*? It's a lot to swallow."

"You think I'm crazy."

"I think you're not yourself. Like I said earlier, that you're not dealing well with how things went down at the Sleep Rite."

The reminder of his betrayal makes my blood simmer, but I refuse to let him get me off track.

"You can't have it both ways, Vax," I say. "Either you believe I did it or you believe I didn't. If you believe I did it, I might as well turn myself in right now." I take a step closer to the bed, holding out the gun, ready to hand it over. "So which is it?"

He meets my gaze. Shame crashes over me when I realize I'm not the only one in this relationship who's gotten screwed lately. Where was I when Vax was pouring his heart out to me last night? Earlier today? My body might have been right beside him, but my mind was somewhere else, like always.

"I believe you," he says.

I'm so relieved tears sting my eyes. I have enough control not to let them fall. "So what do I do now?"

He purses his perfect lips. "When did you say Cassidy pinged you?"

"Right when I got here the first time. So that hasn't changed so far as I know."

"All right, then. You go back to the office, but this time you're ready. You keep your wits about you, and when the guy shows up–"

"I don't trust myself, Vax. It happened incredibly fast, and I was too sick from the penumbra to see straight. I don't think I'd be able to stop him no matter what I do."

"Unless I come with you."

That pulls me up short. Magnanimous gesture, or ploy to catch me in the act? Either way, it's a nonstarter. "You can't go anywhere. And you wouldn't be much use to me even if you could."

"It's not that bad." He lays a hand on his stomach while his face does calisthenics: squats, planks, crunches. He's breathing heavily by the time he's done. "All right, it *is* that bad. Give me a minute."

He ponders, or maybe he's waiting for the pain to subside. Precious seconds tick by before he looks at me again. "So Cassidy knew about us because of me getting shot?"

"Apparently."

"Then it's simple. We go back and make sure it never happened."

I'm about to laugh when I see he's dead serious. "We can't change what happened last night."

"You think it's a knot?"

"I think I don't want to find out."

He looks at me skeptically. A knot – or a NOT, a Non-Operational Temporality or Node of Time, depending on whether you're talking to one of the specialists or a normal human being – is a recalcitrant event sequence that resists tampering. They're called *knots* because that's what agents who've encountered them say they feel like, tangles you can't untie no matter how long you pick at them. I don't know why what happened last night feels like it belongs in that category, but it does. Maybe because I can't stand to watch Vax nearly bleed out all over again, or because I know there are other things about last night that can never be changed.

But I can't tell him that. "I just don't think it'll work. And we have no way of getting there."

"You traveled a few minutes ago, didn't you?"

"So?"

"So how's your core? Anything left?"

I feel around in my gut, trying to gauge whether there's enough juice to initiate another trip. There's more than I expect, possibly because I was exposed to two consecutive penumbras, but whether there's enough to transport both of us that far into the past is an open question. "Three jumps in a day?"

"Two."

"Two and a half. And what about your core?"

He pats his stomach like he just had a good meal. "Never better."

I'm twisting my hands together, doing my best impression of the ugly duckling at senior musical tryouts. If I keep this up much longer, it'll be a moot point, because LifeTime will have tracked me to the hospital and sicced their agents on me. That must be what makes me decide to go for it. Unbearable as the life I'm currently living is, I can't stand the thought of handing it over to Cassidy's goons.

"All right," I say. "I just hope I live to regret this."

I walk to the bed, sit on the edge, and accept his embrace. He's so close and smells so good – no matter that he's been pickling in hospital air for the past day – it's hard to maintain my concentration. I close my eyes for the second time in no time and try to force everything from my mind so I can focus on my core, direct its energy to wrap around us and hold us together for the long ride.

There's a tiny flick inside me, as if my stomach is my Zippo. I open my eyes to find Vax staring at me, and I know he feels the surge building in his core too.

My eyes close again, and I remember the scene with an intensity I've never felt before. That feeling doesn't last long before the pain hits me, the nausea. I have enough awareness to pull Vax tight, and then we're gone.

Thursday, August 31, 2017

The gun.

The awful explosion.

Red in my eyes, red in my mind, red everywhere. Jeremy invisible in all the red.

Hands clutching, voices screaming. Or I'm the one screaming. Sirens. Possible their wail is mine too.

Bright lights blinding me. More hands on my arms, my hair, my face. Voices. An emptiness that consumes the world.

Darkness.

I wake in the room I share with Jeremy. The blinds are down and the nightlight's on, so it must be past bedtime. Mommy and Daddy are sitting in kitchen chairs by my bed. The other bed is empty, the sheets tucked and the pillows and stuffed animals neatly lined up.

When Mommy sees that my eyes are open, she sits on the bed beside me while Daddy stands behind her. She takes my hand and kisses it.

"Sweetie," she says. "How are you feeling?"

"Where's Jeremy?" I ask.

Mommy cranes her neck to look at Daddy. When she looks at me again, she says in a husky voice, "He's not here anymore, sweetheart."

"Where'd he go?"

"He went," she says, then swallows. "Away."

And they both start to cry.

CHAPTER 9

We land in his kitchen.

The two of us at once, which is both good and bad. Good: the bear hug worked. Bad: it feels like someone played Double Dutch with my intestines.

Vax is dry heaving, his injury not helped by my arms squeezing his midsection. Stars dance in the darkness from the dissipating penumbra, but I find the strength to disentangle myself, avoid his eyes, check his wound. Still clean.

"You OK?" I ask.

He groans softly. "I think you tore another day out of my calendar."

"It wasn't much of a day. For either of us."

I poke my head around the island. We're alone. Shadows and moonlight are the predominant décor. My ears ring from the travel, so I'm not sure if there's anything to hear either.

"Could it have been one of us?" I ask him. "If we're here now, could it have been our own penumbra I felt before you were shot?"

He shakes his head. "This is before. Listen."

I train my ears on the low murmur coming from the room down the hall to our left. Voices, two of them. Male and female. One is exactly the way it should sound, the other a bit off, carried through air instead of cartilage and bone.

"Are you still Myriad? Or Miriam?"

"Who would you like me to be?"

"Definitely Miriam."

"Ta-da! Like it?"

"Very much."

"Well, don't just sit there."

Vax – the Vax leaning against the island beside me, not the Vax commencing his virtuoso routine down the hall – turns to me, nodding significantly. I try not to listen to what follows, but now that my ears are attuned to the sounds, it's impossible to screen them out. The nausea from the jump has faded to a dull knob in the pit of my stomach, but eavesdropping on my own mounting crescendo – especially when I know that my lover ratted me out mere hours before eliciting it from me – makes my gorge rise all over again.

"I wish we could travel," the voice that's close to mine resumes. Apparently this horny bitch doesn't realize her soon to be ex-boyfriend is only humoring her, and she's back to scrounge for seconds.

"You've told me that before."

"So is there a problem? With telling you again?"

A moment's silence.

"You wish we could travel," his voice says.

"When we make love."

"When we make love."

"Because then, we could go back."

"To the moment right before."

"To the moment right before. And that way…"

"That way, it would never end."

The voices give way to the expected. I glance at Vax, hoping I'll find sympathy or at least understanding in his eyes, but he's looking the other way. His apparent composure deepens my despair at changing anything of consequence, certainly not anything that will mend the chasm that's opened between us. We might heal his stomach, get me out of the epic mess I'm in, but I can't overcome the feeling that everything else is fixed, set in stone by the choices I've made or failed to make now, after, before.

Always.

A banshee wail from Yours Truly caps the performance. There's a lull of silence. When the voices start up again, they've reverted to a conversational hum, so low I can barely hear them.

I remember the scene, though, word for word. My own voice breaking, the tears that follow. The deep, inaudible vibration of Vax comforting me, even though he knew while he was doing it that he'd hung me out to dry. The clipped words and raised tone when the argument hits its stride.

The bed creaks again, and there's the sound of bare feet padding across the carpet.

"Shh," Vax says. "It's you."

She glides through the living room in his oversized top, ghostlike but substantial enough to break the glow from outside. She opens the sliding door to the balcony, exits, and closes it without a sound. Her almost black hair is a frizzy nest in the halo of city lights. From where we're positioned to the side of the island, I watch her straddle the lounge chair and shake a smoke from her pack. The dancing flame of the lighter briefly illuminates her face, the one I see only in photographs. When she takes her first drag, the burning ember accentuates the hollows of her cheeks, the puffiness of her eyes. She sighs deeply, and I find myself mimicking her, exhaling smoke I never took into my lungs. Then she gets comfortable and I lose sight of her profile, though I can see the blue cloud of smoke scattering into the night air.

Vax touches my shoulder. I jump.

"I have to stay here," he says, laying a hand on his stomach. "You ready?"

I nod. It's possibly the biggest lie I've ever told.

"Almost makes you want to quit, doesn't it?" he says. Before I can ask what he means, he tips his head toward the balcony. "Disgusting, right?"

I take another look at the shadowy figure relaxing in the

lounge chair, her legs crossed at the ankles, her head wreathed
in a smoky mantle shot through with pulses of orange
lightning. Truth be told, it looks pretty good to me, but Vax is
watching me eagerly, his luminous eyes flicking over my face
in the semidarkness.

"Tell you what," I say. "If we make it through this, I'll
consider using the fraidy-cat version you were trying to push
on me."

"Seriously?"

"*Consider* it. I was thirteen when I pledged myself to a
painful, lingering death, and you know I hate to be a tease."

I remove my shoes and rise to a crouch. He touches my hand
lightly, but I jerk away. Checking first to make sure the gun's
ready for action, I duck around the other side of the island and
creep toward the bedroom.

I move like a shadow, which is what I feel like too.

The path to the bedroom takes me perilously close to the
balcony door, where I worry that being seen by my alter ego
will result in permanent blindness or madness for us both. The
woman outside is too wrapped in reverie to notice her noiseless
twin, however. I know what she's thinking. I'm thinking of him
too, but whereas the day-younger me is wondering whether
the two of us have a future together, the current me has kissed
that future goodbye. Though I know this sister-self is no more
innocent than I am, I find myself envying her, the one who
hasn't felt the smack in the fanny of all the doors she's already
stepped through.

And speaking of doors, I'm standing in front of Vax's right
now.

Soft breaths emanate from within. I lay my fingers gently
against the wood and ease the door open, just enough to see
Vax sprawled on his side, legs jackknifed under the sheet. I
could sneak in there really quietly, slide into bed beside him,
and spoon against his back, feeling the solidity of his naked
body through my clothes. If I had a few extra minutes, I could

try to rouse him, entice him to make love to me. I picture the two of us, him doing what he does best, me knowing this really is the last time and clinging to the feeling I fear I'll never have again, the other Vax out in the kitchen hearing us start up and wondering if he made a mistake, wasn't it pretty good, this thing we had, even if his girlfriend is a complete basket case and no time travel can change that, the guilt building inside the kitchen-him while a very different pressure builds inside the other him until he floods me and I cry out, satisfied at last, now I can die happy, now I am at peace. Oh, Vax, it was worth it, it was definitely worth it. If I only had the time, if I only had the time...

The curtains flutter in a non-breeze.

Vax rolls over restlessly, trying out his stomach before settling on his back. Positioned like that, he presents a perfect target for the one who's about to come through the gateway, the intruder stirring spacetime as if it's his personal gin and tonic. Flashes of light appear at the frame of my vision, while the room inside my head rumbles with the staccato snarl of thunder.

No time, I think, no time. Ready or not, here I come.

"Nice try," a raspy voice calls out from the balcony. "But I'll say *no*, no matter how many times you ask."

I push the door open all the way and step into the room.

It's like stepping into the sun.

A blinding penumbra hangs in the air at the foot of the bed, brighter by far than any I've seen. It flashes and roars, so much energy I can't believe the containment field will hold it. So sudden, too: just a second ago there was nothing in the room but sprinkles of pixie dust, and now I'm staring into the heart of a blast furnace hot enough to melt me to slag.

The nausea is overwhelming, but I take a step forward, shielding my eyes with one hand and holding out the Smith & Wesson with the other. The gun shakes as badly as the last autumn leaf on a tree, and my voice is a close second.

"Who are you?" I shout above the roar.

There's no answer as the man steps through. Man, woman – I can't see anything except a shadowy form, warped against the blaze of light.

My peripheral vision catches a blur of movement from the bed, Vax scrambling for his bedside drawer, clumsy with sex-induced languor. The drawer comes free, spilling contents. The figure in the penumbra extends what must be an arm toward the Glock that's landed on the floor, out of Vax's reach.

"Don't move!" I holler, just as the figure raises the gun. "Drop your weapon!"

Two shots sound at once.

I dive for the penumbra as it implodes. The bedroom window bursts a moment later, spraying me with slivers of razor-sharp glass.

CHAPTER 10

Vax is on the floor, motionless. I cry out and fall to my knees, smearing blood across his bare stomach.

"Easy, partner," he says, opening his eyes.

He sits. The blood's my own, bits of glass from the window having embedded themselves in the back of my hands. The penumbra's gone, blinked out like the traveler who arrived in it. I draw a shaky breath and try to hold it together while Vax looks me over.

"What the hell was that?" he says, which is when I start to laugh or sob or both, I'm in no shape to decide which.

"It wasn't a knot," I say. "Thank God, it wasn't a knot."

His eyes narrow on mine. "You've been here before."

It takes some time to explain.

The Vax who throws on clean clothes and leaves the bedroom with me is not the Vax who traveled here from his hospital bed. That Vax seems to have vanished when I saved his earlier self. This Vax, the pre-shot Vax, knows everything up to the present – his present – which means he remembers last night, the love we made and more or less unmade, the showdown at the Sleep Rite Corral, etc, etc. But he knows nothing about the events that followed, including the all-expenses-paid-by-me trip to the ER, our farewell in his hospital room, and, perhaps most crucially, my fatal encounter with Cassidy.

I tell him most of the above, though I'm cowardly enough not to fill him in on our breakup. Nonetheless, explaining to him that I'm from a future where he almost got killed and our

73

boss went the distance is a bit much, even for a traveling man like him.

Eventually, though, he rolls with the punches. That's what we do. No matter how weird it gets, someone's heard weirder.

Where we go from here, though, is less certain.

If Vax never got shot, does that mean no one at LifeTime will discover our relationship? In which case Cassidy wouldn't have called me to his office, and I wouldn't have jumped back to Vax's hospital room after I was framed for murder. But that means I wouldn't have returned to his apartment to stop him from getting shot, right?

Flip it the other way. If I *was* framed for murder yesterday – sorry, tomorrow – then a week from now, I wouldn't have departed for earlier today to reverse the murder-suicide at the Sleep Rite. Vax would have gone with another partner, presumably one he wasn't also sleeping with, while I'd have been either in jail or on the lam. Which means I wouldn't have been here tonight, and, if the assassin struck, Vax would likely have bled out in bed, thereby rearranging the temporal links to preclude my being framed for shooting the boss in the first place.

Paradox: the essence of time travel, and we try not to think about it too much.

All I know is, the gun's in my hand, and my second self – the smoky chick from the balcony – has pulled her own Houdini. I check the living room rug in case she burned into a pile of ashes, but it's so clean Vax must have run the sweeper the day before. That doesn't explain why the only footprints I can find are my own leading to the bedroom, but like I said, you just have to go with it.

I've learned one thing from tonight's adventure: multiple versions of a single person *can* coexist. Or they can until there comes a merge point in the highway of time, where one *you* joins yourself in action. Maybe it's more like an exit ramp, with one driver getting off while the other keeps going.

But what determines the parting of the ways? And does this mean there are countless Miriams running around all over the place, or only that I happened to return to one version of myself in a life I've already lived?

I can't figure. Take your pick.

I do know, however, that the stay of execution I've been granted is only temporary. Yes, in this altered version of events, Vax hasn't sent me packing yet – but he *has* told LifeTime I'm off my rocker, and for all I know, he did that to justify the breakup he was planning for a later date. This night's fling could still be our last night's fling. Plus, I now know what he's capable of, but he doesn't know I know, which erects even more walls between us. I'm like a fortune teller with a cracked crystal ball, and the people who come knocking at my door are going to be mighty peeved when they discover that all I can read is their past.

Vax pulls me out of my reflections. "It's almost midnight. Don't you need to get back to your place?"

"My place?"

"Your apartment. Where your mom is?"

Dutiful daughter that I'm not, I'd completely forgotten about Mom. This is probably because I'd committed myself to being a fugitive from justice and her the inmate of some musty mausoleum of a senior care facility. Thanks to tonight's mulligan, that future has changed too, at least for the time being.

Mom aside, it makes sense to leave. The shooter might come back. Unless I got him, he can always come back. Vax will check into a hotel, and I'll go back to the life I was living. The only difference is I'll be sleeping alone for the foreseeable future. Maybe a stretch of time without my better half will do me good.

"Come on," Vax says. "Don't forget your phone."

My phone. Of course. The one that's sitting innocently on the nightstand, not the one I chucked in the Allegheny tomorrow.

We run a last check around the place to make sure everything's in order. While Vax packs a bag, I walk down the hall to the living room and scan for things I might have forgotten. Speaking of which, I wish I knew where Me #2 ran off to. I'd love to sit her down, have a chat, compare notes.

That not being an option, I open the door to the balcony and stare at the lounge chair, trying to determine if the wrinkles in the cushion bear a resemblance to my body. I touch the fabric, and I could swear it's still warm. That's probably only the sultry air, unless it's the fever heat of my own fingers.

Vax is coming down the hall. "You ready?"

I nod. It's the second biggest lie I've ever told.

He pulls the balcony blinds, then leads the way to the front door. I look back only once, half expecting to see a shadow standing by the balcony. Laughing at me, no doubt. As if she knows something I never will.

CHAPTER 11

Vax pings a robocab. It seems to take forever to arrive. I'm even more fidgety than usual, and he's the first to figure out why.

"Here," he says. "Try this."

He presses the electromechanical vaping thingy into my hand. I was kind of hoping he wouldn't remember my promise – and, this not being the Vax I made the promise to, I guess he doesn't. But my profligate twin made off with what remained of my pack, so he's got me right where he wants me.

While he watches, I suck tentatively on the tube, inhale, and expel a misty cloud. It doesn't smell or taste right, but it does pack enough of a punch nicotine-wise to satisfy my jangled nervous system.

"What did I tell you?" Vax says.

"You didn't tell me it would taste like wild cherry bubblegum."

"It's adjustable." He shows me a dial.

"Does it have plain old tobacco flavor?"

He studies the symbols, but they're like ancient Greek. "Try again. Maybe you'll get lucky."

Tempting fate, I spin the wheel and take another hit. Watermelon this time, I think. "It's like smoking a Good Humor truck."

"Beats hacking up a lung."

"That's debatable."

He turns away to scan the street for the cab. I monkey with the Vape-O-Matic for a few more minutes before resigning myself to its arcane algorithms.

To give my hands something else to do, I ping Chloe and let her know I'm on the way, though I might be a little late. I get mixed up and call her Loretta, then ping an apology when I spot my mistake. Her return ping is her usual chipper self: "Happens all the time. We're pretty much interchangeable around here." When the robocab's headlights wheel around the corner and Vax squeezes into the seat beside me, I feel like I've fallen into the hands of an old accomplice who's intent on returning me to a life I tried to leave behind. At least he's a canny enough crook to turn on his phone's white noise app in case we're being recorded.

"All right," he says. "Now for a plan."

"You mean where I act like I have the slightest degree of control over the future?"

He chuckles in what strikes me as a perfunctory way. "First order of business: stay away from HQ tomorrow. Spend the day with your mom, catch up on some sleep."

"You realize those activities are mutually exclusive."

This time he ignores my bon mot altogether. "No one's expecting you to show up, so you won't be missed. I have to swing by the office to do some follow-up from the Sleep Rite, and if there's a need, I'll ping you. But I honestly don't see why there would be."

"Unless Cassidy wants to meet with me."

The cold glow of the streetlamps slides across his face, turning it into a time-lapse Picasso, alternating layers of blue and gray. "Why would he want to do that?"

"No reason."

Blue Boy looks at me oddly. Though he and I are as far from being married as any two human beings in the history of the planet – and getting farther with each passing second – it seems I've discovered why it's so hard to keep secrets from your spouse. We've been partners for as long as I've worked this job, and previously, everything I knew, he knew. What's it feel like to withhold from *him* my knowledge that he's withholding a major, life-altering tidbit from *me*?

Hint: not good.

"Fine," I say before he pursues the matter. "I stay home and play patty-cake with Mom, and then what?"

"Then we wait and see."

"Seriously? We're just going to live our lives in hopes that this all blows over?"

"*Au contraire*," he says with a heartbreaking smile. "I've been thinking: what if your theory is right? If there's more than one Miriam, then maybe the Miriam whose gun shot Cassidy isn't you."

"Say what?"

"Hear me out on this," he says. "If we're currently inhabiting a timestrand where I didn't get shot, then when Cassidy met with you originally, he met with a different Miriam, the one who inhabited a timestrand where I *did* get shot. The girl on the balcony or whoever. In which case no one framed *you*. They framed *her*."

"But the girl on the balcony *is* me," I say. "Her life comprises a continuous loop with mine: me on the balcony, you shot in the bedroom, Cassidy calling me in, him getting shot by who they think is me, me doubling back to erase the ledger. She's not another Miriam, she's me."

"Arguably," he says. "Except the way you explained it, you and I were there with our doubles up until the point when you stopped the shooter, and then they disappeared, footprints and all. Where did they go? Into the original timestrand, presumably – the one where I *did* get shot. In that version of events, I went to the hospital, you visited me, then you went to HQ, had a tussle with whoever, ran from Therese, tried to escape the posse by jumping back in time, and so on. Maybe it all worked out for that Miriam, maybe it didn't. If it did, fine, she's safe. If it didn't, then Cassidy's avengers are after *her*, not you. Maybe they've found her by now and she's in custody. Or maybe they've…"

"Killed her?"

He shrugs apologetically. "How would you know? Aside from tonight, have you ever felt the presence of another *you* who might be out there?"

Under different circumstances, I would tell him yes, I have felt them – or I feel as if I've felt them, which is basically the same. At the moment, though, all I can do is stare at this new/old partner who spews random gobbledygook like the worst of the tech guys. Say what he will, Vax can't understand that at least in part, I *am* that other Miriam, the one who bears memories he simply doesn't share.

"Why are you doing this?" I ask him.

"Doing what?"

"*This.* I thought you were…"

"What?"

"Never mind."

He reprises the odd look from before. "It's late, Miriam. It'll seem a lot clearer in the morning."

We settle back in our seats. I watch the Strip District dissolve to Downtown, delis and thrift stores blooming into office towers. This late on a weeknight, there's not much else on the road, which enables the robocab to sync with traffic lights to get us where we're going in a hurry. God help the poor soul who climbs into one of these buggies and doesn't want the ride to end. Within minutes, we've pulled to a stop in front of my condo, and Vax pivots in his seat, waiting for either a goodnight kiss or a swift kick in the crotch, who knows which.

"You OK?" he asks.

I'm about as OK as the vanishing lady from the balcony, but I compose my face in the night window and give him my most dazzling smile. "I'm marvelous."

CHAPTER 12

Chloe meets me at the door. She's got her jacket on, a cute little white number I instantly think would look good on Mom, and is reaching for her purse. She doesn't act put out, though. When I apologize, she laughs in a jolly grandmotherly way.

"How was she?" I ask.

"Like an angel. She's asleep now."

"Thank you," I say for about the twelfth time. "It's been a really long day."

"You get some sleep," she says as she breezes out the door in a wave of Chanel no. 5. My brain is muddled enough that I expect her to give me a peck on the cheek, but of course she doesn't.

I throw my things on the sofa: phone, vaping monstrosity, gun. I feel utterly exhausted, even more so than on a typical travel day. Adding it all up, I've lived almost three days in the past twenty-four hours, and I still have to relive tomorrow. It's possible the human body wasn't designed for this sort of thing. If you don't believe me, gals, just wait and see what it does to your period.

I'm on my way to the bedroom when my phone buzzes.

I read the ping, then read it again. I double-check to make sure it's not an old one that Sibyl bumped to the top of the queue. But no, it's timestamped right now, and what it says is this:

Agent Miriam Randle

You are requested to report to LifeTime HQ promptly at 1100 hours tomorrow.

Dr Cassidy will meet you in his office.
LifeTime. Commitment.

I fall onto the sofa, staring at the phone until the words blur. I try to remember if the phrasing's identical to the pings I received at the hospital. But I can't remember, and *those* messages, thanks to the vagaries of time travel, aren't stored on my phone anymore, never were. If I could compare them, would I find some nuance that makes this one less threatening than the others? Should I make anything of the fact that tonight's ping arrived many hours earlier according to Cassidy's timeframe – close to midnight, which seems peculiar in itself – or that it asks for a late morning rather than an early afternoon meeting? Who sent this ping, anyway? It's unsigned except for the corporate tagline. Were yesterday's signed by Therese, or did I just assume they came from her? Practiced as I am at reconstructing the minutiae of crimes that happen to other people, it seems I'm a hopeless amateur when it comes to my own life.

All of these thoughts, however, are overridden by a sticky feeling deep in my gut: *they know.*

True, Vax wasn't shot, but somehow, they still know. Maybe my partner let something slip when he was telling them about my impending nervous breakdown, or maybe they've been watching us all along. The traveler who's trying to kill him and frame me is still out there, and if this truly is an inside job, it's possible he's the one who sent tonight's ping. Whatever the case, tomorrow is *not* another day. It's the same day all over again.

A second ping startles me, but it's nothing – Angel Care debiting me for Chloe's extra hours. I check my crypto to make sure I'm still liquid, then arrange for tomorrow's care, something I'd counted on not having to do. My balance dwindles precariously close to zilch. I guess that gives me a sense of liberation – the kind you get when you're falling off a ladder and can't stop yourself from saying howdy to the floor

– because I follow up that transaction by sending Chloe the biggest tip I reasonably can. Not purely from guilt this time. If I had the funds to put Mom in a nice home, she'd receive more than adequate care from robomeds. But she wouldn't get the human touch, someone who not only cares *for* her but genuinely seems to care *about* her. It strikes me that I know next to nothing about Chloe or any of the Angel Care staff. When I was interviewing them, all of the discussion was about Mom, not them. Is Chloe married? Does she have kids? She seems to be more than usually flexible if she can work a double shift with practically no advance notice, so if she does have family, she must be blessed either with grownup children or an incredibly understanding spouse. I should find out. The next time she's here, I should fix her a cup of coffee and sit with her in the breakfast nook to talk about *her* life. Frankly, I'm sick of thinking about my own.

I jerk upright, discovering that I drifted off for a minute. I consider going out on the balcony for a cigarette, then remember I've got nothing but the vape tube (aka the Vile Smorgasbord of Death). What I really need is sleep. Clear my head the natural way, prepare for tomorrow. With luck, I'll wake up convinced that I'm being paranoid and all Cassidy wants to do is chew the fat about today's job, pat me on the head, and give me a nice juicy bonus for being such a good little worker bee.

I forward the LifeTime ping to Vax to let him know about the change in plans. I include a special love note – *Don't quit your day job, genius* – then turn the phone off before he can ping me back.

I wander through the apartment as I strip down to my underpants, leaving the clothes wherever they fall. My skin feels scabby, unscrubbed. A shower will only wake me up, so I make my way down the hall to my bedroom, where I lock the Smith & Wesson in the safe.

Images from tonight's grand finale with Vax assail me

as I climb into bed. I try to forget them, forget him, forget everything, but now that I've started down that road, I can't stop. If this truly is to be my first night of enforced celibacy, I don't want to be alone. Pathetic, but true. I don't want to be alone.

I kick free of the covers, grab a T-shirt for decency's sake, and tiptoe down the hall to the room next to mine. My phone's on the sofa, so I enter the lock's manual override on the keypad. I've punched it so many times these past two-plus years, my finger moves without my brain registering the code. The door pops open and I step inside.

Mom's snores greet me. Her room's very basic: bed, low profile chair, Berber carpeting in a neutral shade. When I first made arrangements for her to live with me, I was worried about a variety of things – finances, safety, her mental health, mine – but one of my chief worries was how to furnish her room. I wanted it to be pretty, not because I remembered her liking pretty things but because I wanted her to have them regardless. I dropped another bajillion dollars on a woman who specializes in home design for advanced Alzheimer's patients, and I got some very sensible suggestions for my money. No recesses or jutting angles, no cords or throw rugs Mom could trip or slip on, no lamps or dressers that could harm or confuse her. I wanted to put some paintings on the walls, but the woman told me people with dementia can mistake wall hangings for doors and hurt themselves trying to climb through. I settled for a single big window high up on the wall with safety glass to let in lots of sunlight, along with drapes and wallpaper in soothing colors, mostly blues and purples. Add a few throw pillows and stuffed animals to liven the place up a bit, along with recessed lighting to shed a warm glow, and it's not half bad. Everything is meant to stimulate but not agitate or overwhelm. A nursery, really, but there you have it. Whether it's affected Mom's condition I can't say. I'm fairly confident it hasn't made things worse.

I approach the bed. The nightlight shows her lying on her back, hugging one of the stuffed animals to her chest, a blob that's shaped like a mutated cross between a dog and a rabbit. The one thing the therapeutic decorator recommended but I couldn't provide were mementos from Mom's past: photos, a benign knickknack or two. I simply didn't have anything like that, because Dad threw out all her stuff and deleted our albums when she left. Instead, I ordered a needlepoint pillow with Jeremy's name stitched on it. She sometimes sleeps with it in her arms, but she seems just as happy with Mr Dog Bunny.

"Mom?" I say.

She snores on.

I study her face, the face of the stranger she's become. In the whole time she's been with me, that face has grown no more familiar, neither merging with the face of the woman I once knew nor anticipating the face of the woman I might one day be. After what happened – will happen, might happen – tomorrow in Cassidy's office, I never expected to see her again. If tomorrow does happen (again), I might truly never see her (again). It feels like some kind of reprieve, or even gift, to have her back. Even if I don't really have her. Even if I never did and never will.

I fold down the covers and slide into bed beside her. It's the first time I've slept with her since her return. Could it be the first time ever? Probably not; chances are I slept in my parents' bed during thunderstorms or nightmares when I was a preschooler. Certainly, after Jeremy died, I did no such thing. For the five months between his death and her disappearance, I remember little but coldness and distance, the self-protective cocoon I was too young to recognize as grief. Refusing to let herself feel because feeling hurt too much. Tears start in my eyes as I study her impassive profile.

"I'm sorry, Mom," I whisper. "I never meant to leave you."

She doesn't respond. I kiss her cheek, which is cool beneath my lips. Then I curl up to her and rock myself to sleep.

CHAPTER 13

I wake with Mom's arm draped over me, her breath in my face.

Sweet scene, sour sequel. The prickle in my nose means her Depends are full, possibly overfull. I could wait until Angel Care arrives, but damn it, she's my mom, I'm a semi-functional adult, I should be able to change her dirty nappy all by myself. At least that's something I *can* change.

"Come on, Mom," I say in my most cheerful voice. "Bath time."

Her eyelids flutter, then open. Our faces are so close I'm worried she'll get spooked, but she doesn't. Even with our noses practically touching, she looks through me as if I'm nothing more than shower steam.

I help her from bed, where I catch a stronger whiff and discover that yes indeed, she's overflowed her undies and a runny trickle has traced a path down her leg, not to mention staining the sheets. I'll deal with that later, or leave it for Angel Care. I'm determined to get her bathed, dressed, and fed if it's the last thing I do.

Moving her to the bathroom (also locked) is easy. She's both light and pliant, a breeze stirred by a suggestion. I unbutton her nightie, help her into the shower stall, and peel off the diaper, uncovering pasty skin smeared with yellowish gruel. Standing there naked, she looks exposed, utterly at sea. Her breasts are loose and dangling, her stomach hollow beneath her ribcage, her pubic hair so starkly dark against her pallid flesh it's like a black hole between her thighs. The thin, whitish line of an almost invisible scar, some old injury she suffered during her time on the streets, crosses her stomach a couple of inches above her belly button. She makes no attempt to cover herself, just stands there motionless, her arms crooked at her sides where I last put them.

I take a pair of plant-based rubber gloves from the dispenser, wipe the poop off her, and throw everything down the biomass chute before lowering her onto her shower seat and gently sponging the rest of her clean. The water throughout the apartment is set at a constant temperature so there's no chance of it shocking or scalding her, and the way the shower's designed, the spray won't touch her unless I move her directly underneath. I discovered early on that she's terrified of running water striking her skin, and I had to remodel as a result. I have no idea why this frightens her so, but she screamed hysterically and nearly hurt herself trying to twist away the first few times I tried, and I haven't made that mistake since. This turns shampooing into something of a production, so I have the in-home hairdresser keep her hair short, which gives me the option of handwashing it every third day. My dirty little secret is that I know Chloe won't be able to resist and I can generally avoid doing her hair at all.

When she's so clean she sparkles, I guide her to her feet and pat her dry with a fuzzy towel. She sits upright but unmoving on the bed while I pick out her clothes. Though it's summertime, I choose pants and a striped sweater because she gets cold. Like so much else, I have little memory of how my mom used to dress when she was responsible for dressing both of us, so I go with what pleases my eye. When I look at her this morning, I'm happy enough with the results that I give her a kiss on her pale, dry lips. If I have time, I might make her up, which I never do except when we go for a checkup.

"You look beautiful, Mom," I say, and she does. Beautiful and lost and sad, like an evacuee from a war zone in one of those old photos. I would show her to herself if not for the threat of her being startled by her own reflection.

Next stop is the breakfast nook for coffee (me) and cereal (her). She follows as obediently as a shadow. Maybe sleeping together helped cement some sort of mother-daughter bond. I get her settled, prepare my meal and hers, and sit across the table from her, taking sips of coffee between feeding her spoonfuls of Cream of Wheat. She opens and closes her mouth on cue, and I decide after a minute that I can dispense with the bib.

If every interaction with Mom were as stress-free as this, would I feel the need to leave her with Angel Care so much? Would I spend so many evenings with Vax? Since it's likely I won't be spending any evenings with him from now on, period, I tell myself I can learn to do without. Sex can't be more essential to my wellbeing than quality time with my mom. Given the typical progression of Alzheimer's, it's doubtful she'll live more than another year or two, at which point I can reevaluate my options. It's worth thinking about, anyway. I could even find a job with more flexible hours than...

LifeTime.

It's not as if I forgot what lies ahead. Playing make-believe with Mom might have made today's schedule recede from my thoughts, but the invitation – order – from Cassidy has sat in my gut since I woke up, nibbling at my nerves. Now that it's fully reemerged, I set the bowl and spoon aside, take a deep breath, and appeal to the only other person in the room.

"I'm scared, Mom," I tell her. "I'm really scared."

She makes no response. Her mouth is half open, awaiting the next spoonful. A smidgeon of wheat germ mush sits on her upper lip. I pincer it off with my fingertips. The tiny black hairs that nest beneath the morsel remind me she's overdue for a visit from the home grooming service.

"If I lose this job, I don't know what I'll do," I say to her. "It pays really well, and I won't be able to care for you without it. Maybe I could watch you fulltime, do some kind of online work at night. We could move to a cheaper place. It would have to be remodeled, though, and I just don't know..."

Her eyes blink slowly. I watch her tongue wiggle. I wish I could make myself believe she's about to speak, but the only sound is my own heartbeat pounding in my ears. The greater fear, the possibility that the shooter will be waiting for me today as he was the first time, is too terrifying for me to speak out loud, even to a woman who doesn't understand a word of my soliloquy.

"I'm sorry, Mom," I say. "I don't know what to do."

Just then the visitor alert buzzes, startling me. I run to the sofa and check my phone, where the Angel Care logo appears. The time reads almost ten hundred hours, a good fifteen minutes later than I arranged for them to be here. I guess I was having such a pleasant morning with Mom I lost track.

"I'll get it," I assure her breathlessly. Her mouth has closed, as if her internal clock tells her the interruption in her feeding pattern has exceeded its usual limit.

I rush around the apartment picking up the clothes I discarded last night and throwing on a sweatshirt and pants combo to make myself minimally presentable. The alert buzzes again while I'm at it, which isn't like Angel Care at all. But then, neither is being late.

I adjust my phone to the street view, expecting Loretta or one of the other middle-aged women who fills in when Chloe's off. Instead, I find an older woman standing on the sidewalk in front of the main entrance, arms crossed. Condo rules are to question unfamiliar visitors before letting them in, but she must be from the agency for the logo to show up on my phone, so I tap the screen to buzz her up. Given my last-minute change of plans, I can't be surprised they sent a replacement.

A few minutes later there's a knock at the door. That's a bit flummoxing. No one knocks anymore.

When I switch my phone to the hall view, I see that the strange woman is even older than she appeared in the wide-angle street shot. She's considerably older than Chloe or Loretta, probably a half decade or more older than Mom, who turned fifty-eight in March. Her white hair is pulled back in a bun, her nose prominent and hooked. Over the blue Angel Care smock and a light summer jacket, she wears a knitted shoulder bag I hesitate to call a purse. It's so huge it looks more like the satchels newsboys used to carry way back in the early twentieth century. She's reaching up to knock again when I open the door.

She barges in with her head down, seeming slightly out of breath. The knitted bag – or crocheted, I don't know how to do either and can't tell the difference – is black with a red rose design, and it's definitely her own handiwork, because I hear needles clacking inside. She shrugs it off along with the jacket and looks beside the door for a coat tree, which I don't have (safety hazard for Mom). I'm about to take the items from her when she throws them on the sofa, needles chiming.

Only then does she look at me. She's short, about my height, and unhealthily thin. Her face is a maze of wrinkles, her postmenopausal mustache worse than Mom's. She's wearing her Angel Care nametag so lopsidedly I have to stare for a moment before I can read it: *Opal*. She smiles at me, but unlike Chloe's smile, hers doesn't come naturally to her lips. Her teeth are age-and-coffee-yellowed, and her voice creaks.

"Miss Randle?"

"Miriam."

"And where's our patient?"

All the Angel Care workers call Mom their *client* or *customer*. I decide to give Opal a pass on account of her age, but I'm definitely not getting a warm fuzzy feeling with this one.

I look around for Mom. I'm surprised to find that she's risen from the breakfast chair and stands shyly at the edge of the kitchen, watching me and Opal. Or not watching. Mom never truly watches. Her eyes have drifted in our direction, the way they do when she hears my voice. If she must lose this much of her humanity, I wish she could gain something in exchange – at the moment, the ability dogs have to sniff out suspicious visitors. But she's a blank slate, an augury I lack the finesse to decipher. Opal may be bossy and disagreeable, but she's here – late – and I don't have time to waste on a fuller introduction.

Apparently, neither does she. "Let's get down to business," she says, parking herself on the sofa. "Deborah is late stage, I understand?"

I take the chair next to her. "You can call her Deb. She's on the cusp between Stage Six and Seven. She has significant mobility and responds well to physical direction, but she's nonverbal. Receptive as well as expressive. She needs help with feeding, dressing–"

"Toileting?" Opal says, and I swear she wrinkles her nose.

"I just changed her," I say, then remember the disaster I left in her bedroom. "She had an accident this morning. I'll put on new sheets before I go."

If this were Chloe or Loretta, they'd say, "oh, no trouble," and everything would be washed and dried and folded by the time I got home. Opal simply nods, frowning as if I'm the one who can't control her bowels. "Anything else?" she asks.

"She takes a nap after lunch," I say lamely. "And she likes it when I read to her..."

Opal shocks me with a flat-out laugh.

"She's really very gentle," I say. "She can be a handful at times, especially during transitions, but she's not defiant or anything. Just needy."

Opal eyes me skeptically. I'm surprised the agency didn't provide her with more information about Mom's condition. I'm even more surprised that I'm acting like Little Miss Muffet around this battleax. I want to tell her that Dr Deborah Jane Sayre used to be a professor at one of the premier research institutions on the planet, that she lost her only son, that she's my *mom*, for God's sake, and deserves more consideration than to be treated like a piece of hand-me-down furniture her daughter's too sentimental to throw in the trash. But Opal crosses her arms, indomitable, and I'm silenced by that single gesture. As if I'm finally seeing the truth about my own mother through the eyes of this evil bag lady.

"Excuse me," I say. "I'm running a bit late. I'll go change the sheets while you two get acquainted."

Opal looks like I just told her to stick a straw in a pile of horse flop and take a deep snort, but she stands and approaches Mom while I exit the room.

I grab the vaping gizmo on the way. A red light has come on, and when I take a drag, nothing happens. I consider chucking it out the window, but settle for hurling it to the floor. I'm fuming to myself as I strip Mom's filthy sheets and discover that the mess has soaked through to the mattress, so I march to the hall closet and get out the bucket and rubber gloves and sponge and disinfectant spray.

Once the sheets are in the washer and the filthy water has gone down the toilet and I've restored a measure of equanimity to my breathing, I check the time and see that I'm cutting it dangerously close. I take a quick shower and dress in something more professional than the clown costume I donned for Grizelda, then open the safe and stick the Smith & Wesson in my belt, beneath my loose summer top. After a moment's internal debate, I retrieve the vaping machine as well. I'm not sure how I plan to sneak either item past the smart detector, which won't let unauthorized technology into the building. But I don't want to be in that loft without some form of defense.

I return to the living room to find Opal sitting on the sofa and Mom in the chair. Opal's got her needles out – two needles means knitting, I think – and is clickety-clacking away, pale pink wool unwinding from the skein and burgeoning beneath her fingers. Mom watches with apparent fascination, her head bobbing as if she's following the flash of the needles. It's not the level of engagement I was hoping for from her uber-expensive caretaker, but if it keeps Opal's trap shut and her customer occupied, I'll call it a fair trade.

Opal looks up as I enter, though her needles don't pause for a second. "You should get the shot," she says.

"The shot?"

She nods at the device in my hand. "Stop smoking shot. Works like a charm. I haven't had a cigarette in five years."

"Oh." So now this crone is objecting to my personal habits? Isn't that what Vax is for? "I never smoke around Mom."

"Your business," Opal says with a shrug, and goes back to her uninterrupted activity, needles flying under liver-spotted hands.

I glance at my phone. I don't have time for a confrontation, but I've had it up to here with this one. "Excuse me," I say, taking a step toward her. "I'm going to need to see your credentials."

Her head snaps up. "What?"

"Your credentials. You're new, and I–"

"I've been with the agency for six years."

"But you've never been *here*. And I need to make sure "

She flings the needles onto the sofa. Huffs, puffs. Seems about to blow the house down. Instead, she digs inside her gigundous purse and pulls out her phone, then shoves it at me and sits with arms crossed while I read.

Sure enough, she's a licensed homecare worker for Angel Care. A "senior" worker at that, by which I suppose they mean she has seniority, not that she's an old hag. I feel mingled disappointment and relief at the discovery. I'd have loved to throw her out on her ass, but then what would I have done with Mom? I offer the phone as an inadequate olive branch, and Opal snatches it from my hand.

"Now, if I can get back to work," she says with a glare, reaching for her knitting. Which, it seems, is as close to "work" as she's likely to get.

We turn into a tableau. I breathe evenly and uncurl my tightly clenched fists. Opal knits on, vindicated. A shawl, looks like. Mom seems sleepy from the flashing needles. That's probably a good thing.

Before I leave, I run down a quick list with her caregiver. What to make for lunch, where the adult diapers are stored, how to lock the bedroom door. At the last minute, I remember to tell her to use a washcloth instead of running water if she needs to clean Mom's face and hands. She grunts after each item, but says nothing.

When I can't come up with anything else that would allow me to pretend I don't have somewhere urgent to go, I pocket my phone and lean down to give Mom a kiss on the cheek. Her eyes are almost closed, so I'm surprised by what happens next.

She tilts her head to receive my lips.

It's a tiny thing, the kind I wouldn't notice if I didn't scan her constantly for signs. So utterly normal for any mom other than my own, my heart lifts from its funk and I could throw my arms around her and squeeze for joy, Opal be damned. When my lips retreat, she reaches up and touches the spot with her fingertips, and it's all I can do to hold back tears.

"Thanks, Mom," I whisper in her ear.

Opal raises an eyebrow, but I flee before she can utter a parting curse.

CHAPTER 14

Sparring with the sitter means I'm no longer simply pressed for time but positively flattened by it. There are no cabs in sight, so I fast-walk up Seventh Avenue toward headquarters. My ugly-but-functional work shoes would have been best for the half-mile hike, but at least I had the sense not to wear heels. If I can keep up this pace, I should arrive with a minute or two to spare.

I've made it halfway when it occurs to me to check my phone for Vax's response to last night's ping. I turn it on and am bombarded by a barrage of return pings that range in time from immediately after I sent mine to less than five minutes ago. The first one sounds the way he always sounds: calm and confident, cucumber-cool.

Not to worry. Sure Cassidy only wants to clear up some details about the SR.

From there until roughly two in the morning, a series of follow-up pings – each one spaced about fifteen minutes from the previous – echoes that theme, allowing for rhetorical variations.

Nothing unusual about this, right? Event sequences replay all the time.

QC wasn't totally clear on a few points, which is why I have to come in. Must be something like that with you too.

Stay loose. We'll talk later.

It's when he starts pinging again, at around six-thirty, that the messages populate with ever-accelerating frequency and a manic tone I've never, repeat never, heard from Vax. From the sound and pace of them, he must have been busting to send them all night and restrained himself only out of consideration for me. I can't figure out if he's playing some kind of sick game or if he's lost his marbles entirely.

Let's talk before you go. Can't hurt to have a backup plan.

Did Cassidy say ANYTHING about what he wants?

You're taking the gun, right?

If I'd received each ping as it arrived, they'd have been unnerving enough. Reading them all at once, they scare the living shit out of me. As does the very last one, which shows up as I'm scrolling through the others.

Don't go alone. I'll meet you.

No sooner do I read that than a robocab swerves across the yellow line as they're programmed not to do and Vax, true to his word, jumps out. I stop in my tracks, feet throbbing, only to watch the cab roll away to pick up some other fool who's pinging it down the street.

"Miriam!" Vax calls out. "Are you OK?"

"Dandy."

"Did you get my... what's wrong?"

His hands are outstretched as if to catch me before I fall. I have no intention of giving in to any such maidenly weakness, so I shove the vaping doohickey at him.

"Here," I say. "It's broken or something. A light went on."

"The Vape Master?"

"Please tell me that's not its real name."

He studies the torture device for a second, then hands it back. "It needs a recharge."

"It needs a lot more than that."

"Let me..." He searches his pockets, comes up empty. "The charger must be at the office."

"And I must be right here," I say. "So if you'd step aside, I'm going to go get my butt busted by the big boss. In my own uniquely alliterative fashion."

I walk away, but Vax catches up in a couple of long strides. I'd tell him to scram if my lips weren't locked tight. I feel stunned, like a beef cow that got shot in the forehead and hasn't figured out it's dead. Stunned that I was called to HQ, stunned that nothing has changed, stunned that my morning idyll with Mom was spoiled by a refugee from the local coven. Stunned that the man who hinted that he wants to share his life with me could betray me like he did. Most of all, stunned that after who knows how many nights in his arms, I can't bring myself to tell him the truth about anything.

"Listen, Miriam," he says. "I'm sorry if I freaked you out. I just got a little…"

"Freaked out? As I strolled to my doom?"

"I'm really sorry," he says. "I was shacked up in this dive on Route 30, and I couldn't sleep, and I started thinking about getting shot the first time around, and I guess my imagination got the better of me. I still maintain that today's meeting is routine, but I figured we should have a plan just in case."

"And why should *we* have a plan? When it's *me* who's neck-deep in doo-doo?"

That stops him for no more than half a second. "So OK, listen. I'll go in first, then you follow a couple minutes later. You bring the gun?"

I hike up my top an inch to show him the goods.

"Give it to me," he says. "I brought an EFD, and that should be enough to sneak it past the detector. I'll return it once we're inside."

"Where'd you get your hands on that kind of hardware?"

"Long story. Just let me have it, OK? I promise to give it back."

He actually smiles. I'm torn – or to be more precise, I'm ripped down the middle, lit on fire, then fed through the shredder – but the part of me that can't say no to Vax's smile is apparently the only part that remains.

"How are you going to get it back to me?" I ask.

"I'll meet you outside the restroom."

"Good. Because on top of everything else, I have to pee."

We sidle up to an office building in case there's a drone watching while I slip him the gun. Our hands touch briefly, but I'm not going to make a federal case out of that. I've never seen an electromagnetic field dampener before, and I have no idea how big they are or what they look like. I do know they're not the kind of accessory that frontline agents just happen to carry around on their day off. I'm desperate enough at present not to ask questions, but if I survive today's meeting, I won't be satisfied until he spills the whole tawdry tale.

"Let's go," Vax says after we've made the swap.

Time's a-wasting, so we race each other up Liberty toward headquarters. Before we cross Tenth Street, he comes to a stop.

"OK, look," he says. "I'll be one floor down with the QC guys. Ping me at the first sign of trouble."

"My middle name."

"I thought it was Louise."

"Ha, ha."

"We'll go out for a drink afterward. Have a good laugh." And then he says it: "Maybe something more."

"*Something more?*" I say. "There is nothing more, Vax. I thought we made that pretty clear."

His smile falls. "We did?"

"Well, *you* did. When you told QC I'm unfit for service."

He opens his mouth, looking uncomfortably like Mom when she has nothing to say, which is all the time. "I'm..."

"Contrite? Flabbergasted? Spit it out, partner, because I'm just dying to hear."

"I never told QC you were unfit for service. I told them I fucked up the job and you saved my neck."

"Please," I say. "You sat there in your hospital bed and spilled your guts. After your guts got spilled, I mean." When he still looks blank, I add, "Time travel, remember? As in, I was there the day after you got shot?" More blankness. "As in *today*?"

"Miriam." He waves his hands as if he's appealing to my better judgment, something he should know by now I don't have. "I swear to you, I never said anything like that. It wasn't me in that hospital bed. Or it was, but you changed that outcome."

"Nice try, but you had your little chat with QC *before* I fixed things. You're still the *you* you were then. Don't try to make this go away with one of your quantum card tricks."

"That's not what I was doing. I was trying to explain–"

"That you asked me to move in with you three hours after you sold me down the river?"

"That I didn't say what you think I did. You've had a long day. Are you sure you didn't, I don't know, have a bad dream or something?"

"Right, now *I'm* the one who's making things up." I pull the vape machine out of my pocket and practically throw it at him. "I'm sick of this, Vax. We're through."

He says nothing, just stands there staring at the gizmo like it's some kid's toy he doesn't know how to put back together. The traffic light changes, the friendly voice comes on encouraging pedestrians to cross, but he doesn't budge.

"It's two minutes before eleven," I say. "In case you forgot that too."

He looks up from his hands. "So it's over?"

"It's never been anything *but* over, Vax. There are some things in life that can't be changed."

He nods – once, twice, three times, as if he's running a road test on his ability to nod. Just yesterday – today – I would have found it impossible to resist his hangdog look, but it seems he's finally exhausted my ability to forgive him.

"Oh, what difference does it make?" I say. "Let's go in there and get this travesty over with."

He nods once more, but won't look at me. Gun in belt and EFD secreted somewhere on his person, he crosses Tenth Street and vanishes into the revolving-door maw of my soon-to-be-former place of employment.

Which leaves just me, myself, and I, stranded on the corner with my heart hammering and my breath badly out of whack.

I rest my hands on my hips and breathe through my nose until the tightness in my chest subsides. I wish I could ask the big blue genie for something – another chance, another moment, another life – but he's out of wishes so far as I'm concerned. I wait until the light turns against me, then cross the street and enter the building.

CHAPTER 15

The first surprise is that Therese isn't at the front desk. It's some other tall, svelte woman I don't recognize, her dark hair piled high with chopsticks, her face bone-white and her eyes smeared with greasy kohl like a bargain basement Kabuki actor. Her nameplate reads *Sabine*. She looks me up and down with distaste.

"Agent Randle," she says loftily. "Dr Cassidy will see you now."

"Therese out sick?"

"She'll be in later today," is all she deigns to tell me before she points her button nose in the air and turns to her computer.

"I need to use the bathroom," I say inanely, to which she responds as any halfway sane person would: not at all.

I weave across the lobby to the restroom. Just as I get there, Vax pushes open the door and hands me the gun as he brushes past. He disappears without a word or a look. There are cameras all over the lobby, so I play it as cool as I can, ignore him and use the swinging door to block me from surveillance while I tuck the gun securely behind my back.

I really do have to pee, but Cassidy's waiting for me and I can't very well manage the toilet with the Smith & Wesson shoved up my butt. I splash cold water on my face and blow it dry, then exit the room. If all goes well – the shooter doesn't reappear, the boss doesn't revoke my potty privileges after he cans me – I can hold it until we're done.

Déjà vu sets in as I cross the atrium. Marble stairs lead

upward, I hold the polished balustrade, blah blah blah. The only difference is I'm armed this time and even more dry-mouthed than before, when I didn't have any idea what kind of shit storm I was walking into. I check my phone to make sure it's ready to ping Vax if need be, then exit the stairs to Cassidy's office.

Nothing has changed that I can tell. Same light, same view. Cassidy's turned away from me in his swivel chair, same as it ever was. I pound the hardwood and he swivels at my approach, waiting for me to sit. The feeling of sinking into the dunce chair while he perches on his throne is all too familiar.

"You wanted to see me, sir?" I ask, just to switch things up the teensiest bit.

"Agent Randle," he says. "We have a problem."

No fucking kidding.

He taps the desk to activate the screen. I'm expecting my contract to pop up. Instead, there's a still shot derived from body cam footage, timestamped yesterday, Monday, August 31, 2037, at 1235:52 hours. At the top of the screen, across from the timestamp, is the name of the agent who recorded the footage: RANDLE, M. I catch my breath when I realize I'm watching video from the Sleep Rite Motor Lodge, Room 11, just seconds after I entered: bed, lamp, painting, cuckold, all where they're supposed to be, the latter's jowls lit by my dissipating penumbra.

Vax was right after all. This meeting *is* about yesterday's job, not about my extra-contractual activities. Then again, given how badly yesterday's job went, not to mention that QC saw something alarming enough to expedite my body cam footage to Cassidy's desk, I'm not getting my hopes up.

"I've been reviewing the record from yesterday," Cassidy says. "I've noted a number of irregularities in your and Agent Vaccaro's operation that led to its untoward outcome. I'd like to discuss them with you, if I may."

He advances the footage. Vax arrives, and I listen to our

exchange with the husband. I see beyond a shadow of a doubt what I suspected the first time: the not-yet-murderer *was* about to hand the Smith & Wesson over if his wife and partner hadn't entered the scene at just the wrong moment. Cassidy pauses the recording the instant the buck-naked couple appear, which makes me squirm for no good reason.

"Did you notice the irregularity?" he asks.

Other than the fact that two people are about to get their brains blown out all over again? "Well…"

He replays the clip. The spectral light of the screen illuminates his face, but his eyes seem not to participate in the glow.

"Right there," he says, pausing on a shot of Vax, whose body is surrounded by a filmy penumbra. "You'll notice that Agent Vaccaro has taken a secondary position out of compliance with mandated procedures."

"It was a small room."

"But not a small matter, as it increased the risk involved in accessing your target."

"Our target?"

"The offender." He advances the footage, pausing ten or fifteen seconds after the wife and business partner emerge from the bathroom. It seems he loves showing me that part, like a creepy uncle screening a stag film for his sister's kid in the basement.

"Wait," I say.

"You notice the irregularity."

"Play it again. One more time."

He's only too happy to. When he freezes the film and I've determined that I wasn't hallucinating, my face grows clammy with sweat.

"That's not how it happened," I say.

He frowns, and I can't blame him. It sounds insane.

We're watching my own body cam footage, but what it shows me is *not* what I witnessed yesterday. In that version of events, the duo's appearance made the aggrieved husband decide to hang onto the gun. In this one, he places it meekly on the bed and backs away, holding his hands in the air like I told him.

"You can appreciate why this recording has us so concerned," Cassidy says. "Your assignment, as attested to by both yourself and Agent Vaccaro during mission debriefing, was to disable the target and retrieve the murder weapon, peaceably if possible, forcibly if necessary. In either event, without risking the safety of our client. But as you're aware, that is not what transpired."

"Our client?" I ask. "And who was that, exactly?"

He looks annoyed. "The part-owner of the Sleep Rite Motor Lodge."

"You said he was our target."

"The *other* part-owner," he says. "The man with whom we contracted to prevent a repeat of yesterday's murder-suicide."

My head is spinning, and not only from the mismatched body cam footage. So far as I know, LifeTime doesn't *contract* with sleazy business owners; it cleans up murders for the city. Business owners aren't privy to what we do, so how can we contract with them? "I don't–"

"Agent Randle." He folds his hands on his desk like a principal explaining to the class clown why he's failing tenth grade. "As I'm sure you're aware, there's a substantial monetary value – and risk – in matters of life and death. The unfortunate incident that occurred in the Sleep Rite Motor Lodge exposed its surviving owner to substantial legal liability, not to mention lost revenue. When we reached out to him and offered our services, he was eager to restore the balance sheet to its prior status quo."

"But he was having sex with his partner's wife!"

He sniffs. "We don't concern ourselves with externalities. What worries me is that we're in breach of contract due to your and Agent Vaccaro's negligence, and in damage-control mode as a result. This isn't a question of private morality, Agent Randle. It's a matter of the company's bottom line."

I rest my head in my hands, massaging my temples as if that might make his words make sense. I know something about LifeTime's corporate philosophy from the training manual we reviewed the first day on the job. I learned that the feds were on the verge of swooping in and taking over the company for non-civilian applications, but LifeTime successfully lobbied for autonomy on the grounds that we provided a cost-effective alternative to traditional policing. Never in a million lifetimes would I have dreamed that our primary reason for existence was to help insurance cheats and other lowlifes cook the books while slipping it to someone else's wife. It makes me reevaluate all the cases I've had, wondering whose interests I was serving. Has it always been this way, or has something inexplicably changed, the way the footage on his screen has?

"It's not uncommon," he says, and for a second I think he's answering the question on the tip of my tongue. "Younger employees are prone to misconstrue the agency's mission. We don't encourage such misapprehension, but neither do we seek to reeducate those who are passionate about saving lives and righting wrongs. In the long run, most of our agents learn that revolution makes not only for bad life decisions but for bad business. So we let time take its course, confident that, once they've seen enough, our recruits will accept the limitations of what they can change in the real world. Certainly, after six years on the job, your Mr Vaccaro harbors no such illusions."

"He's not *my* anything."

"He was your partner during yesterday's botched job," he says. "And as such, he bears equal responsibility for its outcome."

He advances the recording a few more seconds, to a point where the husband has retreated against the wall, hands in the air, while the wife and business partner come out of their passion-trance sufficiently to realize they're not alone in the room.

And now I'm definitely seeing things.

Because after disentangling herself from her lover, it's the *wife* who picks up the handgun, then stands there stark naked waving it around and screaming bloody murder at her husband while Vax and I try to settle her down. I hear my recorded voice saying, "Ma'am, you don't want to do that," then the husband shouts something the mic doesn't pick up. Vax dives toward the wife, and the next second, there's a shot. Cassidy freezes the video again. I can see the muzzle flash from the wife's gun, but the husband hasn't gone down yet. It's as if the boss's finger is quicker than time, catching the bullet in midflight.

He lets me admire his artistry for a moment, then advances the proceedings a few seconds more. Though my body cam is juddering all over the place and there's so much noise from the screaming and the TV and the shower it's hard to reconstruct the exact sequence of events, the denouement is indisputable: the husband's body slumps on the floor, the wife puts the gun to her temple and pulls the trigger. By ghoulish chance or design, Cassidy freezes the image at the very moment of her death, her lover's horrified face washed out to the point of transparency and his eyes glowing like a cat's in the fossilized burst of light.

Cassidy leaves everything that way for a second before shutting the video off. "Now, Agent Randle. What do you have to say for yourself?"

I'm too shell-shocked to say a word. *That's not how it happened*, I keep repeating in my head, the same way I used to repeat to myself over and over when I was a little girl, *let it not be true, let Jeremy still be alive, let it not be true...* I know time travel plays tricks with your mind. I know events turn out differently when you go back. If they didn't, I'd be out of a job.

But I also know what I saw in that motel room, and it wasn't this. Whose recording did I just watch? Which Miriam lived through that scene? And how could she be the same Miriam who turned in her body cam to QC along with her Beretta yesterday afternoon, then went out for a last tango with Vax?

"Agent Randle?" Cassidy prompts.

"Sir?"

"Do you have any explanation for your and Agent Vaccaro's performance?"

"It was a complicated job…"

He tsks at this. "All of our jobs are complicated. That's why failure to adhere to protocol is an invitation to disaster. You were briefed on mission objectives when you accepted this assignment, Agent Randle?"

"I guess so…"

"And yet you and your partner failed to respond appropriately under field conditions. As a result, the operation was compromised and the company's standing besmirched. All because you declined to follow proper procedures."

"We…"

"Yes?"

I can't continue. Even if I could, this version of Cassidy would think I've lost my mind.

"Agent Randle?"

"We made a mistake. I'd like to ask for the opportunity to go back and set things right."

"That would be a contravention of company policy," he says. "As well as a squandering of company resources. A forensics team has begun the work of reconstructing the events of yesterday afternoon, and, if warranted, a mop-up team will return to the Sleep Rite Motor Lodge at the conclusion of their investigation."

My head is way past spinning by now. It's kissed my neck goodbye and is flying around the loft, buffeted this way and that by the crisscross currents of our first interview and this one, snippets of what I think I remember tangled with language that's almost certainly brand new. That my own responses slip so readily into today's altered reality makes me feel like a marionette dangling at the end of Cassidy's strings, even if he has no idea he's the one pulling them. Who's running this show, anyway?

"In light of the detrimental effect on the company's interests"
– his voice startles me from my thoughts – "I'm afraid we have
no choice but to place you and Agent Vaccaro on suspension
without pay. Effective immediately."

"Does Vax know about this?"

"Agent Vaccaro's case will be reviewed later in the day."

I don't know whether to be thankful or ashamed that both
me and Vax are taking the fall this time. After all I've been
through the past seventy-two-hour-long day, the last thing I
expected was for the boss to turn into an equal opportunity
asshole.

Cassidy calls up a document on his screen and shows me
where to sign. I read it listlessly, discovering that it lays out
the terms of suspension without pay, legal mumbo-jumbo
about how the agent so disciplined can appeal their suspension
through thus-and-such channels and, if denied, exercise the
right to apply for reinstatement after six weeks pending a
battery of psychiatric examinations and a retraining regimen
(at agent's expense), that during such period of suspension
and forevermore into perpetuity said agent agrees to remain
bound by the NDA initially signed upon accepting an offer of
employment from LifeTime Law Enforcement, LLC, limitation
of liability, fine print, boilerplate, the end. But what's it to me?
I sign the thing with a finger – no need to guess which one –
and am getting up to leave when Cassidy stops me.

"One final word, Ms Randle."

Ms Randle. Just like that, just like that.

"It's come to my attention that the handgun responsible for
killing our client's business partner and paramour has gone
missing from our crime lab," he says. "There's no evidence
the storage receptacle was tampered with, but the gun itself
is gone."

"And?"

"We wonder if you might have any insight into its
disappearance."

"Are you suggesting I took it?"

"Not at all."

"Or that Vax did?"

"Ms Randle." He leans forward in his chair. "A key piece of evidence in a criminal investigation has been misplaced. You and Mr Vaccaro were the last persons to handle it before it was assessed by our ballistics team. I thought you might have some clue as to its present whereabouts."

"Well, I don't." I say this with a straight face, which isn't easy considering the handgun in question is currently tickling my fanny.

"Then perhaps you can explain why the gun you delivered to our team was not the weapon involved in yesterday's murder-suicide."

"I beg your pardon?"

He reclines in his swivel chair, a satisfied smile plastered on top of his Teflon tan. Looking like the big bad wolf he is, now that he's got me lined up in his sights.

"When ballistics ran tests on the weapon you submitted," he explains, "it was found that the older-model Smith & Wesson M&P 380 hadn't been fired recently. We're awaiting the results of more comprehensive tests, but based on available evidence, it seems the missing gun hadn't been fired for a number of years."

"That's impossible," I say. "You saw the footage. That was the gun."

"That was *a* Smith & Wesson M&P 380. It was patently not *the* Smith & Wesson M&P 380 that you and Mr Vaccaro handed over to our forensics lab."

I sink back in my chair. The words *this can't be happening* replay in my head, along with the words *that was the gun.* I barely listen through the whispers as he explains that they'll be watching me and Vax very closely from this point forward and that our transponders will be deactivated before we depart the premises to prevent unauthorized travel and that the company prosecutes quite vigorously those who seek to drag its reputation through the mud. That's my cue to split, so I push myself from the chair. "I assume I'm dismissed?"

He does a double-take. I guess he wasn't finished.

"Please report to HR to turn in your badge and schedule the decommissioning of your LifeTime transponder," he says. "And have a nice day, Ms Randle."

He shows me his back. I consider a parting shot, weigh the risks of telling him to drop dead. What are the odds at this point?

I'm turning to go when fate blows me an answer.

CHAPTER 16

Nausea. The shakes. Abrupt depressurization. I wish I could say I was ready for the physiological assault this time.

But I'm not. I find myself on my knees, a hand braced against the floor. I have just enough presence of mind to reach behind me and pull out the Smith & Wesson before I glance up.

Cassidy has turned to regard me. Whether he recognizes the gun is immaterial. His face is mottled red and white. A penumbra pulses behind him.

It's only as bright as the sunbeams piercing the lunette window, nothing compared to the maelstrom from Vax's room. That gives me a clearer view of the figure hanging upside down at its center like a life-size Tarot card. He's wearing casual dress, jeans and a white T-shirt. Long brown hair crackles with static electricity. The penumbra breaks up and the light subsides, but I can't make out the traveler's face in that position.

Then he turns over, revolving in space until his feet touch ground. His eyes open, dark holes in a sallow face. His features are imprinted on my mind with the crystal clarity of nightmare.

His hair is long, just like his body and face. His skin is pale, his eyes shadows beneath his eyebrows.

His jeans are the same, as is his T-shirt. This time, though, he's unarmed.

I point the gun at his face. "Hands up, motherfucker!"

Cassidy's complexion turns purple. When he realizes I'm not talking to him, he swivels and sees the man, the last wisps of the penumbra swirling around him like dry ice. Something that sounds like "regent!" comes from the boss's throat. The word is thick and sloppy, as if he's gagging on it.

Then the traveler launches himself over the desk, kicking the older man from his chair and reaching for me.

For my gun.

He knocks the wind out of me, drives me against the hardwood. His hands are large and oddly cold, steel vises clamping my wrist. No matter that I'm twenty years older than I was that day in the middle school annex. He's still much stronger than I am, and he could easily disarm me if something – the penumbra, the headlong dive – didn't make him clumsy, uncoordinated. I roll hard to the left, landing on top of him, my hand coming free of his grasp. I plant the gun between his eyes, a ring of bloodless flesh forming around the barrel.

"Beg for mercy," I tell him. "You won't get what you wish for."

His eyes find mine. They're dark as bruises, dark as pits.

"I already did," he says.

The floor creaks. Cassidy stands above us, weaving on his feet but brandishing a snub-nosed pistol he must keep in his drawer. My attention's drawn from my adversary for only an instant, but it's enough.

The Smith & Wesson jerks away from the traveler's forehead. He's got my hand in both of his, pointing the gun, squeezing my finger on the trigger.

The blast and recoil give him the distraction he needs to shove me aside. Cassidy's body thuds to the ground, hot wetness splattering my face. I feel like I'm choking on a jug of blood. The traveler stands above me, pointing the gun. He could shoot me so easily. I almost wish he would.

Instead, he smiles. Blood rims his teeth.

"Who are you?" I scream.

"Our name," he says, "is Legion."

A second penumbra opens. There's a sound of thunder played in reverse. He drops the gun and leaps through the portal, and I'm alone.

But only for a second.

Vax catapults over the top stair. Quickly, he assesses the damage. He rushes over, kneels beside me to determine if I'm OK. The bloody mess that used to be Cassidy he doesn't bother to check.

"Miriam—"

Heels click behind him, Sabine understudying for Therese in this encore performance of today. Vax grabs the Smith & Wesson, holds me tight.

"Let go," I say.

"We're out of here," he breathes.

I feel the power thrumming through his core, igniting my own. Gunfire crackles. I don't know who shot who. I try to hold on to the present as my surroundings dim, the memory I'm forced to relive again and again turning the solid world to smoke.

Oblivion enfolds me, but it's never long enough.

Friday, September 1, 2017 – Tuesday,
September 1, 2037

Was there a funeral? Am I in the grave with him?

I remember only the man, the gun, the blast, the red, the dark. The pit I fell into, the one it feels I'm still trapped in today.

And everything in between linked to that one lifelong moment.

The day my brother died, and I with him.

PART THREE
Thief of Time

CHAPTER 17

A week ago.

Tuesday, August 25, 2037. 2212:15 hours.

Vax had the foresight to charge his core while I was meeting with Cassidy, which gave him the boost to jump us back this far. I empty my already empty stomach in a convenient garbage can, then panic at the thought that Mom's alone. I scramble for my phone and check my backdated schedule, discovering that I arranged for her to be with Chloe until midnight. With relief, I remember that Vax and I had just wrapped up a quick and easy case, one that took a mere three days to reconstruct. We'd stopped a guy from depositing a package bomb on his ex's front stoop, and I guess the lurid details of someone else's romantic escapades got our sick little motors racing. That rationale has changed, but we needed breathing room, and now we've got it.

"Give me the gun," I say to him.

"What happened back there?"

"Just give me the fucking gun."

"Maybe I should keep it."

I hold out my hand. He hesitates, but relents. I stick it in my belt. I don't want to feel the metal against my skin.

We wander the near-empty streets of Pittsburgh's East End until we encounter a crappy saloon, basically the grogshop equivalent of the Sleep Rite Motor Lodge. A chrome-railed bar emerges from an atmosphere opaque with smoke, a fifties era jukebox crouches in the corner. There's a vintage cigarette machine by the door, the kind with pull handles, but they've jerry-rigged it to accept crypto. At present, it's out of every brand except Kools – menthol, ick – but I buy a pack while Vax is at the bar, then ignore him when he reminds me we shouldn't leave a credit trace. For once, he says nothing when I tear open the pack, just hands me my beer and selects a stool at a respectful distance, close enough to ward off the speech-slurring clientele but far enough to give me the space I need after what happened ten minutes ago. What won't happen again for another seven days.

I'm halfway through the pack before I finish my beer. I haven't said a word to Vax about my meeting with Cassidy, the temporal anomalies, the fact that, on top of being fugitives from justice, we'll both be unemployed a week from now. I keep downing sips of beer interspersed with lungfuls of smoke until he breaks the silence.

"You saw the guy?"

"I saw the guy."

"And?"

"It was him."

"Him?"

"*Him*. You know, the reason I can't sleep at night?"

"You're sure about this?"

I choke on a mouthful of beer and mentholated carcinogens, both of which seem to have gone down the reverse passageways. "I'm sure."

"And his name was…"

"Eddie. Cassidy called him Regent."

"Eddie Regent. That mean anything to you?"

"No. But he called himself Legion."

"Eddie Legion?"

"It's not a last name. It's a reference to the Bible. The Gospel of Mark. A demon who possessed a man."

"Legion's just a word, Miriam. It could mean any number of things."

"Not to me. He knows."

"Who knows what?"

"He knows!" I say shrilly. The barkeep glances over to see if my date is giving me trouble, but Vax smiles reassuringly and leans close, speaking softly to me.

"Take it easy, Miriam."

"I can't," I say. "I can't. Oh God, he's back. I can't do this again…"

My eyes fill and overflow. Vax edges closer and lowers his voice so only I can hear. His tone is soothing, his words too soft to make out. Maybe they're not even words but just sounds. I hate that he's babying me, but I hate even more that it's exactly what I need. I draw a shuddering breath, close my eyes, and begin to talk.

"It was a few months after Jeremy died," I say. "My mom took me and my dad to this little storefront church in Millvale. It was wintertime, just before Christmas. The preacher scared the hell out of me. He told us we were like the man in the story, and the demon was the evil inside our hearts. My dad had heard enough and refused to let me near the place after that, but my mom kept going until she disappeared the week before I turned seven."

"And you remember the story?" Vax says. "After all this time?"

"That's my problem. I remember everything."

"Do you remember the preacher's name?"

"Everything except that."

"But this guy, this Legion. Was *he* the preacher?"

I shake my head. "Totally different face."

"But you're sure Legion was there? Or at least knew you were there?"

"He'd be a bit too much of a mind-reader otherwise, don't you think?"

"Jesus, Miriam."

"Yeah," I say, and the tears are tracks of fire on my cheeks. "The preacher mentioned him too."

We sit in silence. Vax orders another round. If the bartender notices how badly I'm decompensating, it doesn't stop him from sliding a fresh IC Light in front of me. Through a haze of tears and cigarette smoke, I watch condensation form on the amber glass. I scratch the shiny black and gold label with a fingernail, reducing it to spitball-size beads. Before I know it, the bottle's empty and there's a full one on the coaster, cool mist curling from its neck. Some imbecile puts Pink Floyd on the jukebox, and I listen to synthesized guitar licks and four dead guys croaking about croaking.

Vax is leaning toward me, saying something I can't hear over the screaming music. Or maybe it's my thoughts that are screaming. My core's as empty as the third bottle, but I don't need its surge to travel back to that moment in time. After what happened a week from now, I don't think I ever will again.

The gun. The awful explosion. Red in my mind, red in my eyes, red everywhere. I can't see with all the red. I claw through it, search for him. It's like swimming through fire. A hand reaches in, pulls me free. Someone or something breathes air into my lungs, and that's the only reason I know I'm not dead too.

Just him.

The other shots were fired for show, to clear the halls so the shooter could single out the one he'd marked for annihilation. The child he'd already spoken to, posing as his teacher to get close to him. He could have killed us both in that middle school annex, just as he could have killed me in Cassidy's office.

But he didn't. He let me live, and that's why I want to die.

Ever since it happened, or since I was old enough to understand that Jeremy was no chance victim, but rather the target of a planned hit, I've asked myself why. What had a six year-old boy done to make a grown man want to kill him? The feds were plenty interested in that question too, though they approached it in their typical by-the-book way: what was going on in my family, specifically between Mom and Dad, that might lead to their son's murder? They must have had some theory – a custody dispute, an insurance scam – but they could never turn up any evidence. Later, when Mom vanished, they started all over again, posting unmarked cars outside our house while mysterious voices crackled faintly over our phone line. But again, no dice: they couldn't find anything that implicated Dad in his son's murder or his wife's disappearance, and they couldn't find the shooter based on the school's security camera footage either, so eventually they called it a cold case and let it go.

For years, I've asked myself if there was something they missed. Something *I* missed. Something – inside our family or out – that doomed my brother to die in that school building while everyone else lived. When I was little I blamed myself, believing I hadn't taken care of my day-younger twin the way I was supposed to or that I must have done something terribly wrong to bring this fate down on his head. Later, blame fueled the quest for self-immolation via whatever means I could lay my hands on – pills, razors, booze, cigarettes. But no matter what I tried, the question loomed: why would a random stranger kill a child? And not just any child, but the one who happened to be my twin brother and only friend?

Now I have an answer, though it doesn't help. The random stranger was a time traveler.

That's how he entered the school without being questioned or setting off the metal detectors. How he was exactly where he needed to be exactly when he needed to be there, first in the downstairs hallway and then in the second-floor annex. How he vanished instantly, and permanently, after the deed was done. I should have seen it the moment I joined LifeTime. As usual, though, I couldn't see past the next night in Vax's bed.

And now he's back, and I'm no closer than I was twenty years ago to understanding the *why* of it. In fact, with his reappearance, I'm even farther from having answers to the most basic questions.

Why here? Why now? Why Cassidy?

Why *me*?

Did the traveler hate me for some reason? Did he kill my twin at the age of six so he could watch me kill myself over the next twenty years? LifeTime was incorporated in 2019, so he couldn't have departed from any earlier than then. Could it be that I pissed someone off really horrendously sometime after the age of eight, and that person came back to end my brother's life when he was at his most vulnerable? I've pissed off plenty of people, but none I can think of who'd go to such lengths to pay me back. Who'd want me to suffer so badly they'd forfeit multiple years of their own life to perform the execution.

Unless…

Unless the shooter was one of LifeTime's hired guns, authorized to travel back twenty years to murder my brother in retaliation for me supposedly murdering the boss. Cassidy did act like he knew Regent. On the other hand, Regent is the one who killed Cassidy – twice – so it seems unlikely he's on the payroll. Not to mention that traveling more than a week is a major violation of federal regs. Short of Jeremy getting caught in the crossfire of some convoluted government takeover of private industry, maybe Regent *is* just a random psycho who gets off on shooting people I'm in the same room with.

But even if that made sense, there's one major thing that doesn't.

The killer's face is burned into my memory from that morning in the school. It's the same face I saw in Cassidy's office. The *exact* same face, the wrinkle-free face of a man who has yet to hit his thirties. Which means my personal nemesis, Eddie Regent alias Legion, can travel through two decades of time without aging one single second? *Four* decades if you count from now to then and back?

Impossible. A mere week gives me the shakes. Unless LifeTime recalibrated his core for some reason – and I don't have enough breath in my lungs to dive into conspiracy theories that deep – there's no way a human being could pick up and move from 2017 to 2037 without a scar to show for it. No fucking way.

Unless, unless…

Think, Miriam. Or think: Myriad. How is this possible? What am I not grasping about the inner workings of time travel that makes me unable to square this circle?

I stub out my last cigarette in the overflowing ashtray. My mucous membranes feel like they're coated in minty lacquer.

"The hell with it," I say. "What now?"

"We get out of here," Vax says. I wasn't talking to him, but he seems to have an answer for everything these days. "I'll settle up."

He pays – with cash, smart boy – while I slide off the stool and stumble to the bathroom to drain my bulging bladder. That done, it's back to the vending machine, where the inevitable finally occurs: it rejects my credit. Which makes sense, since I don't get paid until Friday. The red warning light transfixes me like a third eye, but the voice sounds like a robotic Mr Rogers: "I'm sorry, your transaction cannot be processed due to insufficient funds. Please try again. Have a nice day." I'm winding up to break the glass when Vax shoves Puff the Magic Draggin' into my hand and steers me out the door.

It's when we hit the comparatively fresh air of this rundown neighborhood that I realize I'm drunk. Wobbly on my feet, more wobbly in my brain. I feel like I was in the middle of a very important conversation minutes ago, but I either suffered a stroke or underwent maxillofacial surgery in the interim, because I can't remember what it was about. Vax puts an arm around my shoulders to hold me in place. I catch his gaze and try to perform the elaborate gymnastic maneuver otherwise known as a wink, but my eyes jiggle as badly as my knees, and the judges, especially the one from Belarus, give me a sizable deduction for not sticking the landing.

Words are pouring from Vax's mouth. I pick them up midstream. "… with me, Miriam?"

I nod obediently.

"Good," he says. "We have a lot of work to do."

He guides me toward a tiny parklet off a cobbled street. It consists of a bench, swing set, and enough green space for three toddlers to perform jumping jacks without poking each other's eyes out. A single streetlamp illuminates the whole. The standout feature is a large orangish ornament, modeled of concrete or resin to resemble something in the marine mammal family. Presumably it was once a splashing fountain, though rust stains on the surrounding patio tell a tale of woe. Vax maneuvers my heinie onto the bench and sits beside me.

"Steady," he advises.

"Says the man who bought me three beers."

"Four. But you were never this much of a lightweight."

"Guilty as charged," I say, raising my hand. "It's because I don't have any weight anymore. I'm free, get it? Isn't that what they say, the truth will set you free?"

I laugh gaily. Vax studies my face. Either he's drunk too or I'm in even worse shape than I thought, because his eyes seem to be twirling around in his head. When he leans toward me, I tilt my chin and pucker up.

"Miriam," he says.

"Yes, Vax-a-million?"

"I bought us time. A week's worth."

I put on my best schoolgirl simper. Vax doesn't even crack a smile.

"So to begin with, I'd like to know where this church is."

"Church?"

"Church, Miriam. Where you heard the story. Where" – he looks at me as if I'm made of fine bone china and he's made of a ball-peen hammer – "where you and your mom went the year Legion killed Jeremy."

It works. I crack.

While I shed the sorrow my brief bout of drunkenness held at bay, Vax pries the vaping device from my hand and stores it in his jacket. He comes out with a hanky – who carries a hanky anymore? – and pats my cheeks dry, then holds it for me to clear the crap out of my sinuses. I have the most awful taste in my mouth, a combination of mint and cherry and snot, and my scalp prickles like lizard scales. But I'm back in the present, and oh so thankful to Vax for returning me to this misery called life.

"You all right?" he asks.

What can I say? It was fun while it lasted. "Hunky-dory."

"I'm sorry, Miriam. I just–"

"No apology necessary. You're right, it's time I pulled my shit together. What's the use of crying over spilled blood?"

He looks at me closely. Grimaces at what he sees. I'd give anything to know what that is, since at the moment all I can see is Legion's face.

"All right," he says. "The church, then. I'd like to find out about this preacher."

"Sounds like a blast. But won't LifeTime be searching for us now that Cassidy got re-killed?"

"Maybe, maybe not. They're not used to chasing criminals who can travel."

"We're not used to running from travelers either," I remind him.

"But we've got the advantage," he insists. "So far as we know, Cassidy's not dead yet, only to-be dead. Plus we've given ourselves a week's lead. Who's to say they can find us?"

"Who's to say they can't?"

For once, he doesn't have a snappy comeback.

While Vax broods, I pull the gun that Cassidy claims isn't the gun I think it is out of my belt. I handle it, turn it, weigh its pound-plus on my palm. It seems to be a normal enough specimen of its type, not a magical variant that appears and disappears without warning. An M&P 380 holds nine bullets, eight in the magazine plus the spare. Leaving aside everything I know about this gun as well as everything I don't, if it was fully loaded before it fired its single shot the first time I went to the Sleep Rite, there should be three bullets left, subtracting the two that ended up in Cassidy's brain, the two I shot at Therese and the traveler in Vax's bedroom – he had to be Legion – and the one Vax shot at Sabine a week from now. But what reason do I have to assume that this is the gun from that initial trip? Coincidence, that's all. Even if I'm right, how can I ignore the various journeys it's taken through time in and out of my possession? It might have reset when I traveled to Vax's hospital room, gaining back the bullets that hadn't yet been fired at Cassidy or Therese. Or it might have been fired any number of times by the traveler who brought it to Cassidy's office. Maybe this *is* the gun from the video, in which case it fired at least one extra shot. Or maybe there's some other time travel shenanigans going on and it hasn't been fired for years like Cassidy said. If so, who the hell knows how many bullets are left?

I should want to know. An agent should always want to know. I could find out so easily, too. It would take a matter of seconds to pop out the magazine and check.

But I don't, and that's because I *don't* want to know. Whatever it turns out to be, it'll mean I'm going crazy. The chamber indicator shows that there's at least one bullet left, and that's good enough for me.

Vax is talking. Paying zero attention to my quandary now that he's in brass tacks mode. "We'll have to be careful, of course. Wear disguises like they did in *Twelve Monkeys*. Just to be on the safe side."

"Why does it feel as if all your pop-cultural references come from garbage time-travel movies of the late twentieth century?"

"Watched them when I joined the force. Research."

I'm not amused. "And if they know what our disguises are?"

"LifeTime's not omniscient, Miriam. We'll be moving fast. I think we have a shot."

"At what?"

He smiles crookedly. "Beating them at their own game."

I've given up on winning this argument. My newfound sobriety has sprouted a headache, and the thought of reliving the next week with my ex-boyfriend in tow and two murders waiting to be solved – one seven days ahead, the other twenty years in the past – makes my heart feel as heavy as a stone. I don't resist as Vax pulls me to my feet, but I don't exactly whistle for my trusty steed either. The best I can say is that I'm standing.

And then I'm diving for cover as metal dings metal at the same instant a shot rings out. Vax hits the dirt beside me, the bench providing a shield. Whoever fired the bullet came uncomfortably close to killing me – best as I can reconstruct, they hit the frame where I was sitting a second ago. I hold my breath and scan the night, looking for a sign of movement or a flash of gunfire to mark the shooter's position.

Vax has his Glock out and is doing the same. He signals, two fingers pointing right. I mouth *no*, but this is Vax. He's on his feet, making for the single tree that stands guard over the grassy area.

Another shot rips the silence, and this time, I see the flash. I rise hurriedly and fire at the chain-link fence that separates the parklet from the street. There's a grunt, followed by the thud of a body hitting pavement. Vax stops in his tracks and stands there like a spooked rookie before sprinting back toward me.

"Stay down, you idiot!" I hiss at him, but he doesn't slow until he's crouching by my side, breathing hard.

"Sounds like you got him," he says.

"Lucky us. Now what was that you were saying about LifeTime?"

We break cover. A weak gurgling leads us to where our assailant lies on the cracked blacktop of what might once have been a basketball court.

We stand over the body. Blood forms a widening pool of red on black. The would-be assassin is wearing LifeTime riot gear complete with helmet and visor, but my bullet seems to have nicked the left-hand carotid on their exposed neck.

Vax surveys the victim. "Should I attempt CPR?"

"Bit late for that."

I kneel by the person's side and remove the helmet. I'm shocked when it reveals the bloodless face of Therese.

Somehow, she's still conscious. Her eyes bulge, watching the horseman ride close. Pink foam bubbles from her lips. I lean down, catching words as thin as air.

"... not who you think..."

Then she dies.

CHAPTER 18

We drag Therese's body into the alley behind the basketball court and frisk her. Her uniform's regulation: dark jacket and pants, clunky shoes, holster and spare clips. She's got a badge with her picture and alphanumeric ID. The gun in her hand, though, is a model I've never seen. Sleek, lightweight. The word *Raven* is embossed in silver on the grip.

Digging deeper, we find what any halfway-intelligent time-fugitive who's not also a hopeless nicotine addict could have expected: a printed receipt for a pack of Kools registered to the vendor down the street.

Still, there are oddities. That they sent the receptionist on this vendetta is the least of these, considering the aplomb she showed the first time Cassidy got killed. Far weirder is the absence of backup. So far as I know, travel agents never take on assignments – much less assignments to tail the boss's suspected murderer – singlehanded. Throw in the fact that she went for me like a sniper instead of a law enforcement agent, and there's something rotten in this whole business. More rotten than usual, I mean.

Once we've reduced poor Therese to her altogether and found nothing else of note, we take a moment to debrief. I feel a strange reluctance to tell Vax everything about our latest visit to HQ, but this is no time to be coy. He listens intently as I tick off each item: the altered body cam footage, the changes in our assignment, the anomaly of the gun. When I get to the fetching Sabine, he jumps in.

"I figured she was a temp."

"She knew me, Vax. She was armed, too. I don't know what happened when we jumped back to your apartment, but we must have done a real number on things."

"But not on Cassidy's murder."

"No. That seems to be fixed."

He nods sagely. He's obviously trying to figure it out before I do, so I throw one more monkey wrench into his calculations. "Right before she died, Therese told me that Legion isn't who I think he is."

"Why would she tell you that?"

"Beats me. But I have no idea who he is, so telling me he's not who I think he is isn't exactly helpful."

"Think, Miriam. Someone from work, school, anywhere?"

I think. Or try to. It seems I'm not as fully recovered from my barfly performance as I imagined. I am, however, clearheaded enough to arrive at the same answer I did before. "Sorry, Vax. I'm drawing a blank."

He scrutinizes me for a second before looking away. "Maybe it'll come to you."

With that unsatisfying wrap-up, we turn to the more pressing question of what to do with Therese's body.

We review our options. There's no sign that anyone's gotten curious about the gunshots, but I don't want to leave the evidence lying around for the cops to discover first thing tomorrow morning. It's technically possible to hitch a ride on a corpse's core so long as its energy hasn't been depleted, which would enable us to dump her a day or two ago in some less-traveled corner of the city, maybe in one of the rivers. I'm not sure I can handle another trip, though. Counting our original spree at the Sleep Rite, this makes four for me in a two-day period (biologically speaking) plus exposure to multiple penumbras not of my own making, and I fear my next jaunt might be my last.

We debate the pros and cons in hushed voices, but

eventually, we return to the only conclusion that truly exists: leave her and move on.

Not, however, before I don her uniform. That's Vax's idea and, like most of his ideas, I find it hard not to wonder what he could possibly be thinking. Therese is (was) a good six inches taller than me and much narrower in the hips, as well as flatter in the chest. *Lissome* is/was the word for her, whereas I tend more toward the, how you say, *embonpoint*. But Vax has Bruce Willis on the brain, and since the clothes are too small for him – Vax, not Bruce Willis – I make him turn his back so he can't see what he's seen a hundred times before.

I quickly disrobe and slip into Therese's pants and jacket, expecting the cuffs to trip me and the sleeves to swallow my hands. Instead, I've no sooner pulled the pants to my waist than the material shrinks, literally shrinks, until it fits me like Spandex. The same goes for the jacket, which adjusts to my arms, torso, chest. When Vax turns to view the results, he could be staring at a runway model, if a somewhat short and busty one, in hip-hugging pants and form-fitting top.

"Wow," is all he says.

"Get your mind out of the gutter," I answer, but damn it, I know I look good.

I finger the material while he gawks. It has a spongy feel like living rubber. Some kind of organic polymer, but one that adjusts to the body of its wearer. The look in my ex-lover's eyes gives me a fresh grievance against my former employer for letting Therese hog this thing. I feel like I'm wearing a Super Suit, and what girl doesn't want a Super Suit?

After Vax stops ogling me and I stop enjoying being ogled, the next order of business is to dispose of the body. There's a filth-filled dumpster at the end of the alley, and I'm not saying I'm proud of this, but that's where Therese ends up, naked as the day she was born and with my shirt knotted around her neck to prevent her from leaving a blood trail. Vax wants to cremate her in order to spread her genetic material and make it harder for LifeTime to pinpoint the location of the killing, but that's where I draw the line. I do, however, use my Zippo to burn the pants I was wearing. They take a while to catch, but once the flame gets going, it's surprising how quickly a pair of black dress pants can be reduced to smoke and cinders. Let it never be said that I don't take my metaphors seriously.

We keep Therese's helmet and badge. The only thing we can't think of a use for is her footwear, which I chuck in the dumpster. I claim dibs on her Raven and ammo, tucking them into the shoulder holster and mag pouches that come with the suit.

Working together, the whole operation takes us no more than ten minutes. Then we leave the park behind and melt into the night.

And now for the hard part: where to go next.

The church is closed if it still exists, the Sleep Rite six days in the future. As for LifeTime, we agree to give it as wide a berth as possible. Of the several elephants currently occupying the room, Vax chooses the one that's stepping on the largest number of my toes. "What about your mom?"

"Chloe's shift ends at midnight, so..."

"It's twenty-three-oh-five now."

"Right." I pretend to think it over. "We leave her where she is. She'll be put in a home when I don't show up, and I'll never see her again. If all goes as expected, I'll attend her funeral a couple of years from now, provided I don't attend mine first."

Vax chews his lip. "If we sort this out, you'll see her again."

"As the daughter who skipped town and left her to rot? Come on."

"We could always travel back. Make things right."

"When did traveling back ever make things right?" I shake my head, and the weirdest thing happens: the suit ripples around my throat as if it's trying to copy the movement. "I didn't have a mother for almost twenty years. I think I can get used to not having one for the rest of what's looking to be a very short life."

He lets it go at that. I wish I could find it in me to cry, rail against fate, feel *something*. But what choice do I have now that ninja receptionists have been unleashed on my ass? My mother was lost to me long before I could do anything about it. We had one good day at the end. She won't remember, but hopefully I will.

"*Vámonos*," I tell Vax, and we do.

There's a boarded-up building at the end of the cobblestone street. We pull off planks of rotted wood and Vax shines a penlight inside, checking for junkies or riffraff. The light gleams off dusty hardwood floors and built-in bookcases, not a bad family home before the neighborhood went to pot. We creep upstairs and find evidence of prior occupancy, mostly needles and meth pipes. Luckily for us, the squatters seem to have moved on.

Since I'm the one in the Super Suit and I'm too hopped up on nerves to sleep, I take first shift while Vax curls into a corner, using Therese's helmet as the world's least comfortable pillow. Raven in hand, I hunker down on the landing and listen until his breathing turns to swift snores.

My mind is a forest I can't see for all the trees. The prevailing thought isn't so much a thought as a feeling of doom that sifts through cracks in the ceiling and coats the windowsills like flour. Jeremy's murder remains unsolved, and based on what I've learned about its perpetrator, it looks darn near unsolvable. The Sleep Rite grows messier by the minute. Vax has become a distant stranger though I last slept with him – when was it? A day ago? A week? My mom is a faded memory, Cassidy a dead man walking. Possibilities compound beyond the point my brain can hold. Is *this* my punishment for letting my brother die?

I'm jolted from a doze when my phone plays its three-note ascending ringtone. Not a ping but an honest to goodness voice call, the kind I never get. The number that shows up is unfamiliar, but Sibyl doesn't flag it. I'm about to lift the phone to my ear when a shadow swats it from my hand.

"Don't answer." Vax's voice, roughened by sleep.

The phone lies face up on the landing one flight below. We hold our breath and stare. The screen glows, then darkens. Vax steals downstairs and picks it up, returning to lay it on the floor beside me. When I reach for it, the fibers of the suit tighten as if to hold my arm back.

"You can't just take a call," Vax says. "You know that."

"I wasn't thinking."

"They leave a message?"

"Looks like it."

"Play it back. If they've traced us, it won't matter."

Against the suit's resistance, I put the phone to my ear. It reads my skin print and plays.

"Who's it from?" Vax asks.

"Quiet. I'm listening."

The message continues, a voice I don't recognize. I can't stop thinking how strange it is to hear a human voice emanating from this thing that's been silent for years, dispatching and receiving pings but never condescending to say a word.

"It's from someone called Helping Hands," I tell Vax. "Something about..."

"About what?"

"My mom. She's gone."

Vax touches my shoulder. "I'm so sorry, Miriam."

I shrug him off, or maybe it's the suit. "She's not dead. She's just gone. She got out of the building, and no one knows where she is."

The message finishes. The screen dims. The fibers of the suit relax, leaving me limp and lightheaded.

"Helping Hands?" Vax asks.

"I think they used to be Angel Care." I stash the phone, then climb unsteadily to my feet and stand on the creaky top step, hugging myself. "Christ, Vax, what did we do to time this time?"

CHAPTER 19

Chloe is hysterical, which puts me in the odd position of having to comfort her when it's my mother who's disappeared.

"I was right here the whole time!" she wails. "And the next thing I knew, she was gone!"

I pat her hand. Knowing how slowly my mom moves, not to mention the fact that she can't figure out the locks on the front door, I find this version of events unlikely. My guess is that Chloe – and she is Chloe, except she's wearing a salmon pink smock with cupped hands stitched over her heart – is covering for someone or something. But with the cost of the extra bedroom for Mom and the payments to Angel Care – correction, Helping Hands – I've never been able to afford the condo's premium surveillance system, so I have no visual evidence of what occurred.

"She should have been in a home!" Chloe shifts gears. "That's the place for people like her."

She dissolves into tears. I'm feeling guilty enough as it is, but I can't say I disagree with her assessment. Patching together home care while I tried to hold down a fulltime job and a fulltime love life was never going to work. I guess, deep down, I was counting on Mom dying before it got completely out of hand.

And then there's the deeper guilt, the dirty little secret I can't confess to anyone other than Vax: could it have been our latest voyage through the echelons of time that produced the conditions under which a woman of Mom's age and disability managed to give a professional healthcare worker the slip? A healthcare worker, I might add, who no longer works for the agency she did before? I can't fathom how jumping back a week could have altered a company that's been in business for years, but neither can I breathe a word about this to anyone – excepting, again, Vax – without sounding completely deranged. I wish I could blame the entire misadventure on Opal, but she didn't show up until a week from now, so this one lands squarely on me.

While I sit with Chloe, dispensing tissues and shushing outbursts, Vax stalks a path from the living room to the front door. He tried to convince me on the way here that we were making a huge mistake, that this might be a contrivance of whoever's after us – LifeTime, Regent, the undead ghoul of Therese – to flush us into the open. I wouldn't listen to any of it. I'd reconciled myself to leaving my mom in the hands of the state. I'd never agreed to abandon her to wander the streets. So far, the only outsiders who've shown up are two regular cops, guys I don't know who must work the missing persons beat. They're slow but thorough the way their kind always are, and they're not raising any hackles.

"Tell us what happened," I say to Chloe. "As much as you can remember."

"Well," she says, sniffling, "I'd already put her to bed…"

"In her room?"

"Of course." She looks offended, as if I've implied that she puts my mom to bed hanging upside down from the balcony. "She was asleep for a good hour when I went in to check on her, and–"

"What time was that?"

"Almost eleven."

"You're sure?"

"I was getting ready to watch the news. I thought I'd see if she was comfortable before I turned the TV on."

I trade a look with Vax, who's drifted over to sit on the

armrest of the sofa. Eleven o'clock corresponds almost exactly to our faceoff with Therese. Hard to see the connection, but I make a mental note.

"All right," I say. "So you checked her room…"

"And she was gone! I ran around the apartment looking for her, but–"

"Was the bedroom door locked?"

She twists her hands around a tissue.

"Chloe, did you lock her bedroom door?"

"I can't stand to lock the poor thing in!" she blubbers. "She's not an animal! But I searched the whole apartment, and there's no way she could have…"

She breaks down again. I hand her another tissue. I'd be better off handing her a bucket. One of the regular cops comes over and stands behind the sofa, staring down at her. I know what he's going to ask the moment before he asks it, but I'm not quick enough to prepare Chloe.

"Ma'am," he says, "were you using drugs or alcohol prior to your client's disappearance?"

Chloe looks like she's been slapped. "Was I…?"

"It's OK," I say, putting a hand on hers. "They have to ask that."

"No!" she says. "I don't use… I never… I have a glass of wine with dinner on my day off, but not when I'm working."

"Were you entertaining visitors?" the cop jumps in.

"Was I… what?"

"They have to ask that too," I say, but Chloe's a complete wreck, sobbing and incoherently protesting her innocence.

I give her hand another pat then stand.

"Look," I say to the cop, "be nice to her, OK? She's been taking care of my mom for the past two years." Or the past day, depending.

"We have to question her," he says.

"You don't have to make her feel like shit." I could add that there's enough of that going around as it is, but I'm done here. "Come on," I say to Vax. "Let's see what we can find."

The cops converge on their victim while we walk down the hall to Mom's room.

The door stands wide open. I must admit that Chloe's softhearted – and potentially actionable – decision not to lock it as instructed does make me angry. But my anger is leavened by guilt: that I insisted on locking my own mother in, that even that wasn't enough. That I was about to ditch her for good and elope through time with the man who dumped me like a load of cheap bricks. So Chloe left the door unlocked. So what? If I was my mom – which, genetics being what they are, I might be one of these days – I would appreciate the sentiment. Even if it meant my death on the streets of a city that's become an unnavigable maze to my mostly useless rat-brain.

Vax kneels on the carpet outside the room. "Hard to make out a clean print. Probably those two morons tramping around."

"Or Chloe. Mom would have been barefoot, though."

"Check for yourself. I can't see anything."

I lean close, hoping Therese's suit has X-ray vision or something. But it doesn't, and Vax is right: the hallway's been heavily traveled, which leaves nothing to find in the confusion of interrupted fibers. Different problem in the bedroom, where the short, stiff carpeting doesn't hold much of a print. I follow the muddle of blurred tracks down the hall to my room, and breathe a sigh of relief when I find the door locked. For obvious reasons, I've got the only balcony in the whole place, and the thought of what could have happened if I'd left the door open gives me a sick feeling.

When I'm done checking, I return to my mom's room, where Vax has set up shop. He's standing by the bed with hands on hips, trying to look like he's on top of things.

"Any clues?" I ask as a courtesy.

"She a light sleeper? Would she have gotten up on her own?"

"Not normally. It's happened once or twice, but it's pretty

innocent – she wanders around the room until I come to settle her."

"You've got an alarm?"

"Of course."

"Motion detector?"

"Affirmative."

"No video, though."

"If I did, would we be having this stimulating conversation?"

"Huh." He turns a slow circle. "So she gets up, finds the door unlocked, and leaves. And Chloe's, what, in the bathroom?"

"Or somewhere." I scan the room once more, but find nothing. "Let's face it, Vax. We can dust for prints or check for DNA trace evidence or whatever those clowns in the living room do, but we're not going to make any progress until we go looking for her."

"Which is exactly what anyone hoping to nab us would love to see happen. You and me out on the streets, searching for your mom, paying no attention to anything else..."

"And your alternative is what?"

"Let the guys out there handle it. They'll take Chloe in, question her, find out what really happened. We'll lay low as planned, keep an ear to the ground in case anything turns up."

"You honestly expect the Keystone Kops to pull this off without us?"

His answer is cut short by Chloe's exclamation – more like a shriek – from the living room. It sounds as if they're done with the nice part and are ready to book her on suspicion of transporting a dementee across state lines. The suit grows hot for a split second then cools. Or was that my own temperature spiking?

"I have to see what they're doing to Chloe," I say, and leave.

What they're doing to Chloe is helping – manhandling – her into her coat. She throws a pleading look at me, but there's not much I can do. Super Suit or no Super Suit, I'm not regular law enforcement. They'll hook her up to the poly, and assuming she didn't do anything drastically wrong, she'll be fine.

Which is what I tell her. "There's nothing to worry about. If they give you any trouble, just call." That last part is nonsense, which is why I say the next thing. "Thank you for caring for her, Chloe. You've been a godsend. She couldn't find the words to say it, but I know she trusted you and loved you."

Chloe bursts into tears. The cops are unmoved. The one whose head resembles a flatiron exits with the quivering mass of protoplasm formerly known as Chloe. The other one (head shape: indeterminate) stays to sniff around the apartment. I return to the bedroom to confer with Vax.

He hasn't budged. He turns and squints at me – in sympathy, apology, who knows what. I detect a headache coming on and consider going to the kitchen to brew a pot of coffee, then feel like a horrible person for worrying about my own physical discomfort when my mom's life is in imminent peril.

"You OK?" Vax says.

Another hot flash runs through the suit as I push past him. Is there such a thing as sympathetic menopause? I look at the shape of my mom's body in the sheets and remember the connection we almost made the last time I was here. And now she's gone, vanished as surely as she did the first time, as surely as the agency that used to care for her. Did *I* do this? Through an accident of time travel coupled with some unconscious evil wish? If I never see her again, how will I forgive myself? How will I know if my mom, that transient, formal visitor from my past and present but apparently not my future, ever thought of me? Remembered me? Loved me?

All I have is absence, not evidence.

"I'm not OK, Vax," I say. "I've never been OK."

He places a hand on my shoulder. It turns into a hug when I try to push him away. I fight him, and there's no longer any doubt that I'm wearing a bona fide Super Suit™, because strong as Vax is, he can't keep his hands on me. I don't want him to keep his hands on me, except I do, a realization that makes me fight all the harder. He tries to grab me one more time, but I whirl loose so violently that I trip and fall onto the bed, bringing him down on top of me. I swear to God, if he tries anything while we're lying in the bed where I last slept with my mom, I will scream.

But he doesn't. He lets me go.

"The bed," he says.

We stand. I run my fingers over the bottom sheet, then pull it aside. There, in the middle of the mattress, is a shallow depression I've never seen the likes of. It's almost circular, except the edges have a melted look, like ice cream you've pressed your lips into. I touch it, and I'll be damned if the suit doesn't react by giving me a shock. The current races up my arm to my brain, and the lightbulb goes on at last.

"She didn't walk out of here," I say. "She traveled."

CHAPTER 20

Vax talks to the remaining cop, who stations himself by the door in the event my mom finds her way back. To my thinking, this is about as likely as me finding gold bullion under the sofa cushion. But Vax likes to feel useful, so I decide not to rain on his parade.

"How much did you give him?" I ask as we take the elevator down.

"No big deal. He owed me a favor."

"Stop right there. I don't even want to know."

My life having officially become a crime scene and not simply a train wreck, there's no way I'm going to be able to sleep in my apartment. Since Vax's place is out of the question too, we check into a hotel. Not a cheapie like the Sleep Rite. Vax splurges on the Fairhaven, the Steel City's equivalent of the Ritz-Carlton. Finger bowls in the dining room, piano player (human, and really good) in the lobby. It's the kind of place where newlyweds consummate their vows before they have time to reconsider. Vax's rationale is that no one will expect two lowlifes like us to choose such swanky accommodations. However, as if to emphasize that no consummating of any kind will occur tonight, he books a room with twin beds.

The whole way up the elevator and down the hall to the Vestal Suite, he keeps trying to convince me I'm crazy. Most days, convincing me I'm crazy wouldn't require much effort. This time, I stick to my guns.

"Look at it logically," he says. "For your mom to travel, she'd have to be equipped with a core."

"Who says she isn't?"

"Plus she'd have to possess the mental resources to formulate the intention and select the destination."

"Unless another traveler initiated the trip."

"In which case there'd have to be a reason for someone to take a cognitively impaired person on a ride through time. Pretty unlikely scenario, it seems to me."

"OK, Sherlock. Then how do *you* explain the crackling pit of doom in her bed?"

"I don't have enough evidence to explain anything. That's why I'm keeping an open mind while I sort through the possibilities."

"One of which is simplest of all: she didn't *leave* the apartment but was *lifted* out of it by a traveler who came barreling in like a Monster Truck and deposited his skid marks on the bed. The same traveler who's been going out of his way to muck up my life for the past twenty years. Wonder who that could be?"

Vax sighs dramatically as he sits on the bed closest to the window – the one I was about to pick, not that I'm trying to be difficult.

"I'm never going to change your mind, am I?" he asks.

"Is that your purpose in life? To change my mind?"

He looks up. A light glints in his eyes, a reminder of the Vax who came this close to asking if he could carry me over the threshold of a place exactly like the Fairhaven. It feels like years since I've been with that Vax, and I guess it feels the same way to him, because the light is gone as quickly as it came.

"So, what do you want to do?" he asks.

"I want to get some sleep. Then start searching for her."

"Fine. You can take the bathroom first."

I glare at him for no good reason. He's got his phone out and is paying no attention to me anyway.

After removing my holster and setting my things on the nightstand, I breeze into the Marie Antoinette-size bathroom, only to find my heart pounding. All the while that I'm washing my face with lavender-scented soap and brushing my teeth with the gold-handled electric toothbrush that pops out of a nook beside the gilt-edged mirror, I try to think soothing thoughts, but there are none to be found. What's to soothe me if not a cigarette before bed, which I'm out of, and a sensual massage from Vax, which I can't ask for?

I do discover one thing: the Super Suit is becoming more super by the minute, because it softens as if by magic – probably by brainwaves – into material every bit as comfy as the monogrammed PJs in the bathroom cupboard. I'm excited to explore its other properties tomorrow. The thought of its former owner rotting in a dumpster disturbs me far less than I wish it did.

Vax does no more than nod when I return. It's only after the bathroom door closes that I look down and realize the Super Suit has become practically a negligee. *Brainwaves*, I think, and pull the covers to my chin as I sink into the impossibly luxurious bed.

He's a long time in there. He comes out wearing only his boxers, but there's not much to see since he's dimmed the lights and crosses my path of vision quickly. Once he's in bed he rolls toward the window, leaving me no compass points to navigate his body except the dark blob of his hair. Not to be bested, I turn to face the wall.

Now we truly are an old married couple. Twin beds, no conversation, no sex.

Exhausted as I am, I can't sleep. A single thought keeps running through my head: What could I have done differently? With Vax, my mom, my life? Time travel is such a con. Once you start pulling that lever, how do you stop? When do all the tumblers fall into place so you can finally say to yourself, *enough*?

I roll onto my back, glance his way. No change. "Vax?"

"Mm."

"You asleep?"

"Trying to."

"You really think I'm wrong? About my mom?"

"It's late, Miriam."

"I can't sleep. It's a simple question."

"It's not so simple."

"I promise I'll shut up if you answer."

He sighs, but doesn't speak. Probably he's in that automatic place right before sleep where your brain doesn't know what your mouth is saying. Where you're floating peacefully down the river to dreamland, and the last thing you want is to be tethered to the shore of consciousness and grief.

"I think he's out there," Vax says.

"Do you think he'll kill her?"

"That would seem to defeat his purpose."

"Which is?"

"To kill you."

I mull that over. Jeremy's been dead for twenty years, or not quite twenty, given my most recent sojourn through time. All those years to be nothing, to not be. Much as I've dwelt on death for the past two decades, I've never been able to wrap my head around the concept. The one visit I made to church certainly didn't clarify it. I wonder now if it's something like time travel. Without the puking. If Eddie Regent kills me, will I travel to a time when my brother is still alive?

"He doesn't want to kill me," I say.

There's a pause before Vax responds. "How do you know?"

"I just know. He's had plenty of opportunities, but he's stopped short every time. Killing me is exactly what he doesn't want to do, because what he wants to do is make me suffer. Over and over and over. I don't know why, but he wants to break me down, tear me apart. Make me crawl."

A breath. "You going to?"

"Not a chance."

"What, then?"

I think it through. The answer's always been there, but I see
it more clearly now than ever before.

"I'm going to end this," I say. "I'm going to track him down,
and I'm going to stick his own gun in his face, and I'm going
to pull the trigger. I don't care how long it takes. From this
moment forward, that's what I'm living for. If I die in the
process, so be it. Just as long as he dies first."

I throw the covers off and climb out of bed. Vax is turned
the other way, and when I peer down at myself, I find that
the suit has adjusted to my mood once more. Very prim and
proper, nary a fraction of skin unless you count my ankles.
Perfect for an execution, not a seduction. I search through the
items on the nightstand until I find the Vape Master, then plug
it into the hydra-headed lamp between the beds. In the red
glow of the charging light, I run a finger over the Smith &
Wesson, assuring myself that it still has at least one bullet left.

"Goodnight, Vax," I say, and pull the covers to my chin.

He doesn't answer. The room is bathed in red. The prospect
of a life without cigarettes, without sex, without him makes
my heart want to curl into a ball somewhere in the vicinity of
my pancreas, but the image of my brother's killer with a hole
between his eyes comes to my rescue.

Watch yourself, Regent, I say silently. *Or Legion, or whatever your
real name is. I am coming for you, and when I find you, you're going
to be the one who crawls.*

I'm about to pivot toward my favorite wall when Vax
rolls over. I see half his face, one eye covered by the pillow
but the other glowing like a laser pointer. His smile isn't the
come-hither one I'm used to, but it sends a thrill through me
nonetheless.

"Atta girl," he says.

CHAPTER 21

Morning light streams through the blinds. I shake Vax on the shoulder.

"Rise and shine," I say. And then, an expression I remember my mom using way back when: "Daylight in the swamps."

He mumbles, rolls over. The covers slip, revealing the muscular expanse of his back. I can't express how weird it is to have slept in the same room with him without actually *sleeping* with him. Maybe there's still hope for a rapprochement. I could convince him it doesn't have to mean anything. Just two consenting adults burning off steam before hitting the streets to track down a time-traveling serial killer. Two or three hours of mindless pleasure, then right back to business.

But I know that's not going to happen, and when I think about it, I realize it's not what I want. Ever since we started seeing each other, all it's taken is a look from Vax's smoldering eyes to make me feel like the sexiest woman on earth. Right now, I'd give up a whole day of steamy lovemaking for a minute of simply touching him, holding him, feeling the solidity and safety of his arms.

But that's not going to happen either, so I chase the thought from my mind and open the blinds even further.

Vax protests, tries to cover his head with the pillow, but eventually gives up and gets up. He stumbles to the bathroom, losing the bulge in his boxers on the way. I swear I only took a little peek.

While he's in there, I return to my roost on the balcony,

where I set up a workstation sometime after three in the morning. I was too anxious to sleep, so I spent the predawn hours high above the city, sipping coffee and inhaling licorice-flavored vapor to ease my headache and queasy stomach.

First thing I did was track down the church in Millvale via the national satellites since the local feed, "Burgh's Eye View," didn't come online until 2034. I spent a good two hours bopping from satellite to satellite, hoping to catch a glimpse of six year-old me entering the front door with my mom and dad. But the resolution from those days was too low, the interval too long.

When I switched to the local I discovered that, lo and behold, the church was still there, a bright red door among a row of storefronts. The placard on the wall was clearly legible at the highest resolution:

Resurrection Bible Temple
Worship Services Sunday
Hourly from 7 AM
All Welcome
God Bless

I wondered if it could be the same preacher after all these years, spending his Sundays at the podium every hour on the hour. He had to be at least sixty when I went there as a child. Maybe doling out the good word keeps a guy young.

The shower goes on. Fearful that Vax might start belting out arias from *Rigoletto*, I close the balcony door and go back to scrolling through the feed.

Today's Wednesday, August 26, so the church is shut, but the street it sits on is bustling with activity. When I rewind to last Sunday, there's a steady stream of parishioners coming in and out, all dressed in their finery. I see girls about the age I would have been, hair pulled back, skirts and blouses crisply ironed. There's no sign of the preacher. The church has no website, so I ask Sibyl to chase him down, but she can't find anything, not even his name. I wish I could search the criminal databases to see if his face shows up, but there's a chance LifeTime might be able to trace me if I try. I throttle my impatience and return to the room.

The shower's still running, so I sit on the bed and glance at the badge I stole from dear old dead Therese. Her expressionless face stares back. On an impulse, I lay my fingers on the photo and close my eyes, then open them to see if it worked.

Bingo.

Where Therese's face was, there's now mine.

I've added an alias I came up with on the spot: *MEREDITH, RANDI.* According to the badge, I'm a lieutenant working for the Pittsburgh Police Investigative Division, Missing Persons Bureau. The fibers of the suit and its accoutrements must operate along the lines of cuttlefish chromatophore cells, except they're surely genetically engineered, probably nanotech enhanced to boot. What's almost scary is how quickly they linked up to my neural network – starting the moment the suit shaped itself to my body, I'd guess. Obviously they can't change my actual mass, but I've seen what they can do to my appearance: slim my waist, reduce or boost my bust. Plus the suit's reinforced in some way that makes me stronger. If it can't entice Vax, it can give me the extra muscle to do without him.

He exits the bathroom. Shaved to perfection, hair slicked and curling beneath the ears. His body ripples with pecs and abs, since he forgot to take a change of clothes with him and is wearing nothing but yesterday's dirty boxers. That should be a turnoff, but when have I ever been turned off by Vax's dirty anything? I tamp down the naughty thoughts while he ducks back into the bathroom to change. By the time he returns, I've calmed myself enough to focus on the task at hand.

"Ready to go?" he asks.

"I'm going alone."

The predictable frown. "What if Legion's waiting for you?"

"Then I'll kick his ass. Get over here."

He joins me at the little table in the room. I take the chair across from him, plant an elbow on the table top. He looks at me patronizingly, but locks his hand around mine.

The second we engage, the microfibers of the suit tighten in concert with my muscles. Vax's expression changes to surprise right before I slam his knuckles down so hard the table rattles.

He massages his hand. "What the fuck was that?"

"The suit," I say. "I've never been defenseless, Vax. In this thing, I'm damn near invincible."

"Or someone wants you to think you are."

"If so, they're about to find out who's right."

He lectures me. Like Cassidy, or one of the trainers at the academy. He lays it on pretty thick, some half-baked harangue about how Legion has taken me by surprise twice already and I don't know what he's capable of and when did I decide it was a good idea to go on a job without my partner? I deflect him with alternating snorts and silence. This has nothing to do with my job. This is revenge, plain and simple.

"I'll be fine," I tell him. "I need you to scan the databases, see if Regent shows up. Do it in a roundabout way in case LifeTime is trolling for us. The Sleep Rite rehappens on the thirty-first, and we need to cover as much ground as we can before then."

"What's going to happen then?"

"Just a feeling."

"Miriam—"

I dismiss him with a flick of my hand. He chews his lip but says nothing while I strap on the Raven, shove the Smith & Wesson in a handy pocket that's appeared on my hip, and tuck the Vape Master in a pouch on my other side. The bulges blend into the material so you'd never know they're there.

Vax holds the helmet out like a peace offering. "What about this?"

"Gives me hat hair. I'll ping you when I'm done."

I'm out the door before he can say a word. If he thinks he can stop me, he hasn't learned his lesson about messin' with a girl in a Super Suit.

CHAPTER 22

Millvale is one of those neighborhoods time forgot.

Narrow streets crowded with worn storefronts rise steeply from the river. Defunct trolley tracks are embedded in the cobblestones, forming occult designs that put me in mind of crop circles. The racket of bad mufflers and the smell of gasoline hang in the air from ancient jalopies someone's found a way to keep on the road. No sign of flip phones or boomboxes, but I wouldn't put it past the place.

I've set foot in Millvale exactly twice before, once at the age of six and once my junior year in high school. The latter visit occurred when my favorite local band, Junkheap Chariot, opened for The Sporadic Jerks at a venue on Hays Street, and I went with Larry, the twentyish pothead I was sleeping with at the time. (Mostly for the pot.) The theater was a converted Eastern Orthodox church, its proscenium where they used to hang their god in all his mangled glory. I dipped into Larry's private stash before the show, then proceeded to scream myself hoarse and dance myself dizzy before returning to his place for a private curtain call. He was no Vax in terms of technique, but I didn't know back then that lovers like Vax existed, and what with the weed and the post-show rush, I had no cause for complaint.

The time before was a nightmare. I don't know if I was more terrified of the fire-breathing minister or of my own mom, who bowed and scraped like a doll in the hands of a malicious toddler. Mom was never the emotional type that I can remember, but that day she was a zombie: vacant, slack, soulless. A prefigurement of the brain-ravaged shell she would become years later.

The LeMon (short for All*egheny*/*Mon*ongahela) drops me off at the bottom of Lincoln Avenue. Vax, who must handle his personal finances better than *moi* if he can afford a night at the Fairhaven, shifted some crypto into my account, so I opted for a private ride rather than one of the bugged municipal cabs. From here, it's a ten-minute walk uphill to the business district, which gives me a chance not only to burn some calories untarnished by a post-workout smoke break but to test the powers of my Super Suit as well.

I know that I have enhanced strength and speed, but when I press my hand against a brick building, it turns out I lack wall-crawling abilities. I can, however, camouflage myself against just about anything – not automatically, but as a conscious act. Further experimentation proves I can use this trick to disguise things I come in contact with, which means if the need arose, I could make my gun look like nothing more than my hand. I can also change the appearance of the suit at will, so I've opted to shed the attention-grabbing cop clothes and dress like your average small-town girl out for a stroll in shorts and T-shirt. For kicks, I tell the suit to reproduce the Chariot logo from ten years past.

No sooner thought than done. The fabric tingles, and a broken-down Caddy with fins and wings unfurls across my chest.

"Glory be," I say. Now that I'm about to get religion and all.

I'm not the slightest bit winded when I reach the top of Lincoln and turn right onto Grant, the main drag. A few blocks down, I spot the bright red door nestled amongst its comparatively bland neighbors.

Jitters set in as I step up to it. The door's locked, the painted wood peeling so badly it looks like it's been clawed bloody. There's no buzzer or knocker. I rap with my knuckles, wait for a response, try again. When there's nothing, I put my ear to the door and listen. I think I hear pounding from inside, but that's probably my heart in my ear. Sadly, the suit doesn't come with a Spider Sense either.

"Looking for Reverend Hitchens, honey?"

I turn to find a middle-aged woman watching from the sidewalk. Like many of her fellow pedestrians, she's flouting the city's no smoking ordinance, and her voice is correspondingly gravelly. I'm instantly suspicious of her, but I decide to treat her like a regular human being instead of an alien pod person. "Do you know if he's in today?"

"This is God's house," she says with a snaggle-toothed smile. "He's in every day."

"I was hoping to talk to him."

She takes a step closer, which alerts me to another of the suit's properties: infrared. I feel her body's warmth, plus the pinpoint of focused heat in her hand.

"You in trouble, honey?" she asks.

A phone appears in her hand. She pings, tucks it away. Smiles beatifically. This is why I don't trust people. In her eyes, I must be pregnant or strung out or just plain lost, and it's her job to fix me up with the man who'll put me on the straight and narrow.

"He'll be right down," she says. "God bless."

"Screw you," I say quietly enough that it could be a benediction. But she's gone, off to search for the next easy mark.

I wait, taking deep breaths to calm myself. A few locals glance my way from across the street, but I can't read their expressions. Could it have been one of them who told my mom that all of the answers were behind the red door? I look down and find that the suit has assumed its most kickass form yet, a single-piece black leotard with long legs and sleeves. I make a fist, and it becomes a regular cop outfit just in time for the door to creak open.

Considering my expression, the man who materializes from behind the door doesn't look particularly put out. I remember the preacher as huge, room-filling, but this guy is no taller than I am and quite a bit thinner. Wrong church? Child's-eye-view memory? Replacement minister? The face is familiar, pinched and simian with mandalas of wrinkles around the eyes, but I feel as though I've seen it more recently than twenty years ago. It's a second before I make the connection.

The old man in the hospital.

Has he recovered? Or no, that was six days from now. Maybe he suffers a heart attack in the interim. Maybe I shoot him today. Just give me a reason.

"May I help you, my child?" he asks.

That's almost reason enough. I flash my badge. "Lieutenant Randi Meredith, Pittsburgh Police. We're investigating a possible abduction."

"At my church?"

"The missing person was one of your... customers."

"I see."

He ponders. Lips pursed, eyes beseeching the heavens. I keep trying to make his face align with the firebrand from age six, but it's not a perfect match, possibly for the simple reason that twenty years of Sundays have passed for both of us. He's wearing a typical geezer outfit, much too warm for the weather: corduroys, vest, flannel shirt. I remember a flowing robe. Or did I add that detail when I saw pictures of popes and cardinals and other religious figures in the news?

"Let's go inside," he says. "Where we can talk."

He reaches out a seamed hand. There's a quiver of palsy. I draw back, but he's only gesturing for me to follow him into the church. Whether or not this is the ogre from twenty years ago, he's nothing but a weak old man now. So why am I so squirmy?

He leads me into the dimly lit interior. The church must have been a dance studio at one time. There are horizontal bars on the paneling, folding chairs lined up in neat rows on the scuffed hardwood floor. The mirrors have been replaced by painted scenes of Christ and his disciples. Or are those the Stations of the Cross? A wooden lectern stands at the far end of the room, a crucifix suspended overtop of that. Even with all the religious trappings, the place could play host to an AA or grief counseling meeting, complete with coffeemaker and Styrofoam cups in the corner. I feel as if I've entered a frozen bubble of time, where miracles like internal combustion engines and extruded polystyrene foam are as plentiful as Christ healing the blind and making cripples waltz down the street.

The preacher – Hitchens – offers me a chair. It requires some doing for him to lower himself into his own. There's definitely something wrong with him; his hands won't stay still in his lap. I'd better get this over with before he cashes in his chips right in front of me.

"The investigation involves a woman named Deborah Sayre," I tell him. "Fifty-eight years old, Caucasian. I have a picture," which is true thanks to the Department of Human Services. "She suffers from early onset Alzheimer's and was found missing from her domicile last night. We're checking up on all of her contacts, including this church."

He holds the ID card at arm's length – farsighted, apparently – to study it. Upside down, so do I. My mother's black-to-gray hair frames her fish-belly face, while her eyes stare at the camera with no awareness of what it was for. Truth be told, I'm not sure why we went through the hassle of getting her picture taken in the first place. It's not like the state sends us flowers on Mother's Day.

"I remember Deborah," the preacher says. "But that was years ago."

"You're positive about the identification?"

He passes the card to me, his hand trembling. "I make it a point to remember everyone who visits my church. I'm so sorry to hear about her disappearance."

"When did you first meet her?"

"Oh, a good nineteen, twenty years back. She came here one Sunday in, I'll say early December of twenty seventeen, and she was a regular for the next two months or so."

There's no longer any doubt this is the guy. His memory is striking, I'll give him that much. Could *he* be a traveler? Someone who works for Regent? I wish I could remember the face of the orderly who was pushing his bed in the hospital, but the guy was masked, and I barely glanced at him. "You haven't seen her since?"

"I'm afraid not. If I might ask, what gives you reason to believe she was abducted?"

"We're not at liberty to discuss that."

"I understand."

There's silence while I try to figure out my next move. The man's slick as greased butter, and he doesn't seem fazed by my tough-gal-cop routine. I could waste all day trying to trip him up.

"Do you have any additional information about the time she spent here?" I ask. "Any contacts she made, any conversations she had with you?"

He loops his hands around a knee, maybe to keep them from moving on their own. "We had a number of conversations in those days."

"About what?"

"Lieutenant... Meredith, is it? You have your code of conduct, and I honor that. But you must understand that there are a great many things spoken within these walls that stay within these walls."

"This is a criminal investigation."

"And this is a church. A place where people bare their souls as they cry out to God. I'm privileged to hear those cries, but I have no authority to divulge their contents."

"Reverend, I don't think *you* understand," I say. "If you have any information that might lead to Deborah's recovery, I'd expect you to divulge it willingly. We're not talking about God here. We're talking about a woman's life."

"It was God who gave her that life," he says. "God who led her to my doorstep. Wherever she is now, God holds her in His hand, and He won't let her fall."

I've had more than enough of this pious jagoff's doublespeak, but I'm at a loss for what to do next. At LifeTime, we investigate murders that have already happened, using rules tailored to that very special category of crime. I've never had to learn all the ins and outs of standard criminal procedure, and I don't have clue one what the law says about a minister's right to withhold privileged information. Much as it irks me to play nice with this man, I see no other option.

"Reverend Hitchens," I say. "Deborah Sayre has a family. A child. I'm asking you to help restore a mother to her daughter. I hope you'll see that as a matter of conscience too."

He sighs deeply and leans back in his chair. For a long moment, he looks away – toward the pulpit, toward his God. I wonder if he hears an answer. I also wonder if he's figured out who I am. He remembers Mom from twenty years ago. Can it be possible he remembers me?

"Deborah was a lost soul," he says at last. And then, turning back to me: "A lost soul."

"How do you mean?"

"When she came to my church, it was obvious she'd never sought God before. She was a college professor, accustomed to searching for answers in the microscope, the laboratory. But she'd found that those weren't enough. Human devices never are. Not when we come to the great crisis of our life."

"And that's why she was here?"

"Oh, yes. Yes, indeed."

I wait for him to say more, but I can't wait until the saints come marching in. "Did she tell you she lost a son?"

He rubs his chin. "She never mentioned a son. She came

here once with her husband and little girl, but after that, she always came alone."

I'm that little girl, I want to say, but something – chalk it up to the Super Suit, which tightens around my throat before the words are out – stops me.

"He was murdered," I say instead. "Her son. When he was six years old. I thought – maybe – that was why she came to you."

He studies me keenly. Tears are on the verge of making themselves felt in my eyes, and no Super Suit can hold them back. When he speaks again, his voice is as gentle as if he never stood a mere five paces away, thundering about sinners and devils and eternal hellfire.

"I took it that she was grieving," he says. "But for what, she never told me."

I bow my head to collect myself. When I look at him again, I'm astonished to find tears in *his* eyes, as if my suit transferred them across the negligible distance between us.

"Did she tell you anything else?" I ask.

"She had no need to tell me," he says, still in that gentle voice. "Her actions spoke what her heart could not bring itself to say."

"I don't–"

"I told you she always *came* alone. I didn't say she always *left* alone."

I'm stunned, but I get the words out. "There was... a man?"

"A man, yes. A fellow parishioner who met her here on her first day. It was my understanding he'd showed her to this place, though I'd never seen him before. But God works in mysterious ways."

"Were they" – I don't know how to say this – "involved?"

"I've learned not to pry into my parishioners' private lives," he says. "I made that mistake with Deborah after she'd attended services long enough that I thought I might approach her about the matter, but I found that my words were not welcome. From that day forward, she never visited my church again."

"This man." I feel as if I'm strangling, as if the tens of thousands of cigarettes I've smoked in the past thirteen years have knotted into a single cord around my neck. "Was his name Regent? Eddie Regent?"

"He never gave a last name," he says. "But he introduced himself as Jonathan. That's as much as I learned of him, though one comment Deborah made when we had our talk led me to believe they'd met as coworkers."

"Is this him?" I ask.

My hands tremble worse than the old man's as I shove my badge at him. On the back, I've told the Super Suit to render a picture of Regent's face. A snapshot is what it looks like to Hitchens, a printout of a digital photo. There's no way he can know it's the image that owns more than half my brain, more than three-quarters of my life.

"That's the man," I hear him say. "It's possible I've misremembered his name."

"Or that he was using an alias." The strangling sensation stops me from saying anything else except, "Excuse me."

I throw myself from the chair and run for the rear of the church, hands cupped over my mouth like a sorority girl during rush week. I barely have time to open the bathroom door before puke gushes from me in a rainbow arc. Fortunately the room is small, and most of the discharge finds its way into the toilet. I gag, cough, spit, but nothing can wash the foulness from my mouth. When I stand and look in the mirror, I see that the suit has tidied itself, but the woman staring back at me is as pale as a reflection in a night window.

Reverend Hitchens taps discreetly on the door. "Is everything all right, Lieutenant Meredith?"

"I'll be out in a minute," I say, and I don't care that my voice catches.

I rinse my mouth, splash cold water on my face, and use the

crank-operated paper towel dispenser to pat my cheeks dry. My eyes are red but my skin has returned to a semblance of its normal shade by the time I exit the room.

Hitchens allows me a polite distance. There's no way he hasn't figured out who I am. "I'm sorry to have upset you, Lieutenant Meredith," he says.

"That's OK. I'm just..." Pregnant? On the rag? Suffering from withdrawal? "I should go now."

"I understand. I'm sure there are other leads you have to follow up on."

He says this with a straight face. No irony, no cadge. He's been in the business long enough to know that if I'm going to come back, I'm going to come back. Hell, if the day arrives when I'm as battered and beaten down as my mom, there's no telling what I might do.

He escorts me to the door, opening it to bright sunshine. He takes a sudden breath as if he's as startled as I am to discover that there's still a world outside.

"Best of luck to you, Lieutenant Meredith," he says. "God bless."

I'm on the sidewalk when I turn back to him. The door's open, the dark interior of the church visible. "Can I ask you one more question?"

"Of course."

"Do you believe in fate?"

"The ancients believed in fate," he says. "I believe in God's plan."

"There's a difference?"

"To the Christian, there's no bigger one. Without Christ, there is *only* fate. With him, there is *faith*."

"Like the faith of knowing you're going to drop dead six days from now?"

He makes a sign with one quavering hand. If he suspects I'm from his future, he doesn't say. "The faith of knowing you're going to be reborn into new life, my child."

CHAPTER 23

I'm not dealing with this well.

It's early evening. I pinged Vax and followed his directions to our new place. If possible, it's even sleazier than the Sleep Rite, a ramshackle two-story motel a few miles from the airport that might as well hang a sign for the annual opioid abusers' convention. I literally have to step over passed-out guests on my way up the stairs. It seems Vax isn't as flush as I thought, either that or our spree at the El Swanko put a major dent in his pocketbook.

I sit in the imitation Adirondack chair on the wraparound balcony, rest my feet on the railing, and pull out the Vape Master to indulge my own addiction of choice. Vax was dying to tell me something the moment I got here, but I wasn't dying to hear it. Plus, I drained most of the vape cartridges before I arrived, so I sent him out for refills. I don't give a shit what they taste like at this point, because everything tastes like ashes.

I can't get the image of Mom with Jeremy's killer out of my mind. Not because of the apparent infidelity. Lieutenant Randi Meredith is hardly the morality police, and if I could bring myself to believe that my mom found a moment of release or even bliss in a lover's arms, I'd be thrilled for her. But to know that it was Legion who deceived her, who made her think she was escaping something – memory, grief, life – while all the while he was dangling her like a worm on a hook… It makes my heart ache. No accompanying pain or numbness in my neck and jaw; I should be so lucky. It's just heartsickness, pure and simple, for the woman who bore me, the woman whose torment I never knew.

Oh, Mom, how could anyone have hated you so? What did he believe you'd done to him that he could rob you of your child, your family, your pride? And that even now, when you're utterly ruined, he could come back to rob you of what little peace remains to you before it's all over?

I've tucked my knees under my chin to stare into the twilight when Vax returns from his shopping trip. He hands a dusty box to me, which I open to reveal a twelve-pack of cartridges suitable for the Vape Master and other Vape Genie products. He seems insulted when I toss it back.

"They don't make those anymore," he says. "I had to run all over the city before I found one in the back of an old newsstand."

"Lovely. So now I can die from black mold instead of lung cancer."

I collect my things while he pouts.

Inside the room, I sit on the less saggy of the two beds while Vax takes the other. He reaches into his shopping bag and pulls out a Plantplastic container with four bulbous, very green muffins.

"St. Patrick's Day was five months ago," I point out.

"They're pistachio."

"I do not like them, Sam I am." But I nibble one to make him stop moping.

"You find out anything?" he asks.

"False lead. You?"

He looks at me strangely, but doesn't comment. "Plenty."

Now that he's got me captive, he drops his big reveal. I pick green crumbs off the soiled coverlet and listen with every ounce of my world-renowned patience while he tells me what he's discovered or, to be more precise, what he hasn't.

"There's no Eddie Regent matching the description you gave me in the local or national databases," he says. "I saved the closest matches I could find in terms of age, race, criminal history, et cetera, but they don't look promising."

He pings the images to my phone, and he's right: none of the dour mugshots bears any resemblance to the face branded into my memory. I consider telling him that the man we're after might have gone by the name of Jonathan, but that would require an explanation I'm not in the mood for. "This is all?"

"Far from it. I also located drone footage from the twenty-fifth of August between twenty-two hundred and twenty-three-thirty hours, which is the rough timeframe we suspect the abduction took place. There was fairly heavy coverage outside your place that night, so I figured one of the vidcams might have picked up any suspicious activity."

"Except Regent traveled in."

"Correct. But take a look at this."

He sets aside his half-eaten Shamrock McMuffin and pings me a video clip timestamped 22:09. I watch from the drone's multiple points of view as it hovers outside my condo for the next couple of minutes, cameras recording the crisscross streets of Downtown, the moon, the stonework of the building. A self-driving bus rolls through the frame. A few seconds later, the drone swoops around back, where Mom's room is. There's a shot of her window, curtains closed for bedtime.

"And I'm watching this because...?" I ask.

"Just wait."

The seconds tick by. There's only so long I can watch a closed window. The timestamp reads 22:12, give or take, when there's a muffled sound plus a quick burst of light through the curtains as if someone took a flash photo. I play the moment back twice, then set the phone aside to find Vax looking at me.

"So, what do you think?" he says.

"I think it's mighty peculiar the drone was right outside her window just then."

"It probably detected a sudden drop in air pressure. But

get this: I checked my chronometer, and the time you and I traveled to corresponds precisely to the time on the video."

"So?"

Apparently, this isn't the response he was looking for. "So you were right. Regent no sooner left Cassidy's office than he jumped back to the same day and time as us and made off with your mom."

"Bully for him."

"I thought you'd be happy."

"You thought I'd be *happy* that my mom is in the clutches of a time-traveling psychopath?"

"That's not what I meant. We know she's with him now. We find him, we find her."

"Just like that, huh? A man who can jump through decades without aging a day? Should I look him up under Daughters of Dementia Delivery on Demand?"

"Miriam. What did you find out at the church?"

"Nothing," I say. "A big fat nada. The minister's dead, and the church was converted to a dance studio. I did a couple of quick pliés just to stay in shape then came right back here so I could listen to you spout your usual nonsense."

He could check his phone and figure out I'm lying about the church, but he doesn't. "So OK, we search for Legion the old-fashioned way. We hit the streets and–"

"And what? Hope he's got a piece of toilet paper stuck on his loafers?"

"Miriam…"

"We don't have the first idea where to look for him," I say. "And you don't have the first clue what I'm feeling. So stop telling me how *happy* I should be that you spent all day hunting down a worthless piece of drone footage that proves my mom could be anywhen in the world with the man who killed her son."

He stashes his phone. "I was just trying to help."

"You were just failing to help. You really want to help, stay the fuck out of my way."

He stands. The Super Suit registers prickly heat – Vax's anger or embarrassment, no doubt. I've gotten good enough at reading the suit's moods to know that I'm bristling with enough anger of my own to leap onto his shoulders and crush his skull between my thighs, but what would that accomplish?

"I'm going to CMU tomorrow," I tell him. "Alone."

"Fine." He gathers trash. "I'll be back later."

He slams the door. I sink into the concave mattress and stare at the ceiling, where a water stain spreads like an intricate fungus. I'm too tired to think, too tired to sleep. One of the junkies is stumbling around on the balcony, moaning about his miserable life. Next thing I know I'm out there with him, the Raven pointed at his head.

"Your choice," I tell him. "One way or another, you're checking out."

He stares in horror before backing away, hands raised. I guess even junkies have something to live for.

At the door to the room, I pause to look out over the parking lot. A single streetlamp illuminates the weed-grown blacktop, but Vax is gone.

CHAPTER 24

The CMU psych department is housed in Baker Hall, one of many enormous beige-colored buildings that give the campus the look of a prison or at best an office park. Being here feels nothing like a homecoming. I was thankful to the school for giving me a full ride – something they didn't need to do, considering my mom was an employee for all of a semester before becoming a missing person – but I took the majority of my classes online, joined no clubs, made an appearance mostly for the off-campus bars. I'd forgotten the bizarre statue that sits on the front lawn, the one with a bunch of people trotting off into space. It seemed pretty stupid back then, and that was before the same thing happened to me.

Vax never returned last night. I got worried that he might have been jumped by a junkie biker gang, but I relieved my guilt with the reminder that he can handle himself. I'll ping him once I'm done here, and assuming he's all right, we'll lurch through another episode of *Breakup Blues*. That's the last thing I need, but my crypto's maxed out from all the robocab rides, so I can't do without him.

A gaggle of undergrads eye me nervously as I enter the building. I ignore them – relax, Skippy, I'm not here to bust you for last night's kegger – and then take a look around to reorient myself. The sterile interior is an accurate reflection of the department's no-nonsense approach. Upstairs at the Cognition and Artificial Intelligence Institute, they're busy building better brains; across the breezeway at the newly built

Neuroimaging Center, they're crunching data from one of the most powerful MRIs on the planet. I take the stairs to the second-floor faculty offices and walk down the row, wishing I knew which door used to be my mom's. When I searched the faculty directory, I couldn't find any of the professors whose classes I had to take for my Criminal Justice major, let alone anyone with the last name of Regent. I did see one name I recognized: Dr Ayesha Mahmoud, who worked with my mom as assistant director of the Learning and Memory Program (LAMP). We did a videoconference the year Mom resurfaced, during which Dr Mahmoud effused in a very unprofessorial manner about her former boss. When I pinged her this time, she sounded eager to reconnect.

Now that I'm standing in front of her office in my cop clothes, I feel a moment's misgiving. She probably thinks this is a social call. Do I have the right to drag perfectly innocent people into the cesspool of my life?

I knock anyway. It's too late to abort now.

Dr Mahmoud opens the door and does one thing that doesn't surprise me – flashes the mouthful of blinding white I remember from our video call – and one thing that does: wraps her arms around me and pulls me close. She's about my height, and has on a bright red hijab and a flowered tunic over black slacks. From the complete absence of wrinkles on her face, I assume she's younger than my mom. Still, the hug is unnervingly intimate, and I find myself squirming like a schoolgirl who doesn't want her hair braided.

"Miriam," she says, holding me at arm's length. "It's so wonderful to see you again."

"Thank you," I say awkwardly. "For agreeing to meet with me."

"Of course."

She lets go and leads me into the office. It's filled with the typical academic clutter, gadgets that look like they're for experiments strewn all over her desk, framed diplomas and posters of lit-up brains on the walls. There's a small bronze statuette on the windowsill shaped something like a lamp, the kind Aladdin might have tinkered with. I expect Dr Mahmoud to retreat behind the desk and point me toward the straight-backed wooden chair for students who are failing her classes, but she scoops a tower of very old-looking books from a divan and beckons for me to sit beside her. When she reaches out to take my hands, I feel like a criminal being interrogated by the world's nicest cop.

"It's been years since we talked," she says. "How have you been?"

"Fine," I lie. "I've been working, and..." My shrug covers Mom, Legion, Vax, Cassidy, the Sleep Rite, and much, much more. "Other things."

"And you're a police officer?"

"Private law enforcement."

"How wonderful." She glances at me conspiratorially. "I assume you can't reveal your employer's name?"

"Actually, that's one of the reasons I'm here."

She smiles a psychologist's smile as she translates that into the truth. The *only* reason I'm here. "Is there some problem?"

"It's my mom," I say. "She – this is hard, Dr Mahmoud, but–"

"Call me Ayesha. Has Debbie's condition worsened?"

Debbie. The only time I heard anyone call my mom that is when this woman said it during our video call. Over and over. *Debbie had such a beautiful mind. Debbie was on the verge of major breakthroughs in the field. Debbie could have done anything she wanted with her life, but she chose to help other people.* Her hands tighten on mine, and maybe the psych department practices hypnosis or past life regression after all, because the words that come out of my mouth are as small as if six year-old me is the one speaking them.

"She vanished, Ayesha. A couple of days ago. She'd been living with me, and then she was gone."

"Oh, my dear." She draws me to her for a quick hug, releases.

Her black eyes sparkle. "And your employer assigned you to locate her? Her own daughter?"

"I wasn't assigned, exactly. I just thought…"

"I understand." She nods briskly. "Wandering is very common for people with your mother's condition. I take it she wasn't chipped?"

"No." I swallow, feeling like a fool. "I never thought to have it done." Translation: I thought about it but never set aside the time or money to actually do it. "And it's not that simple. We have reason to believe…"

She watches me closely. Something – my training, my native suspicion – tells me that this interview is going all wrong, that I'm the one who's supposed to be asking the questions, not her. How many shrinks did I see in the years before my dad decided he was wasting his hard-earned money and could better spend it on highballs at the gentlemen's club? How many techniques did they go through in their attempt to peel open the top of my head and catch a peek at the festering morass inside? Ayesha is no doubt a lovely person, concerned for my mom, as well as for me. But enough is enough.

"I'm conducting a criminal investigation," I say. "There's reason to believe my mother was abducted, and one of the persons of interest may have been a former member of this department. Possibly the same man responsible for her prior disappearance. I wanted to reach out to see if you have any pertinent information. Since you were here when she was."

I take out my phone. I've scanned Regent's picture – from my brain to my suit's chameleon ID to my screen, so effectively, I *am* showing her the inside of my head. Her expression clouds as she leans close to look. "What is the name of this person?"

"We believe he may have gone by the name of Regent. Eddie Regent, or some variation of the same. Jonathan might be a first or middle name as well."

"He's not familiar to me," she says, shaking her head. "But then, twenty years…"

"He might have been considerably younger than her," I say, and have to grit my teeth to force the words past the obstruction in my throat. *Debbie was such a delightful colleague. Debbie was a lost soul. Debbie was having an affair with the man who killed her son.* "A grad student, maybe."

"I can check the university's database," Ayesha says. "But the name isn't one that brings a particular person to mind."

She pulls out her phone. I guess there are perks to being the supervisor of the memory project, because she calls up a directory of everyone who's ever worked or studied at CMU since it was founded by Andrew Carnegie in 1900. The name check draws a couple of hits, but Edward Regent, a Philosophy major who graduated in 1951, and James "Ed" Regent, a maintenance worker who retired in 2003, look nothing like Legion. I ping Regent's image to her phone and she searches again using the school's facial recognition software, which bears the all-too-cutesy nickname "See 'Em You." This time, the search comes up empty.

"The database is not one hundred percent complete," Ayesha says as she puts her phone away. "The plan is to create a comprehensive record, but it's a time-consuming process, and there are some individuals for whom photographic evidence is unavailable, which forces us to generate AI reconstructions based on secondary sources. If the man you're searching for attended or was employed here under another name in recent years, I'd have thought the database would contain his image. But it's possible he slipped through the cracks."

In time, I say to myself. "Are there any other repositories I might check?"

"All of the existing archives have been integrated into our network," she says. "If he doesn't appear here, I'm afraid I wouldn't know where else to look for him."

The room grows quiet. I'm still holding my phone as if to record a confession, so I stash it inside my jacket. My fingers brush one of the two guns I'm carrying – not the Raven, but the one that killed Cassidy. The same one that might have killed an estranged couple in the Sleep Rite Motor Lodge. Or not.

Eddie Regent. Jonathan. Legion. Why do I feel I should know him? Why do I feel I never will?

"I'm sorry I couldn't be of more help," Ayesha says. "If further questions occur to you, please, please don't hesitate to reach out any time of day or night. And of course, if there's news about your mother, I hope you'll let me know."

"Thank you," I say. "I'll be in touch." Translation: I won't.

She ushers me to the door. Though she looks so young, moves so gracefully, she's got to be in her forties at least to have worked with my mom. In a way, she knew my mom better than I did, mourning the loss of a friend she remembered, whereas all I could do was fret over the absence of a stranger I forgot. I'm not sure why I feel as if I owe her something, but I find the words coming out of my mouth nonetheless. "What were you and my mom working on? Before she vanished the first time?"

She smiles another oracular smile. "Our work involved the neuroanatomy and neurophysiology of trauma. In particular, in the realm of memory."

"Through LAMP?"

"The clinic has been engaged for the past two decades in mapping the human memory system. Your mother was brought on to head up the project, and I inherited her position when she went missing."

"And trauma? Is that because of…"

She shakes her head. "The relationship between trauma and memory formed the basis of Debbie's doctoral work, years before your brother's murder. Here."

She goes to her file cabinet, which it seems professors still use even though practically everything's digital these days. She pulls out a long wooden drawer and rifles through it with a practiced air that makes me think she's consulted this particular file many times over the years. After a moment, she removes a dog-eared, coffee-stained folder and places it reverentially in my hands. I flip it open and am startled by the title of the manuscript inside.

Mind out of Time: Post-Traumatic Stress Disorder and Temporal Displacement Mechanics

"This is the paper Debbie presented when she interviewed for the directorship of LAMP," Ayesha explains. "I was new myself at the time, but I remember her presentation to this day. Her thinking was unorthodox, to say the least – speculative in a way the department doesn't typically acknowledge or reward. I wasn't a member of the search committee, so I can't speak to the deliberations that took place there, but obviously, they found enough promise of future scholarly achievement to recommend her for the position. This paper, however, was never published in the short time prior to Debbie's disappearance."

"What's it about?" I ask, holding the folder out to her. I feel like a typical undergrad trying to make the teacher do the work for me.

Ayesha's been around the block too many times to fall for that. She smiles and touches my hand lightly with her fingertips.

"Read it and see," she says.

CHAPTER 25

That afternoon I'm holed up in our latest pay-as-you-go hideaway, sitting by the window on the leatherette love seat with my mom's paper in hand. Vax didn't answer my ping at once, which started me down the road of blame and shame I've been walking most of my life, but when I heard from him an hour later, his reply was civil enough. It guided me to our new place in Dormont, a decent hotel in an area devoid of obvious criminal activity. The room was unoccupied when I arrived. What I'll say to him when he shows up is an open question, so I've chosen to put it out of my mind.

I had an epiphany on the ride from campus, possibly a reaction to meeting with a certified genius like Ayesha. I reasoned that if the Super Suit is an extension of my being, a second self that reacts to my body and brain, maybe I can use it to reinforce my resolve, amplify calming thoughts, that sort of thing. I have no clue if it works that way, but merely coming up with the idea gave me a mood boost. I've got a cup of coffee by my elbow, Sibyl to jump in for words and concepts beyond my Intro Psych recall, and the Vape Master fully charged just in case, but all things considered, I'm feeling pretty good about myself for a change.

Then I start reading my mom's paper, and I realize that next to Deborah Jane Sayre, PhD, I'm a complete moron.

The neuroanatomical and neurophysiological substrates of post-traumatic stress disorder (PTSD) have been subjects of increasing scrutiny in recent decades. Acute as well as protracted trauma, it is

now widely acknowledged, actuates drastic, cascading temporal-limbic
events, altering the hippocampus and its functionally related structures
including the orbitofrontal cortex, retrosplenial cortex, anterior
cingulate gyrus, entorhinal cortex, and hypothalamic-pituitary-
adrenal (HPA) axis in ways that possess significant implications for
pathognomonic symptomatology and other maladaptive sequelae…

That's just the first two sentences. It gets worse as it goes,
with so many terms I've never heard of it's like Sanskrit
encrypted by sadistic alien IRS agents. *Neural connectome.*
Default mode network. Hippocampal N-acetylaspartate. Brodmann
area 11. Voxel-based morphometry analysis. MNI echoplanar imaging
template. There's a section titled "Review of the Literature"
where she lists a ton of published studies by researchers with
names like Lucent and Miranda and Delph and Yu, but when
I glance at a couple of their papers on my phone, I can't make
heads or tails of them either. Smack in the middle of the
thing is a section full of charts and brain scans and formulas
composed of mathematical symbols that look like slug trails.
Sibyl's hauling ass to keep up with my nonstop requests, the
result being that I get more and more confused as I sink into a
bottomless sea of psychobabble. What are *alexithymic responses*
and *psychoform dissociation*? What's the difference between
idiothetic and *allocentric* memory? (Hell, *is* there a difference?)
I have the vague sense that my mom's laying out some grand
theory of something – or of everything – but when I try to pin
it down, it dissipates into thin air. Thank goodness I only had
to live with the woman, not take a class from her. Not only
would I have flunked, but I'd probably have developed a bad
case of *Hebbian neuroplasticity* or fallen victim to *corticotropin-*
releasing hormone (CRH) as well.

After an hour of reading and rereading the first fifteen pages
and getting nowhere, I set the paper aside, close my eyes, and
take deep breaths to calm myself. I'm determined to do without
nicotine unless the literal apocalypse arrives, and it seems the
suit catches my drift and gets to work creating the appropriate

mix of alpha and beta brainwaves. When I open my eyes, the room has stopped doing cartwheels. I'm about to go back to the beginning of the paper and try again when I remember what my research methods teacher told us junior year, and I flip to the section titled "Summary and Conclusions" right before the reference list. Begging the suit to come to my relief, I read:

Since the earliest, quasi-experimental studies of Charcot, Janet, and Freud, the basic model of traumatic memory has not changed significantly. When the brain is exposed to terrifying or overwhelming events – particularly in childhood – the autobiographical memory system may become disordered in predictable ways. The ability to situate the traumatic memory within a coherent narrative of the evolving self breaks down; the traumatized person may remember only emotionally charged fragments, sensations, and images divorced from a particular place and time. Yet for this very reason, these stored event-traces prove unusually vivid, pervasive, and durable, such that they seem to the traumatized person to be active, ever-present, occurring in an eternal, inescapable "now." In effect, persons suffering from severe PTSD as measured by the Standardized International Trauma Index (SITI) become unwilling and unwitting time travelers, compelled to "return" to the site of experience(s) that form the basis of an extended trauma network. In short, such persons are never not revisiting the spatiotemporal locus of the trauma; they are never not traveling into the past.

By identifying the specific anatomical and physiological alterations within the autobiographical memory system responsible for these subjective sensations, this paper suggests that effective Temporal Displacement Mechanics (TDM) technologies must operate on two interdependent tracks, coupling the material rearrangement of spacetime with the activation of specific neuronal centers within the brain of the putative traveler. Absent this critical second component, one might theoretically develop a mechanism to travel through time, only to find that the human mind is unprepared to negotiate the "trip." Learning from the brains of traumatized persons thus offers the clearest pathway to overcoming this challenge.

Difficulties arise, however, in translating theory to practice. One such impediment is ethical rather than mechanical: were it possible to send traumatized persons to the past, the prospect of retraumatization looms large. On the practical side, the strong likelihood exists that such persons could not travel at will to designated targets but must always return to the site of the foundational trauma. Possible means of surmounting the latter difficulty include: stimulating the requisite regions of nontraumatized persons' brains to reproduce the effects of traumatic memory-reconstruction; suppressing (in some as-yet-undiscovered way) the emotional content of the traumatic experience so as to facilitate free movement through time; and/or engineering TDM technologies that draw on traumatic memory-processing in such a way as to redirect time-traveling subjects to specified coordinates. Needless to say, given existing technologies, not to mention ethical norms, such experiments must remain to be conducted in the indefinite future.

I sit up in the chair, reading those three paragraphs over and over. Even without Sibyl's help, their meaning is clear.

Mom wasn't studying time travel as a metaphor for trauma. She was studying trauma as a mechanism for time travel.

Does that mean she was working with Cassidy? *For* Cassidy? Given her background in neuroscience, I doubt she was involved in developing the strictly technological aspects of the process: the core, the chamber, the energy source. Her mega-brilliant brain's contribution was the discovery that, without the psychological component – unlocking the traveler's memory to make the time and place to be visited *feel* real – the technologies would be worthless. That explains why so much of the work LifeTime does involves forensic reconstruction, because without a solid mental image of the *where* and *when*, there'd be no way to return to the scene of the crime. It also explains why, even without the chamber, agents are able to travel on a charged core: because it's *necessary* to the process for our minds to link us to the past. That's the reason I flash back to Jeremy's death every time I travel. Someone, whether my mom or one of Cassidy's people, figured out how to *draw on traumatic memory-processing in such a way as to redirect time-traveling subjects to specified coordinates.* To *use* trauma as a ticket to lapsed time.

Is that how it works for everyone? Do all travelers – Vax, Therese, Eddie Regent – have a history like mine?

Too many questions. The unpublished paper in my hand stops short of answering them, so I tell Sibyl to search for everything my mom ever published, every audio- or video-recorded presentation of hers that's been archived, every citation of her research that's been made. I'm frankly ashamed that I never looked into her scholarly legacy before, but I guess that's another thing about her I was trying to forget.

Within a split-second, my faithful AI retrieves thousands of results, the vast majority of them consisting of references to her work by, among others, Dr Ayesha Mahmoud. It's far too much material for me to delve into even if I understood half of what it was saying, so I skim a few articles instead, finding that some of Mom's published research dealt not with PTSD but with Alzheimer's. From one of these, I learn that the inability to make sense of space – what she calls *hippocampal topographical amnesia* – arises from damage to the same brain centers in people with both conditions. The paper links me to a lecture of hers from 2016, and I startle when her face appears onscreen: the woman I barely remember, unlined and intense, speaking in a matter-of-fact tone about the illness that will gut her mind years later. Viewing the lecture, I want to scream a warning, jump twenty-one years into the past and rescue her from what's coming. Instead, I watch her wrap up her talk and snap her briefcase shut, her shoulder-length black hair obscuring her face as the video fades to black.

I've lost count of how many hours have passed. I lay the paper facedown and switch tactics, instructing Sibyl to search Mom's acknowledgments and bibliographies for the name *Regent*. My AI pal takes only moments before perkily telling me, *Word not found, showing results for "regret,"* which annoys me so much I shut her off and activate manual searching. When I do, I discover that there's not a single instance of the phrase *time travel* in the entirety of my mom's published articles or recorded talks – not in the tens of papers she wrote or delivered before she joined CMU, not in the two short commentaries she published afterward, both of which have to do with mainstream PTSD research. I search for *TDM*, *Temporal Displacement*, and all of the related terms my comparatively puny brain can come up with, but there's nothing there. It's as if, other than the brief detour into weird science that helped her land her first superstar academic gig, my mom spent her abbreviated but productive career toeing the line her employers expected her to.

But was that the real her, or only a role she played? If she was researching time travel *before* Jeremy was killed, why would she drop the issue *after* she had a deeply personal reason to want to change the past?

Still too many questions. With Sibyl off nursing her wounded pride somewhere in cyberspace, I decide to reach out for the kind of help only a fellow human being can supply. I look up Ayesha's name in my contacts and ping:

I read my mom's paper. Was she trying to travel through time?

And then, because I don't want a Psychology professor to think I'm a total loony tune, I add:

lol

Ayesha's phone must be optimized for subvocalizing, because her lengthy return ping arrives almost instantly.

Debbie's work had two main facets. Her primary objective was to advance our understanding of the etiology of PTSD so as to make possible the development of effective long-term therapies. At the same time, she was engaged in the work of constructing an enhanced map of the brain's memory and learning centers that could be used for any number of applications. If she'd only had more time, I'm sure she would have succeeded at both endeavors.

This seems heartfelt, but I can't help noticing it's not exactly an answer to my question. I ping back:

Then why talk about time travel at all? If she wanted to highlight her cutting-edge research on PTSD and memory, she could have done that without delving into TDM.

She subvokes immediately:

What is memory but time travel? What is time travel but memory?

I'm about to inform her that time travel is a hell of a lot more – or less – than memory, but then her message continues at length. She must have been subvoking at breakneck speed while I was preparing my response.

As your mother's work illustrated, PTSD comes closer than any other form of psychopathology to the precepts of theoretical, mechanical temporal displacement. The literature is filled with first-person testimony from sufferers of severe PTSD claiming that they felt as if they were "back in the past," "at the scene of the accident," "physically transported through time," and so on. It was Debbie's research that first mapped the specific neurological aberrations that produce the condition, and as such, it was her research that first suggested effective interventions by which such persons could be freed from the past and restored to full functioning in the present.

Still not really an answer, but I ping back:

And now that she's gone? Have you been able to develop the interventions she was looking for?

She responds:

We've significantly expanded the memory map and its accompanying database. We've made great strides in treating patients with PTSD and Alzheimer's disease, using SSRIs and more recently developed neuroregenerative medications. It saddens me to think what we might have been able to do to address your mother's condition had we caught it earlier. But I comfort myself with the assurance that, if she were cognitively capable of appreciating the work we've accomplished, she'd be proud to have been its founder.

I picture Ayesha sitting in her cluttered office on the CMU campus or her beautifully appointed high-rise in Shadyside, trading thoughts about memory and time and loss with the daughter of a woman who's lost her memory and, if I'm right, is currently lost in time. I've got one more question for her, and I don't expect an answer to this one either, but I've got to ask.

I'm about to ping it – *What about time travel? Have you managed to accomplish that too?* – when my screen glows with her response to a message I haven't sent. Her latest ping consists of six words and a winking emoji:

What do you think, Agent Randle?

CHAPTER 26

Here's what I think.

Regent is an asshole.

Cassidy was/is/will be an asshole.

Ayesha – sorry, Ayesha, I'm just calling 'em like I see 'em – is an asshole, albeit a time-traveling asshole who thought it would be nice to check in periodically on her boss's victim's daughter from somewhen in the future.

My mom wasn't an asshole. At least, I'm pretty sure she wasn't. She was just a woman who got mixed up in events much bigger than she realized. Must run in the family.

I ping Ayesha back, only to discover that her number's out of service. The CMU robosec tells me curtly – these bots can get an attitude – that they've never heard of anyone named Dr Ayesha Mahmoud. Which means either she's been using an alias for the past twenty years or she's figured out how to pull some kind of temporal switcheroo à la Helping Hands. It makes me wonder if the papers I found online are by her or some other, non-traveling Ayesha Mahmoud whose identity she stole.

I ping the cops to see if my mom's status has changed, but they tell me she's still missing, no news on where she might have gone. I consider asking them to put out an APB on Ayesha Mahmoud, but realize I have no basis for anything so drastic. Plus I'm sure that Ayesha, or whatever her real name is, has scurried back into the crannies of time. *Any time of day or night* was code for *I'll be sitting by my phone waiting for my chance to twist the knife into you*. Now that she's performed her assignment, I'm sure she's got her feet up on the coffee table and a glass of Bordeaux in her hand as she shares a good laugh with Legion.

I'm staring blankly into space, trying to use my suit-enhanced mind-powers to perform an act of clairvoyance, when the doorknob rattles and Vax stumbles into the room.

He looks terrible. Pale, bleary-eyed, unshaven. I've known my share of men his age, bachelors or divorcés with no reasonable prospect of getting married on the immediate or distant horizon, and they're an unkempt bunch as a rule. But Vax has always been the most kempt man I can imagine. The sight of him tripping over the doorstep of the Heartbreak Hotel into the darkened room – when did it become night? – is painful to watch.

"Where have you been?" I ask.

"Out," he says. I can smell the booze on his breath from across the room. "Wha's it to you?"

He fumbles with his shoes, gives up and slumps onto one of the beds. His hands seem too big for his body, his shoulders too heavy to shrug.

"Find anythin'?" he mutters.

"Plenty," I say. "I'll go over it tomorrow when you're in shape to listen."

"'m sorry."

"To say the least. What ever happened to keeping on our toes and all that?"

His hand goes to his throat. It seems he's trying to undo his tie with an index finger, but the impression is of someone tightening a noose around their neck.

"Well, I'm hitting the sack," I say. "Want me to get you anything?"

He shakes his head.

"Good. Use the balcony if you need to puke."

He makes a small sound, a gulp.

I glance over and see that he's crying. Face contorted, snot running down his chin. Men crying is never a good look. With him, it's like watching Michelangelo's David turn into a baboon.

"Don' care 'bout me," he says. "Never did."

"What are you talking about?" I say. "I cared enough to save your ass at the Sleep Rite. Not to mention stopping you from bleeding out in your apartment."

"'s not enough."

"Vax, look." I retrieve the manuscript, stand and shake out cramped legs. "I've never pretended it was anything other than what it is. I'm sorry if you thought it was more. But right now, I'm a little too busy trying to save my mom to expend time and energy on your hurt feelings."

He cries harder. Face bright red, eyes squeezed shut, the whole nine yards. The sole advantage to this is that I can't at the moment picture what it was that attracted me to him in the first place.

"You should be thankful," I tell him. "By tomorrow, you won't remember a word you said."

He heaves himself erect and comes at me like some kind of golem. The Super Suit reacts instantly, changing into an armor-plated exoskeleton that's a cross between King Arthur and King Kong. It's a little bit of overkill considering Vax can barely stand straight, but I catch hold of him, swinging his one-hundred-eighty-three-pound body so hard he flies across the room and collides with the wall. Luckily he's too drunk to tighten up, because his neck might have snapped in two. As it is, he's out cold, breath coming thick and sloppy. His face is terribly pale and haggard but, without the tears, there's a chance for some of his rugged beauty to show through.

I kneel beside him to check his pulse, pull up his shirt and palpate for injuries. There are none to be found. If I hadn't jarred him, he would have passed out on his own.

I hesitate a moment before stripping off his pants and shirt and pistol, then drag him to bed. Disgust rises in me at the smell of him, the whiskey patina I associate with my dad's infrequent nighttime appearances in the house we shared. I cover him quickly and turn away.

His rumpled clothes are draped where I threw them over the desk chair. For reasons I can't understand, I dig in his pants pocket and pull out his phone. I take his hand, press his finger against the screen until it switches on, and stare at the picture that appears.

It's us from early last year. The flower arrangement on the table reminds me that we were at some fancy restaurant in Mount Lebanon. According to him, we were celebrating the one-year anniversary of our first date. Truth be told, I didn't remember. We look happy, arms around each other, smiling for the camera. In the picture, Vax is his usual self, restored to the man I used to love to watch, in bed or out. I, on the other hand, look less like me than like an ingénue from central casting, with big soulful eyes and my hair in the pageboy I was experimenting with. It lasted all of three weeks before I got sick of it and let it grow.

Funny. You try to be someone else, the *you* you think others want to see. In the end, though, you're always who you are. Miriam, Myriad, it makes no difference. I'll never be what this man wants, just as he'll never be what I need.

I put the phone back before I'm tempted to pry further. Vax's snores fill the room as I slip into the bathroom to change.

CHAPTER 27

As predicted, Vax has no recall of what happened last night. What he does have is a colossal hangover.

He curses, flings an arm over his eyes to block the sunlight, complains at the slightest sound I make. I don't have time for this, so I yank the covers aside and give him a cup of black coffee. He burns his tongue on the first sip.

"Feeling better?" I ask.

He glances at me, frowning as if he's trying to reconstruct the chain of events that might have prompted such a question. Once the coffee kicks in, he pulls it together enough to stand and shuffle into the bathroom. To shower, nothing worse.

I sit by the window, breathing deeply until I fall into a rhythm. I got up early and read a few articles on smoking cessation, discovering in one of them that Opal's miracle shot blocks nicotine receptors in the brain. The last thing I need is for less of my brain to work, so I'm sticking with Plan A, trying to train the suit to calm my nerves. It's a strange process, binding this nonliving being to my flesh in hopes it'll hold me together, but at present, it's the best I can come up with.

Vax looks almost like his old self when he emerges. He's shaved, his hair slicked, his tie knotted to a T. The only difference is the paleness that comes with the hangover. Or I shouldn't say that. The biggest difference is that when I look at him, I see nothing but a good-looking man standing in my hotel room, not a lover who for the past thirty-two months

– shattering my previous record of six weeks – was the only person on earth I cared to share a bed with.

"Let's get to work," I say.

He pours himself another cup of coffee, his hands not shaking that I can tell. "What's the agenda for today?"

"A little visit to an old friend."

"Come again?"

I'm not keen on airing my family's dirty laundry, even (or especially) to Vax, but I remind myself it's now or never. He listens intently while I tell him what I've learned these past couple of days, or most of it. Regent's connection to the church, my mom's research on time travel. If Vax figures out the part about the affair, he's too discreet to say anything. The mystery of Ayesha intrigues him.

"So she's a traveler?"

"One of many. Legion isn't doing this all on his own. He's got associates: Therese, Ayesha, maybe Hitchens, though he claimed he'd never seen Regent-alias-Jonathan before he met my mom at church. Maybe others as well."

"Chloe?"

"Possibly. The one I'm interested in right now is Cassidy."

"I thought we agreed to steer clear of LifeTime."

"Changed my mind. I need to find out what he knows about Regent and my mom."

"And it has to be today?"

"Might as well be. The way Cassidy keeps dying, we'd better get to him while we can."

He ponders. Now that we're not frittering away our resources on some middle-school melodrama, I'm surprised to remember that Vax isn't just my ex-lover. He's my partner, the guy I work with, plan with. He's smart, savvy, solid. It almost makes me wish we'd never fallen into bed in the first place. That would have meant a significant decrease in out-of-this-world sex, but a corresponding upsurge in comfortable conversations like this one.

"So OK, we go to LifeTime," he says. "You figured out a way to get Cassidy to talk?"

"I've been working on some ideas, yeah."

"Then let's saddle up. You can fill me in on the ride over."

We bustle around. Our movements are the way they used to be in the old days, a single machine with finely orchestrated parts. Vax drains his coffee, packs his bag. I clean. This shocks both of us, because I only dirty. The Super Suit flirts with an *au pair* number, but fortunately, Vax's back is turned. In the end, it settles for my blandly unisex LifeTime outfit, and that's just fine with me. My head is clear for the first time in a long time, my guilt where it belongs.

I holster my weapons last thing before we go, and Vax raises his only real objection of the morning. "I don't have the dampener anymore."

"You lost it?"

"Told you it was a loaner. How're we going to get past security?"

I think about it for less than a second before shaking my hair out. The suit responds as desired, rippling from my shoulders downward until I'm clothed in black feathers and scales like a latter-day Quetzalcoatl. Vax blinks as I spread my wings and fade into the room's vine-patterned wallpaper.

"Personally," I say, "I don't think it's going to be a problem."

CHAPTER 28

The day is just getting started when we arrive at HQ. There's a trickle of employees entering through the revolving door: techs, forensics, random people in suits whose names and purpose I don't know. The robojan is visible through the glass, tootling back to its alcove after stocking the bathroom. From the look of things, today's an average day at the ranch. No thrills, no chills.

That's where we come in.

Vax stops across the street from HQ. I've been tagging along behind him. Though I'm not strictly invisible when I'm in motion, I'm as close to invisible as a non-invisible person can get. Someone staring straight at him might see a distortion at his back, a ripple that makes his dark suit seem to be breathing, but that's about it.

"Let's review the plan," he says in a whisper.

"Such as it is," I respond in a normal tone of voice. Let people think he's talking to his imaginary rabbit friend. "You go in there. Figure out how to shut the cameras off. Then come back out and get me."

"How will I find you?"

"You won't. I'll find you."

I ease up to the nearest building and fade into the brick, the suit's tendrils reaching up to wrap my face and hair. Vax's eyes search for me, but standing still, I truly am invisible. He shakes his head and laughs, then trots across the street and disappears into headquarters.

When he's gone, I take deep breaths and review the plan to myself. I've got nothing else to do, and my partner won't be back for another twenty minutes. The suit has definitely figured out what I want from it, so much so that I threw caution to the wind and stashed the Vape Master in Vax's bag, which he secreted in a back alley on the way over. Despite the heat and traffic noise and my own morbid thoughts, I feel relaxed, almost floating. As if there's nothing on my schedule to stop me from standing here for hours, soaking up the sun, enjoying the day.

Except Vax is back in less than five minutes. He hustles across the street, looking for me. I remove my shield long enough for him to spot my face, then vanish again as he joins my invisible self beside the building.

"News flash," he says. "Our friend Therese is there."

"The Therese I killed?"

"So it seems."

"What about the cameras?"

"I thought you'd be more interested in how poorly Therese's demise stuck."

"I've given up trying to maneuver around speed bumps like that. I just drive right over them."

"In that case, the cameras are controlled from the reception area. If you sneak around behind the desk, you'll see the display. I assume Therese's headset turns them on and off. Or some mechanism under the desk."

"Good enough for me," I say. "Walk slow. I'll hang onto you so you know I'm here."

There's a moment's hesitation where I'm afraid he's going to chicken out. Then he offers an arm and sets off with me in tow.

We enter the revolving door as a single larger-than-Vax unit. Both of my weapons are secreted beneath the fabric of the Super Suit and, as I'd hoped, there's no reaction from the smart detector. Vax's Glock is registered, so he's authorized to carry it in and out. If the detector had sensed my contraband, the door would have locked us inside, trapping us in the perfect position for an interrogation or an arrest.

I see Therese the moment the door spits us out.

She looks the same as always, no more wan or winded than usual from having died three days ago. Her presence is far more unsettling than I'm willing to admit, but after Ayesha's little stunt, I suppose it's not out of the realm of the possible. Nor is it necessarily an impediment to what I have in mind. Someone would have been at the reception desk. I'd prefer to do this without recourse to violence, but if I have to kill her twice, I'm sure she'll come out in the wash.

I pinch Vax's sleeve. "Distract her."

"How?"

"Sweet-talk her. Pour on the alleged charm. Worked with me." I wish I hadn't said that.

"Where will you be?"

"Wouldn't you like to know."

He approaches the desk, which means I'm obliged to stop blending into him and blend into the lobby instead. But it's child's play by now. I simply focus on my surroundings and imprint what I see on the suit. The process is continuous, the optic feed shifting moment by moment as I move. The only tricky part is that I can barely see myself, so I have to be careful my feet don't scuff the floor and give me away.

Vax is leaning against the reception desk, chatting in his heartiest baritone, the object of his unexpected attention looking not just tickled but positively smitten. Wouldn't have expected that from a cold fish like Therese, but then, Vax can be a smooth operator. I circle the desk as he keeps up his patter, some line of bull about the casino on the other end of town and how he likes to go there on weekends when he's not working a job. If I didn't know better, I'd believe he's asking her out for real. But why shouldn't he? She's about my age, and there's no sign she's married. No smell of decomposition either, so why not? I'm mildly surprised that it never occurred to me how attractive my former flame must be to other women (and men) in the office, but the time to be petty is past. All that matters is that Therese is listening intently enough that she's paying absolutely no attention to the shadow-sister who's slipped into the reception area behind her.

Until the Smith & Wesson is pressed against her temple, that is. Then she's paying attention.

"Hands where I can see them," I whisper. "Nothing obvious. And don't dream of going for the alarm. Come to think of it, I'd like the headset off."

She removes it casually, as if she's merely adjusting the strap. You'd think voices feed her commands out of the ether every other day.

"Agent Randle?" she says in a tight undertone.

"Or somebody."

"How are you doing this?"

"Funny you should ask. As it happens, I inherited a Super Suit from a corpse. I'll give it back after I get it dry cleaned."

Vax aims a significant look somewhat in my direction. "Time."

"Right." To Therese: "Cameras off. Every last one of them. And no bright ideas. I'd hate to have to add another corpse-suit to my collection."

I expect her to put up more of a fuss, challenge me on the likelihood that I'll fire an unlicensed handgun in broad daylight in the main lobby of LifeTime. But all she says is: "I need the headset."

"Ask and thou shalt receive," I say, passing it back to her. "But remember, just the cameras."

Our hands touch, which spooks her enough that she shivers.

Without putting the set back on, she speaks the shutdown command into the mic, and the screens behind the desk go dark. She's smart enough to give the headset back without being asked.

"Cassidy have a separate feed?" I ask her.

"I don't know."

She's lying, that much is sure, but I have no time to probe. With luck, the good doctor is too busy counting Krugerrands to check the feed.

"Do something about her," I say to Vax.

He produces a roll of duct tape. Such a clever lad. In a heartbeat, Therese is down, hands cuffed. Just before the tape goes over her mouth, she looks in my general vicinity and says acidly, "You won't get away with this."

"I've gotten away with worse," I say. Vax shoves her beneath the control panel and dons the headset, taking her position behind the desk.

"Dr Cassidy will see you now," he says, a dead-on imitation of her deadpan voice.

"No he won't," I say, and though he can't tell that I'm smiling, he grins back.

I glide up the stairs. At the top, I glance over my shoulder to find Vax manning his post, just as cool as can be. He's handing a brochure to some clueless soul who wandered in off the street thinking we're the kind of business our name implies. As soon as the clueless one leaves, he'll ping the number Vax gave him and be connected to an automated system that will book a cruise for him and his fiancée, all without him knowing there's a bound body beneath the desk and a girl in a Super Suit about to give the boss the surprise of his life.

I exit into the loft. Take three.

Cassidy isn't behind his desk this time. Instead, he's pacing in front of the lunette window, thin and sepulchral in his undertaker's suit, hands locked behind his back. I wonder why he appears so agitated, but it's not my problem. Another feckless employee, no doubt. I've perfected the invisible girl routine with Therese, and I'm prepared to repeat the procedure with him.

Floorboards creak with my next step. Cassidy stops and turns toward the stairs, but it's obvious he can't see me. I curse silently, then take another, more careful step.

And drop to the hardwood in a blaze of pain, my body making a very unladylike thump. The Super Suit becomes nothing but a regular agent's uniform, and the Smith & Wesson falls from my deadened hand. I try to get up, but all I can do is flop like a beached tuna, eyelids twitching and tongue stuck to the roof of my mouth. Cassidy appears overhead, and he can sure as hell see me now.

"Agent Randle?" he says, not sounding surprised. "I can't imagine how you came into possession of a skinthetic body armor prototype, but as you can see, it's not invulnerable to electric shock."

I like *Super Suit* a lot better than *skinthetic body armor prototype,* but even if I could tell him that with my tongue on the fritz, I'm not feeling very super at the moment.

His face dips uncomfortably close as he leans down to scoop the Smith & Wesson from the floor and remove the Raven from its holster. I can do no more than twitch in protest. The pain has subsided to a dull fire, but I can't concentrate hard enough to recover my camouflage, much less perform Jujutsu on the beanpole waving the M&P 380 in my face.

"This is not a regulation sidearm," he says sourly. I'm reminded that we're still several days shy of the initial occurrence at the Sleep Rite, which means he has no reason to associate this gun with anything in particular. "Explain yourself, Agent Randle."

With an effort, I roll over, take a breath, and stiffly sit. I listen for Vax, but there's no clank of my knight in shining armor storming the citadel to rescue his lady fair. I wish I'd told Therese to keep the feed open so my partner could monitor my progress or lack thereof. Yes, this certainly was a brilliant plan.

"Agent Randle?" Cassidy repeats.

"Ah vessa," I say thickly through my buzzing tongue, "vessigadusha." *I'm investigating an abduction.*

It doesn't make any more sense to him than it does to me. Frowning, he moves behind his desk, the Smith & Wesson leveled. He sets the Raven down and checks his screen, which shows Vax at the reception area. Things are unraveling fast, and I can't stop them.

"Agent Randle," he says in mock disappointment.

"Ma muvuh," I say, almost articulately. "She vash." *Vanish*, damn it. "I try a fine huh."

"So you and Agent Vaccaro conspired to sneak into the office, disable our receptionist, and confront me with deadly force?" He shakes his head. "I'm calling security. This is beyond the pale."

"Wait," I say. "My mom was studdin" – I pause to collect myself – "studying time travel. I thought you might know what happened to her."

"You were wrong," he says, a finger hovering over the call button. "Very, very wrong."

Before he can bring the finger down, the lunette window rattles and there's the sound of a heavy object striking home. Cassidy collapses face down on the desk, revealing the penumbra hovering behind him.

It's much smaller than normal, not nearly large enough to contain a human being. What it does contain is Therese's Raven, which floats a foot above the desk, rippling weirdly as if it's underwater. I've never seen anything like this, and though I feel a tickle in my core, the penumbra's apparently too tiny to induce the nausea of its full-scale cousin.

The gun nudges Cassidy, who slides from desk to floor, limp but breathing. I must admit, it's been a rough few days for LifeTime top management.

The Raven turns toward me, and I tense for the shot.

Instead, it flicks to the side a couple of times like a hand beckoning me near. I rise on quivering legs and approach. I've figured out that the gun must be in the grasp of someone wearing the same kind of suit I am, though how they're reaching only their hand through the mini-penumbra is beyond me. In any event, they're much more adept at the camouflage function than I am. Even when I'm standing behind Cassidy's desk an inch away, I can't see the hand that holds the floating Raven.

I can, however, see one of the buttons on his screen illuminate. I glance at the gun, which tilts up and down as if it's nodding, then angles downward toward the boss's swivel chair. I settle into the seat, my eyes glued to the screen.

The penumbra purrs beside me as an image forms.

CHAPTER 29

It's an image of this room, but not this moment. The recording was taken at night, with a single desk lamp forming a bubble of brightness in the shadowed loft. The lunette window reflects the light like a blind eye.

The camera hangs high overhead, giving me a bird's eye view of the two figures sitting on opposite sides of the desk. Cassidy, the Richard M Nixon of dirty bosses, occupies the chair I'm currently sitting in. It's the person across from him who draws my notice.

Mom.

She's not visibly older than she was in the lecture I watched yesterday. Dark-haired, dressed to kill, she looks every inch the professor. But where Cassidy's face is as artificially well-preserved as at present, hers is pale and worn.

Was this video recorded after Jeremy's murder? Did she come here to plead for a chance to travel back to the day it happened? I can't remember my mom pleading with anyone for anything, unless she was pleading with God that day at the church. Maybe this isn't her first nighttime visit to Cassidy's office.

Then I see the timestamp.

August 28, 2017.

It's the day exactly twenty years ago that Dad brought me and Jeremy from Lancaster and we moved into the home Mom had been living in for the past two months. We spent the next several days exploring the house and neighborhood,

Dad away working his new job, Mom indulging the two of us before we started school on August 31. I don't recall her looking so careworn, but then, I was preoccupied with my own childish cares at the time.

Her hands are folded in her lap. That doesn't stop them from twisting nervously.

"Please, Norman," she says. "Let me show you the data again."

"We've gone over this many times, Deborah," he says. "The technology has been ready for months. You were brought here to oversee the human trials, but you've failed – refused – to disclose the process of memory reconstruction and retrieval. My associates are growing impatient, and you alone hold the key to satisfy their demands."

"I can't," she says, her voice little more than a whisper.

"If you're concerned about the ethics review board..."

"It's not a matter of ethics. It would be... dangerous."

Cassidy raises an eyebrow. "Dangerous?"

"Extremely dangerous," she says. "Much more than I realized. These people you propose to test, these subjects..."

"Yes?"

"They're unhealthy. Psychologically deranged. Dislocated in space and time."

"Which, according to your theory, is what makes them capable of time travel."

"And also what makes time travel so hazardous. To tap into trauma as a mechanism for temporal displacement–"

"Again, precisely what your model proposes."

"–is to traumatize the very foundations of time, can't you see that? I wish it weren't so, but it is."

Cassidy leans back in his chair, steepling his fingers beneath his nose. "Why the sudden change of heart? You seemed convinced before."

"I failed to take certain factors into account," my mom says miserably. "That's the nature of new research."

"Don't patronize me, Deborah."

"I'm trying to be honest."

"It sounds as if you're merely getting cold feet."

"That's bullshit, and you know it," she says. "You'd get *cold feet* too if you'd seen what I've seen."

"And how, exactly, have you seen what we haven't yet achieved?"

"I've foreseen it."

"Please, Deborah."

"You don't believe me?" she says. "Then let me tell you that I've seen travelers carrying their trauma histories with them wherever and whenever they go, revisiting nightmares every bit as vivid and raw as the first time they happened. I've seen the travelers' reactions: anxiety, panic, violence. If we open that box, if we allow what's inside to escape, we'll have no way of calling it back. Every temporal scenario you can imagine, every moment in time from now to eternity will be infected by the distortions and delusions of the travelers' minds."

Cassidy scoffs. "You're overanalyzing this."

"I'm doing what you brought me here to do," she says. "You directed me to examine every nuance of temporal displacement from the perspective of the minds you were proposing to let loose in time, and I've done exactly what you asked. My research has led me to one inescapable conclusion: it can't be done without an unacceptably high level of risk."

"Risk is my business," Cassidy says coldly. "The higher it may be, the more carefully we plan for it, that's all."

"And the more profitable it is."

"We're on the verge of offering a service with the potential for significant social benefit. A service we've invested substantial capital to develop. Don't you think we're entitled to something in return?"

"I can't do it, Norman. I'm sorry."

He leans forward, his voice softening. "Deborah, I urge you to reconsider. We'll take every precaution, follow any protocols you recommend. If it's a matter of employing test subjects without trauma histories…"

"There's no way around this," she says. "If we tap the mechanisms in unaffected brains, we'll *produce* the trauma we're seeking to avoid. No matter what we try, the outcome will be the same."

She hangs her head. She's not crying – just exhausted, defeated. Afraid. More like terrified, and that terrifies me. *Every temporal scenario you can imagine, every moment in time from now to eternity will be infected by the distortions and delusions of the travelers' minds…* Did she *know* that, or only fear it? How could she have *foreseen* what wouldn't happen until two years later, when LifeTime opened its doors for business? For that matter, how did LifeTime run the human trials necessary to launch its operation if she held some sort of secret she wouldn't let them use?

The video has frozen with my mom in her hunched position, Cassidy's mouth open to make another point. A new button on the desk lights up as an unseen finger touches it. The video disappears – I cry out when Mom vanishes, I can't help it – and the desk-screen fills with long columns of data, a spreadsheet in glowing green pixels. The invisible controller scrolls through the list, and I see that it consists of words accompanied by numbers – dates – along with a final column that reads *Status*. I press the button to stop the scroll, my hand briefly contacting whoever's there. I shiver as badly as Therese did, and then I start to read.

Subject IA. History: battlefield trauma. First date of travel: 9/7/17. Temporal destination: 9/6/17. Physical destination: LifeTime headquarters. Mission: rendezvous with TDM team. Status: mission failure, subject's whereabouts unknown.

Subject IB. History: battlefield trauma. First date of travel: 9/9/17. Temporal destination: 9/8/17. Physical destination: LifeTime headquarters. Mission: rendezvous with TDM team. Status: mission failure, subject's whereabouts unknown.

Subject IC. History: battlefield trauma. First date of travel: 9/11/17. Temporal destination: 9/10/17. Physical destination: LifeTime headquarters. Mission: rendezvous with TDM team. Status: mission failure, subject's whereabouts unknown.

It goes on like that, each subject sent a day back in time two days after the previous failed mission, only to fail at their mission objective as surely as the travelers before them. Clearly, these first travelers weren't assigned to change the past, just to show up at HQ as evidence that the process had worked. But they never did.

Where did they go? Did the mere fact of traveling produce an altered trajectory where they were marooned, unable to find their way back to the location from which they'd started? Or did they physically disappear, their bodies torn apart by the forces of temporal displacement?

I scroll down the list, wondering who these nameless "subjects" were, what happened to them on the battlefield. How Cassidy got his hands on them. It takes three weeks for your body to recover from core-implantation surgery and your mind to attune with the hardware, so for him to send out so many so quickly, he must have equipped them all with cores beforehand, then held them ready, waiting for my mom to reveal her secret. Which she must have done no later than September 7, 2017.

A week after Jeremy was killed. When she was most vulnerable, when she didn't care anymore. Or when she cared so much she was willing to risk other people's lives on the chance that it might be possible to alter the past.

The list of unsuccessful missions continues to the middle of October 2017. There's a weeklong pause, maybe to work on some technical glitch or other. When the missions resume, the "Status" line starts to read like this:

Successful mission, traveler reconnected with timeline at designated coordinates.

Successful mission, traveler reconnected with timeline at designated coordinates.

Successful mission, traveler reconnected with timeline at designated coordinates.

Mission failure, subject's whereabouts unknown.

Successful mission, traveler reconnected with timeline at designated coordinates.

Successful mission, traveler reconnected with timeline at designated coordinates.

There are still no names, but there are additional changes to the basic procedure. For one, not everyone on the list is marked *battlefield trauma*. Some are identified as having experienced *childhood sexual abuse, surgical awakening, natural disaster, live burial,* and more. Subjects who complete their first mission are sent back more than once, each trip a day deeper into the past until they max out at a week. A few of these longer missions fail, the subjects disappearing like the earliest travelers. Most, however, succeed, which leads to another innovation: sending travelers two weeks into the past. Clearly a preliminary to scheduling longer and longer trips: a month, a decade, a century... I can practically hear Cassidy's cackle as he imagines the possibilities. The power he'll wield when he's master of all time.

Except that's when he hits the wall. The longer trips fail, the travelers vanishing without a trace.

The trials grind to a halt in late November 2017. There's a short gap where the technicians must have been trying to figure out the problem, followed by a few last-ditch attempts.

All of them fail. In the end, a note pronounces glumly: *Safe window for temporal displacement appears to be of extremely short duration. Recalibrate business model pending unforeseen advances in TDM technology.*

After that, there are no more long trips.

I pause to consider. When I joined LifeTime, the training manual said that the one-week limit was imposed by government regulators to prevent us from monkeying with the distant past. Now it seems as if there's something inherent in the process –

the strain on the mind or body, perhaps? – that cuts people off at a week. If so, that makes Legion's twenty-year jumps even more incomprehensible. Does he know a secret Cassidy didn't? A secret even my mom didn't? Or is he somehow unique, able to withstand trips that doom everyone else?

I return to the list. The trials resume in December 2017, again with new wrinkles. This time around, travelers are sent not singly but in cohorts of as many as twenty. And they're sent not to LifeTime HQ but to places farther afield, the mission objective being to rendezvous with satellites in other cities. It doesn't take a genius to figure out Cassidy's strategy. If he can't control the farthest reaches of time, he'll widen his influence across space.

And he does. Almost all of the physically distant trips are successful. Interestingly, most of their subjects are marked *no trauma history*, which means LifeTime must have figured out how to do what my mom's paper suggested: duplicate the mental activity of trauma in nontraumatized people. I begin to suspect that Ayesha was lying about that paper too, that Mom read a perfectly conventional research study on memory to the CMU search committee while saving the time travel bombshell for Cassidy's eyes alone. Whatever the case, the pattern is clear. Two years before LifeTime's public emergence in 2019, fifteen-plus years before my own first trip, Cassidy was using my mom's knowledge to seed travel agents throughout the country. Travel agents *without* trauma histories, the very people he'd offered my mom when she sounded her warning about traumatizing time.

The invisible finger that's pressing the buttons touches another, and a second dataset pops up beside the first. This one is marked *Restricted Access* in red, and there are three columns following the traveler's alphanumeric ID. The first contains a date, the second a brief history. The third is headed, somewhat ambiguously, *Further Outcomes*. But there's nothing ambiguous about the outcomes themselves.

Suicide.

Homicide.

Unknown.

Arrest for arson.

Double homicide.

Vehicular homicide.

Homicide-suicide.

Mass shooting.

Disappeared.

Disappeared.

Arrest for rape.

Homicide.

Suicide.

Unknown…

It goes on like that for hundreds of entries, the results never changing: homicide, suicide, arrest, disappearance. I try to convince myself these are first-round failed trials, but the dates are more recent than those recorded for the earliest instances of successful travel. A few come from as far back as 2018 or 2019, but most are from the following decades, including the past two or three years. Some of these travelers have trauma histories, some not. It doesn't seem to matter to the *further outcomes*.

I linger on one of the entries from late March 2035 listed *suicide*. Something about it sparks a memory, but I can't quite connect the dots. Then it comes to me, and I stare at the entry until the words blur.

"Oh, my God," I say.

At my shoulder, the Raven nods in agreement.

It's a date from my first year at LifeTime, the evening Vax and I were sent to stop a drug deal that turned deadly on the South Side. The same evening we watched a suicidal teenager launch herself from the top of the Birmingham Bridge, her body folding on impact with the dark water.

I'd always assumed it was a simple screw-up, a case of bad research or bad targeting. But it wasn't.

I double-check the ID tag. Sure enough, it corresponds to a nontraumatized subject who completed her trip more than ten years before the date of her death. When I cross-check others, it's the same: they're all successful travelers. Successful, that is, except for the *further outcomes* that awaited them down the road.

The list stops scrolling. The gun settles on the desktop, as if it's shown me everything I need to know. And in a way, it has.

LifeTime has been sending agents back to clean up its own messes. They transported a bunch of people – traumatized or not – back in time, and all of the travelers seemed to survive the experience, until they started cropping up as killers of themselves and others. Does that mean the husband and wife in the Sleep Rite were renegade travelers? There's no record of them on the spreadsheet, but of course there wouldn't be, because that hasn't happened yet. Could *all* of my assignments over the past two and a half years have had to do with time travel gone wrong? Or were some of them – at least, the ones Vax and I were given complete and accurate information about – routine homicides we were assigned to reverse in order to keep the company in the black?

It doesn't matter. Whatever Cassidy's original intentions may have been, his *recalibrated business model* turned out to be a goldmine, enabling the company to rake in cash and burnish its public image by correcting chaos of its own making. If the effort to fix the past sometimes failed, as it did with the girl on the bridge, so what? One less headache to eliminate, one less canary who could sing. One less person who signed up for time travel with a visibly normal brain and came out of it wanting nothing more than to end a life.

Mom was right. As usual. *No matter what we try, the outcome will be the same.*

I rest my head in my hands and close my eyes. I need a moment to think, to puzzle out pieces that don't make sense.

The girl on the bridge, for example. She was eighteen years

old when she died, more than ten years after her first trip. Unless Cassidy was sending schoolchildren out as travelers, does that mean there are others like Legion who can move through time without aging?

And what about the ones who vanished in the earliest trials, as well as those who disappeared when they made journeys of more than a week? Their IDs don't correspond to anything on the second list. Could they still be out there, waiting to strike? Could Ayesha, Therese, Chloe, the random stranger I passed on the street an hour ago be the next killer I'm called in to stop?

Could Legion?

The thought is tempting despite the lack of evidence. I wouldn't be surprised if he was one of the first travelers, those with battlefield trauma. It would certainly explain why he hates my mom so much, why he keeps gunning for Cassidy. Who wouldn't want revenge on the two people responsible for sending him into the hell of his own past?

And OK, not to make this all about me, but what about *me*? If time travel turns people into maniacal killers, will the agents who are currently being sent back to stop other travelers eventually go rogue themselves? I don't feel like killing anyone at the moment – at least, not anyone I don't have good reason to. But what lies in my future? If I'm a ticking time bomb like the rest of them, when will I go off?

There's a tap on my shoulder. I spin, expecting LifeTime security, but it's no one. No one visible, that is. The Raven floats beside me again, its barrel pointed at the screen. It seems impatient, for a gun. I return my attention to the list of names, wondering if there's something I didn't catch. The muzzle is close enough that I hear the metal singing with the mini-penumbra's energy.

The data on the screen fades. It's replaced by the video I watched before, though the timestamp reads a few minutes later.

Cassidy is alone. He's out of his chair, pacing in front of the whited-out window the way he was when I entered the loft today. From time to time he stops to glance at the stairs, then resumes his course. I realize a second before it happens what he's waiting for, and with that realization comes another.

Everything I've thought about LifeTime up to this moment has been both right and terribly, terribly wrong.

Footsteps echo on the stairs. A shadow rises into the loft, crosses the floor to Cassidy's desk. When the shadow enters the circle of light, it reveals itself to be a young man with long hair, sallow skin, and eyes like craters. He sits in the scolding chair, extending his legs to rest his ratty tennis shoes on the boss's immaculate desk-screen.

"What did she say?" Regent asks.

Cassidy has lowered himself into his chair, a thin veneer of sweat visible on his pale cheeks and forehead. He removes a handkerchief from his pocket – OK, *he's* the kind of guy I'd expect to carry a handkerchief – and wipes his face, then balls the hanky and tries to shove it inside his suit. He misses twice before lining it up and sending it home.

"She won't talk," he says. "She absolutely refused."

"You explained the situation to her?"

"As much as I could."

"And?"

"She texted me her resignation after she left."

"Effective…?"

"Immediately."

Regent lowers his legs and sits forward. "This is a problem, my friend. For me, but even more, for you."

"I can contact the IRB. Perhaps, with pressure from that quarter…"

"Always thinking inside the box, aren't you? You going to threaten to pull her funding next?"

"I've tried everything," Cassidy says, and despite his outward calm, his voice breaks. "If we attempt to expose *her*, we risk exposing ourselves. Our clients..."

"The only client you need to worry about at the moment is me."

"Please, John," Cassidy says. Or is it *Jon*? "We've reached an impasse with Deborah, but it's not insurmountable. Give me time, I'll figure something out–"

"I don't have time," Regent says. "You know that."

"But there are options," Cassidy persists. "Another practitioner in her field, someone younger, more ambitious..."

"No. She's the one. The key to it all. And the clock's ticking, my friend," he adds, tapping his wrist even though he's not wearing a watch. "There's far less time than you might like to believe."

Cassidy spreads his hands in appeal. "What do you want me to do? Just say the word, and I'll do it."

"Not if it might be traced to you, though, isn't that right?" Regent says with a scornful laugh. "You're just lucky killing you doesn't serve my purposes at present."

Cassidy cowers. Regent stands, paces a few steps in front of the desk, then turns to his business partner. The smile I remember from the school annex forms on his thin lips.

"Maybe we haven't taken the correct approach with our reluctant genius," he says. "Given her the proper motivation."

"What do you mean?" Cassidy asks, his voice trembling.

"I think you know what I mean."

"No, John. No. I can't–"

"You won't have to do a thing. Leave it to me."

"John, please. She has children..."

"Exactly what I was thinking."

Cassidy's eyes widen. "You can't mean..."

"She's the trauma teacher, right?" Regent says. "Maybe it's time we took her out of the classroom. Showed her what it's really like."

"John, please..."

Regent waves a hand dismissively. "You've always been a chickenshit, Cassidy. Full of scruples, never willing to go all the way. I was the one who fronted the money, made the contacts you were too petrified to make. I even tracked down the great Deborah Sayre for you, and all I asked you to do was find out what she knows. And you couldn't even do that."

"She was afraid," Cassidy says. "Afraid of what might happen if she told me."

"I guess she wasn't afraid enough of what might happen if she didn't."

"John…"

Cassidy half-stands, groping across the desk as if to detain his partner. The younger man looks at him contemptuously, then reaches for his back pocket. Cassidy flings his arms in front of his face.

But Regent doesn't withdraw a gun. He simply nods, pats the pocket in satisfaction, and heads for the stairs. At the top, he turns to the man behind the desk. His face is in shadow, and his words seem to emerge from the darkness all around him.

"You're recording this?" he asks.

"Of course."

"Good. Don't try to erase it. If you do" – he levels a long finger at his partner – "I'll know."

Cassidy recoils as if the finger is an actual gun. Regent chuckles hollowly.

"You won't see me for a long time," he says. "But the next time you see *her*, she'll be on her hands and knees begging to tell you what she knows."

He makes his way down the stairs. Cassidy raises his hands in an attitude of prayer before sinking into the chair and burying his face in his arms. His shoulders shake as he cries.

They can't be shaking any worse than mine.

The mini-penumbra has vanished. Whoever was inside it has taken the Raven with them, but they've retrieved the Smith &

Wesson and laid it on the desktop. The end of its barrel rests on another button. Tempting me, torturing me.

I know everything I need to know, don't I?

Regent killed Jeremy to force my mother's hand. Fearful as she was of time travel, she was desperate enough after her son died to accept the personal risk. Her brainchild was born, and with it, Legion.

Do I need to press this final button? Do I need to know where things went from there?

I reach out, lightly tapping the screen.

The video fades. In its place is a single line of text, providing the itinerary of a single traveler. Unlike the others, this one has a name.

Deborah Jane Sayre.

Her history tells me she was equipped with a core on January 25, 2018. That she took her first and, until three days ago, only trip a week later, far less time than she needed to adjust to the core.

But she didn't travel back in time. She couldn't.

Maybe she was too stricken with grief to volunteer for the earlier trials. Maybe she implored Cassidy to add her name only to be rebuffed. It doesn't matter. By the time she got her core, after months of self-blame, bargaining with God, and trifling with the man she couldn't have known was her son's killer, LifeTime had learned that anyone who tried to travel back longer than a week would be lost. She'd missed her chance to save her son, to save herself.

So she didn't go back. She went *forward.*

Almost twenty years from the time she left. To August 31, 2037.

To the Sleep Rite Motor Lodge.

CHAPTER 30

The Smith & Wesson sits on the desk beside me. Cassidy is still in la-la land. It would be so easy to put him out of his misery right now.

But what's the point? He's a pawn in this as much as any of us. Besides, he'll get his soon enough.

I holster the gun and head downstairs. Vax glances up from his station, worry written all over his face.

"Where have you been? It's almost–"

"I'll tell you on the way there. Let's move."

He comes out from behind the desk. "What about Therese?"

"Leave her. Cassidy's down for the count. By the time someone notices the receptionist is missing, we'll be gone."

"Where are we going?"

"To the chamber."

"You want to go back *again*? Where to?"

"Nowhere. I want to go forward."

That stops whatever he was about to say. "Can we do that?"

"Why not? The future's there, isn't it? We've already been."

"But..."

"But nothing. That bastard Legion moves back and forth at will, showing up whenever he chooses. Twenty years ago, yesterday, tomorrow, he's there. Unless he knows something we don't, there's a way to do it."

"You said he doesn't age."

"Not that I can tell."

"So he *does* know something we don't."

"Except he's not the only one. My mom did it too."

"Traveled forward? When?"

"Almost twenty years ago is when. Wait until you find out where."

I tell him. The worry on his face deepens.

"Did she age? When she went forward?"

"How am I supposed to know?"

"Is that what made her sick?"

I'm hurrying toward the door that leads to the lower level, but Vax almost collides with me when I come to a dead stop. "You think time travel caused her dementia?"

"It's a possibility."

"So you're concerned we'll lose our minds if we skip forward to the Sleep Rite?"

"Also a possibility."

"I'm going," I say. "You can come with me if you want. I don't have all day to stand around shooting the breeze."

"And you can't wait three days until it happens again?"

"I can't wait three seconds until it happens again. The Sleep Rite took place twenty years to the day after Jeremy was killed, and it's where my mom went the first time she disappeared. It's also where everything started going haywire for us: the job turning bad, you and Cassidy getting shot, Legion coming back, timestrands changing in unpredictable ways, Mom disappearing a second time. I've *got* to go there. I've got to know what's going on."

"Could be you don't *want* to know, Mir."

It seems like he hasn't called me that in years. If I can reset me and Vax, why can't I reset other things as well? "No matter how bad it is, I have to know. I don't expect you to come along."

"You kidding? A chance to see the future? Where do I sign up?"

"Except this future is already past."

"Not yet," he says, and that closes the deal.

We make our way to the basement, where the labs and servers and travel chamber are. We move fast, so there's no time to give Vax anything but the highlights-reel version of what I've learned. Someone's bound to notice sooner or later that the reception desk is unoccupied, and then they'll discover Therese, and then they'll take the chamber offline and put the whole building on lockdown. I wish we could travel manually, but Vax's core is depleted and mine has only the tiniest of boosts from the mini-penumbra, and there's no way that's enough juice for both of us to travel forward three whole days. If, that is, we can travel forward at all.

"Got your Glock?" I ask.

He pats his pocket.

"I have no idea what to expect when we get there," I tell him. "Just play it cool and be ready for anything."

"Always am."

I vanish against cement and cinder block. With Vax in the lead, we exit the stairwell and make our way down the hall to the travel chamber. The tech and security guard are lounging in the cubicle just outside, and they don't exactly jump to their feet and salute when they see Vax rounding the corner.

"What's up, Vaccaro?" the guard asks.

"Traveling today."

"You're not on the manifest," the guard says, yawning.

"Special delivery," I whisper in his ear, right before bashing him on the head with the Smith & Wesson.

He drops to the floor. The tech reaches for the alarm, but decides better of it when he finds Vax's Glock in his face.

"Set the coordinates," Vax says to him. "August 31, 2037."

"But that's..."

"The future. You must have been first in your class."

"We can't do that."

"I've got a hunch you can."

The guy fusses with the screen until he figures out how to pull up a future date. He looks amazed that he can. "What time?"

Vax glances at where he supposes I am. He's way off, but I answer. "1235:50 hours."

"Hear that, champ?" Vax asks the tech guy, who's looking around for where my voice came from. "Not getting any younger here."

The tech grumbles, but finishes inputting the data. "Where to?"

"Sleep Rite Motor Lodge, I-376. Room 11." When the guy frowns, Vax gives him a nudge. "Little getaway. With the missus."

I stifle a laugh. The guy fools with the equipment some more, pulls up a satellite map, homes in on the location. The network grid has the same accuracy the Pentagon achieves with guided missiles, which is what we're about to become. It makes me wonder who the mysterious *clients* Cassidy referred to might be. Domestic or foreign? Either way, I'm going in there to get my mom, the rest of the planet be damned.

"It's ready," the tech says.

Vax double-checks the screen to make sure everything's kosher. It must be, because he gives me – or the air three feet beside me – the thumbs-up. Keeping his gun on the tech in case the guy tries anything foolish, he gestures with the other hand for me to go first. Always the gentleman. How he's going to keep the tech at bay for his own trip is anyone's guess, but it's not my problem.

The door to the chamber hisses open. It's small, about the size of an MRI, which means it can't hold two bodies at once. Its dimensions are just right for a casket, now that I think of it. The smell of ozone washes over me. The light is set to green, so I squeeze in. I've dropped the camouflage mode, but the black suit's barely visible against the gunmetal-black interior of the tube.

"Don't be long," I say to Vax.

"Right behind you."

The machine powers up before I have time to question if

we just engaged in some kind of double entendre. The hum pierces my feet, my bones. I close my eyes to focus on my task and reduce disorientation upon launch. Despite my own warning, I can't help wondering what I'm going to find when I get there.

A klaxon screams, and my eyes fly open.

Someone must have discovered Therese. Either that or the tech is sneakier than we suspected. Vax shoves him aside and slams his hand down on the primary booster. He turns to me, shouting a single word over the noise of the alarm.

"Go!"

Bright light wraps me. Heat blazes in my gut. Vax is fading, along with everything around him.

"How will you be able to follow?" I want to ask, but the winds of time pick my words to pieces before they can leave my tongue.

Monday, August 31, 2037

Bright light. Nausea. I clutch my stomach like a woman giving birth.

A jumble of images floods my mind. Fragmented, disordered. There's no way to place them, pin them down.

The school. Jeremy. Gunfire. All I can see is red.

Cassidy's office. The lecture. He's not my anything.

The church. Christ on the cross, the old man in the hospital. Ayesha.

The park. Therese dead.

Mom. Dad.

Razor blades against my arm. Smoking. Sex. (With Vax?)

The bridge, the girl, the fall, the impact.

Chloe, Loretta, Opal. Needles blurring, skein spilling from the bag, forming itself click by click into a long pink garment.

Eddie Jonathan Regent.

A penumbra opening wide. Legion stepping through it again and again and again. Eyes like holes.

Mom disappearing in a blink. Everything disappearing.

My whole life lived and unlived in less than a second.

Then.

The arrival.

Spacetime squeals as it folds in two, squeezing the air from my lungs, pulling my guts tight. My head spins from the violent dislocation in where I'm meant to be.

I look around, but everything's too hazy to discern. Reflexively, I check the readout on my chronometer.

Sleep Rite Motor Lodge. August 31, 2037. 1235:50 hours.
I breathe.
Right on time.

PART FOUR
The Dark Backward

CHAPTER 31

Everything looks the same.

Bed, lamp, painting. Daytime soap. The shower hisses. Sunlight works its way around the blinds.

I let out a sigh of relief. I've arrived with not only my body but my brain intact. At least that I can tell.

A man in a rumpled suit stands in shadow beside the bed. He turns at the sound of my breath, and I catch a glimpse of his lean, sickly face, bloodshot eyes, and mustache blending into grayish stubble.

It seems I spoke too soon.

"Dad?"

It's him. Alive.

He's wearing the same misshapen brown suit the husband wore when I traveled here with Vax. The same suit I watched on Cassidy's screen. I can't remember my dad owning that particular suit, but it's been a while.

Could it have been him all along? The husband was much beefier than the man I shared a house with for the last ten years of his life, but if I add eighty pounds to my dad's wasted frame, would he be the man I saw the previous two times? If those pounds were to melt away like a summertime mirage, would he be the man who stands before me now?

But the name wasn't the same. It couldn't have been. The husband's name was–

I can't remember.

I rack my brain but come up blank. Same with the wife and

lover. It's as if I never knew their names, as if I didn't read them a thousand times on the forensics report when I was preparing for the jump I first took on September 7, 2037. I can picture myself poring over that report with Vax, setting the report aside and poring over him, but everywhere the names should be, there's an ellipsis, a redaction in memory.

So it's possible the husband *was* my dad from the start and I forgot that too. Or it's possible I'm not where I think I am – wrong room, wrong date, wrong affair.

Wrong Miriam.

"Dad," I say again.

He blinks, head wobbling. He's unarmed. And very drunk. He leans against the wall to keep from falling. The alcohol reek of his breath fogs the air between us. He mumbles something, but I can't make out the words.

My penumbra's gone, faded into the general haze of the room. The nausea's gone too. Vax should be here by now. The chamber couldn't have shut off when the alarm was tripped or I wouldn't be here either. Panic strikes me at the thought that he tried to make it through the doorway just as it closed. That his body was ripped to atoms and sprinkled all over the cosmos, never to return.

But I can't think about that now. I came here for a reason, though I'm no longer sure what it is.

I take a breath to steady myself, then point the Smith & Wesson at him, holding it with both hands. That doesn't help. They shake as I speak the words.

"Dad," I say, "you're under arrest."

"Wha' for?"

"For," I say through clenched teeth, "attempted murder."

"Din' kill anyone."

"Not yet."

He tries to stand on his own. Bad idea. He loses his footing, falls. Something comes from his mouth on the way down. When he climbs back up, lumpy puke coats his shirt front and loosely knotted tie. He wipes chunks from his chin with a sleeve.

"Who're you?" he says thickly.

"It's me, Dad," I say. "It's Miriam."

He stares at me, slack-jawed. "Mir'am?"

"Yes," I say. "Please, Dad, don't make this any harder than it has to be."

He tries to take a step toward me, but loses the battle with gravity once more. He falls onto the bed and lies face up, staring at the ceiling, breathing heavily.

I approach the bed. The smell of sweat and puke clings to him like a film. Hesitantly, I reach out toward him, this wreck of a man I never thought I'd see again, never wanted to. His eyes have closed. I notice how papery thin his eyelids are, purple veins outlined beneath his skin.

Then he heaves himself upward faster than should be possible for a man in his condition. My synapses try to sync with the suit, but it fails to armor up. My father's hands are on my wrist, fumbling, uncoordinated. I could shoot him easily. But I don't, and a second later my elbow collides with the headboard and my arm goes numb.

When we roll off the bed and stand, him on one side and me on the other, he's holding my gun in violently trembling hands.

"Dad," I say.

"Lea' me alone!" he bellows. "'m here for her!"

"Dad, please, give me the gun."

"Kill 'er! Kill 'em both!"

"Daddy," I say, for the first time in however long. The thumb safety's off, and my dad, actuary and alcoholic Jules Randle, is aiming at me like a sharpshooter.

Before he can pull the trigger, the bathroom door bangs open, and the gun swings in that direction as a shape parts the curtain of steam.

One shape, not two. It's a woman with long dark hair, gray

eyes, and a smooth complexion. An inadequate bath towel is wrapped around her chest, exposing the triangle of black hair below her hips. She should be shocked to find two intruders in her motel room, but her face shows nothing. She walks straight toward her husband as if she doesn't notice the gun he's waving around, removes the towel, and lays it on the bed. Beneath her full breasts there's a closed surgical incision where her core was implanted, its edges angry red against her pale skin. She turns from us without a word and takes a brush from the desk, running it through her long, shiny hair.

"Mom?" I say.

No reaction. The brush moves rhythmically, loosening tangles. Her naked body is fit, the muscles of her back bunching beneath slick skin. She seems to be the age she was when she vanished the first time, but she acts like the passive, oblivious woman who disappeared from my apartment three days ago. Correction: six days ago.

I watch her face in the mirror above the desk. It's a blank.

"Mom," I say. "Please, Mom."

"Deb!" my father cries, but his voice isn't enough to penetrate her trance.

She pauses, her hand motionless, her head cocked as if listening. Then her eyes widen and she spins toward the bed.

The air crackles and hums. My dad falls into the corner beneath the TV, bringing the lamp down with him. The bulb shatters. This would be the perfect opportunity for me to retrieve the gun, but the penumbra that forms above the bed is so powerful it crushes me to the carpet like a bug.

My mother darts to the door, her hand closing on the knob. She rattles it frantically in its frame, but it won't open. She whirls, takes in the room, sees exactly what I see: no way out. A look of terror crosses her face as a human figure forms inside the penumbra.

I'm praying for Vax.

What I get is Legion.

He leaps to the floor. He's wearing jeans but no shirt, and his skin is sallow, long arms striped with veins, ribs distinctly visible. The glowing threads of the penumbra crawl over him like grave-worms eating their way out of a corpse.

My mother hesitates only a second before she charges at him, the brush raised like a hammer. He catches her wrist as the blow comes down, then uses his other hand to pry the paltry weapon loose. She reaches for it, but he dangles it just beyond her grasp like a bully taunting a much younger child. Her hand closes around the brush for an instant before a mini-penumbra swallows it, her fingers flying to her mouth as if she's been burned. Legion releases her and she falls to the bed. She wraps her arms around herself to cover her nakedness while he stands above her, his head thrown back in a soundless laugh.

Then he turns to me.

He's not at all winded from his fight with my mom. I try to stand, only to be squashed by the waves of power emanating from him. I crab-crawl toward the door, sending desperate signals to the Super Suit, but it won't arm. From my position in the corner of the room, I lock eyes with my dad, who's wedged against the wall beneath the weirdly flickering TV. A single word escapes him.

"Same!" he says, or maybe it's *shame*.

Legion pays him no mind. He takes a step toward me, smiling the way he did in Cassidy's office, the way he did twenty years ago. He holds out an open hand, and a penumbra blooms from his fingertips. The fiery disc grows rapidly until it fills the room like a supernova. I squeeze my eyes shut while the pressure builds in my ears until I feel my head will explode.

Then it stops. I open my eyes to find the room returned to darkness. The last traces of the penumbra wink out like a cloud of glowing dust motes, and he's gone.

I stand on liquid knees and approach the bed. My mom lies on her stomach, limbs splayed like a rag doll. Her face is turned toward me, but her eyes are sightless. I reach out hesitantly to touch her wet, flushed skin. A floral smell saturates her, and I understand at last why her older self is deathly afraid of the shower.

But is this her? The real her? Legion took her as a fifty-eight year-old woman from my condo, so who is this stranger from my distant past? And how did she get here?

"Mom," I say.

Her eyes focus on my face, but it's obvious she doesn't know who I am. How could she, when I'm nearly twenty years older than the little girl she left behind? I lay a hand on her head and stroke her still-damp hair, overcoming the shudder in my chest to talk to her in the measured tone I perfected during our time together.

"Mom," I say, "it's me. It's Miriam."

"Who?"

It's the first word she's said to me in almost twenty years, and it just about rips me in half. "Your daughter. Miriam Randle. Do you remember me?"

She shivers. "You're so old."

"I grew up. I've come to take you home."

"You can't. He keeps me here."

"I won't let him."

"You don't understand," she says. "He came to me. Showed me the future. Warned me. Told me to meet him here. I came, and he wouldn't let me get away. I've tried to fight him, but he's too strong. Every time I close my eyes I think I'll wake up somewhere else, but every time I open them I'm still here."

"You're trapped," I say. "In some sort of time loop. Do you remember the first day you came to him?"

"No," she says. "It's always the same."

I sit on the bed and wrap my arms around her. I glance at the heap of gabardine that used to be my dad, but he's out cold, the gun dangling between his legs. My mom doesn't resist when I lift her partway from the bed. Her face is frozen, her eyes fixed on nothing. I let go of her with one hand to retrieve the Smith & Wesson.

When I do, she shoves me away from her and dives for the gun. Before I can recover my balance, she rises from the floor, the barrel pressed against her temple. Her finger is on the trigger, and her hand doesn't shake at all.

"It's too late," she says. "For everything."

Her eyes have glazed over. Her face has regained the look of smooth emptiness, as if she's willing herself to be hundreds of miles from where she is. My mom, caught in this hell for an eternity, tortured by a demon in human form. Never to be free of this place, except possibly in death.

"Mom," I plead, "you don't have to do this."

Her head turns to the side. A penumbra's coalescing in the darkness above the bed. She closes her eyes, and a single tear slides down her cheek.

"He's here," she says.

The penumbra flares suddenly, so bright I can't see a thing. I flinch at the sound of a gunshot. When the light subsides a second later, I find her face down on the sheets, blood spurting from her head.

"Mom!"

I pull her to me, drenching myself in her blood. The entry hole isn't where I expect – it's at the back of her head, not her temple where she was holding the gun.

It takes me a second to realize what that means.

The penumbra's fully formed. I can see the shadow of the man who occupies it. His arm is extended, the gun that killed my mother a dark blot against the light. Taking the Smith & Wesson from her unresisting fingers, I rise to face him.

"No more hiding," I say. "It's just you and me this time."

He steps through. I aim at a spot between his eyes. All I want is to see the fear there, then I'll pull the trigger.

"Miriam?" he says. "What are you doing?"

I watch as Vax's face forms out of the glow. His Glock is leveled, but he lowers it when he sees me.

I leap at him. "Murderer!"

He grabs me, pulls me close. There's a wildness in his eyes I don't recognize. Therese's suit is still out of commission, and his hands are no longer the gentle ones I remember. He pins my arms, relieves me of the Smith & Wesson, tosses it aside. I'm crushed against his chest while I fight to free myself.

"You killed her!" I scream. "You killed her, you bastard! You killed my..."

The word fails on my tongue. I see the woman lying naked on the bed, sheets stained red in a pool around her dark hair. Her face is plainly visible despite the dimness of the room.

It's not my mom. It's Ayesha.

"It was her!" I say. "I swear to God it was her!"

Vax tightens his grip, pulling me against him until I choke for breath. I keep fighting, struggling to free my hands so I can claw his face. I have to get to the woman on the bed, have to see who she is. My mom, Ayesha, the wife in the Sleep Rite, I have to know. Have to convince myself I'm not crazy. Or maybe my last hope is that I am.

Vax spins me around. His eyes are stern. For a second I think I'm looking at my father's face, and I spit at him. It catches him in the forehead, drips into his eye. He wipes it away, then raises a fist and brings it down.

The punch snaps my head to the side and makes my cheek pulse with pain. He hits me again, his knuckles landing so hard it feels as if he broke the ridge above my right eye. Stars dance like a penumbra as he shoves me away from him, onto the bed, the blood. I'm choking on it, drowning in it. I can't see anything, can't tell who the woman is. Vax's shadow looms above me. I curl into a ball, dreading the next blow.

He laughs. He actually laughs. I raise my head to see his beautiful face twisted with malice.

"Your armor won't work here," he says. "Want to try again?"

He pulls out the roll of duct tape he used on Therese. Carelessly, he shoves the dead woman to the floor. She lands with a thump. Before I can stand, he grabs my wrist and drags me to the headboard. The Glock is in one hand, the tape in the other, but even with all the gear, he's much stronger than I'll ever be. He picks at the tape with his teeth, pulls out a long strand, and tears it off. His knee is braced against my chest, trapping me beneath his weight while he wrestles to loop the tape around my wrist. My mouth is full of blood, my own or someone else's. It's possible he knocked out a tooth.

"Hold still," he growls in my ear.

My right wrist is taped to the headboard. He leans across me to catch the other.

"Vax…" I gasp.

"Shut the fuck up."

"… not alone…"

He squints at me in puzzlement. A face appears over his shoulder, outlined in a crown of glowing light.

"Pretty weak, Vaccaro," the voice says. "Need a hand?"

Vax loosens his hold to look. I aim a knee at his nuts, and I don't miss.

He emits a choking sound and goes limp, falling on top of me. I sink my nails into his crotch to make sure he won't be getting back up and then bite his hand, the Glock landing on the floor. Legion makes no attempt to retrieve it. His body shimmers, becoming see-through. I roll hard to the right, pitching Vax on top of the man in the brown business suit. I fish with my left hand for one of the two guns, close my fingers around the first one I find. I straighten and fire blindly at the penumbra as it folds in on itself like puckered lips.

It's gone. The sound of the TV blares. I didn't realize it was still on. I tear the tape from my wrist, then stand.

Vax is cursing feebly. My dad lies dead beside him, a bloody hole in his chest. I never heard the second gunshot. Maybe Legion ripped his heart out with his bare hands. I'm holding

Vax's Glock. The Smith & Wesson is gone. The dead woman, whoever she was – my mom, Ayesha, the wife – is gone too, only a puddle of gore left to mark the spot where she fell.

He's taken her again. What more can he want with her, now that she's dead?

I press the gun under Vax's chin. He groans, but can't muster the will to push me away. The Super Suit is nothing but a plain LifeTime agent's outfit, except it's covered in blood. So are my ex-partner's pants where I came close to emasculating him.

"Playtime's over, you son of a bitch," I say. "You're going to tell me everything you know."

CHAPTER 32

Vax is churlish, uncooperative. Also too nauseous to put up much of a fight when I spread-eagle him on the bed and tape his wrists to the headboard. The best he can do is try to hurt my feelings.

"You have no idea what a chore it was to fuck you," he says. "Little nympho with no clue how to please a man."

"Well, that was uncalled for."

I yank his pants down and duct-tape his balls. He whimpers but doesn't struggle.

"First things first," I say. "Who are you?"

He won't answer. I pinch the ball-tape, peeling it back slightly as if I'm ready to give it a good hard pull. His eyes bulge. For the record, Vax has very hairy balls.

"Again," I say. "Who are you?"

His face shifts. "My name is Martin Vaccaro."

"Which one?"

"Which one do you want me to be?"

"Fuck you, asshole. How long have you been working for Legion?"

"Johnny Lee."

"What?"

"He calls himself Johnny Lee."

Keeping the Glock on him, I open the desk drawer and take out a pen and notepad, both of them stamped with the Sleep Rite logo. I scribble a name and hold it up to Vax. His eyes cross as he reads.

LEE, JON

"Legion," he mumbles.

"Congratulations. Now, again: how long?"

"Six years. Before I joined LifeTime."

"*Six* years?"

"Yeah. He got me the job."

This is unexpected, but I roll with the punches. "What were you doing with your life before then?"

"Teaching. Seventh-grade social studies."

"Perfect," I say. "So you were screening video clips about the Battle of the Bulge to a bunch of horny preteens, and then this Johnny Lee character shows up. What did he say he wanted?"

"He told me you'd be joining LifeTime a few years from then, and he needed me to have enough seniority that I'd be partnered with you. He wanted me to get close to you." An eyebrow goes up in a way that would have made me melt not long ago. "Really close."

I suppress an urge to pull the trigger. Just thinking about the two of us in bed together makes me want to take a shower for the rest of my life. "Did he tell you he was going to shoot you?"

"He mentioned it."

"And you were willing to do his bidding because...?"

"Because he's a time traveler. Who happened to know a few too many things about my past."

Much as this intrigues me, I can't head down that rabbit hole. Wherever it leads, it must be something so atrocious Vax was willing to ransom his freedom to keep it under wraps. "And what did he hire you to do with me, other than ruin a good night's sleep on a semi-regular basis?"

He shrugs, or tries to, what with the tape immobilizing his arms. "Whatever he asked. Take you here and there, tell you things. Make sure you didn't give up the hunt. He said you'd never doubt me after I got shot, and he was right."

I feel like a gullible fool, but I can't let him know that. I putz with the tape around his wrists so he won't be able to read the embarrassment in my eyes. As with my mom, I have no idea which Vax I'm talking to, the shot or unshot variant, but it seems it makes no difference in terms of his basic odiousness.

"For what it's worth, I did try to find a way out," he says. "Except every time I thought I'd given him the slip, he was one step ahead of me."

"That's the thing with time travelers. What was your plan?"

He says nothing, only lowers his eyes and licks his lips. He looks like a little boy who got sent to his room for pulling his sister's pigtails or some other such horseshit, but all I can see is the face he wore right before he clobbered me.

"You wanted *me* to kill him," I say. "Is that why you made me wear the suit? So I could tag Legion?"

He looks up sullenly. "I thought you might do it, yeah. The suit's from the future. He must have given it to Therese."

"You complete idiot," I say. "It never occurred to you that a guy who can transport Super Suits across the eons might be on to your little scheme?" I would laugh if my mouth didn't hurt so much. "*That's* what Therese meant – not Legion, but you. *You* weren't who I thought you were."

I let him stew on that for a while. The pieces are starting to come together. The erratic behavior, the drunken sob-fest, the crypto he always had handy. The on again, off again romance, the dampener that came and went with just as little explanation. The freak-out pings and tissue-thin lies, not to mention the mind-bending lessons on time travel that did nothing but confuse me. That were *meant* to do nothing but confuse me. Well, bravo, Mr Vaccaro. You played me like your own personal glockenspiel, and now I'm stuck in this crummy motel room with a malfunctioning Super Suit and a double-dealing ex-lover who's modeling the latest in adhesive jockstraps. Story of my life.

"So what about this place?" I ask. "How'd my mom and dad get trapped here?"

"*How'd Mommy and Daddy get trapped here?*" he mimics. I go

for the tape again, and he cuts the comedy. "The way Legion explained it, this room is outside the normal flow. A pocket where he can control the circumstances, bring travelers in and out at will, replay the loop as often as he wants."

"Travelers? So my dad had a core too?"

"Everyone who matters did. Even Cassidy."

I think back to the boss's physical reaction in the video when Regent arrived. He *did* look like someone suffering from the effects of a penumbra, which means Regent must have traveled back to that moment *after* my mom revealed the secret he'd traveled back to force her to reveal. Nifty trick, that. "Go on."

"Like I was saying, Legion created this place years ago. There's an actual Sleep Rite Motor Lodge, Room 11, and bad shit happens in it like the triangle we broke up, but this is a self-contained bubble."

"Which is why I can't remember the names of the husband and wife from regular time? Why antique guns can be fired without evidence that they were fired and futuristic battle armor won't armor up?"

"Presumably."

"How does he have the power to do that?"

"Ask him."

"I'm asking you, lover boy. If Legion's the one who made this place, how did the chamber send us here?"

He looks at me curiously. His expression is something like the Vax I know, the Vax I thought I knew. Except there's a hardness and calculation in his eyes I never saw before.

"You really don't understand how any of this works, do you?" he asks.

"How any of what works?"

"Time travel."

"I understand just fine. I hop aboard the cosmic carousel and get jerked around by creeps like you."

"I'm serious, Miriam. Time travel's nothing like you think."

"Enlighten me."

"Well, for starters, it's all fixed. You can't change a thing."

"Bullshit," I say. "I saved you from getting shot. I killed Therese at the park. Angel Care became Helping Hands. All of those things happened outside this place, and they wouldn't have happened if not for me."

He shakes his head. "That's an illusion. Each timestrand is its own knot, and you can't untie any of them. All you can do is jump to a different strand where there's a different outcome."

"What do you mean, a different strand?"

"Don't play stupid with me, *Myriad*," he says. "Your half-assed theory was more right than you knew."

I have too many half-assed theories at this point to keep track of, so I need a little more help with this one. "Just tell me, Vax."

"Fine," he says in a pissy voice. "The way LifeTime explains it to field agents, we jump back to earlier points in the existing timestrand – the one we've been living in all along, the one we started out from – and introduce changes into the past. According to this way of thinking, when we make a choice and change an outcome, we overwrite the *before* version with an *after* version, correct?"

"Um… correct?"

"But that theory is bullshit. The reality is that you – and me, and all the travelers who've ever worked for LifeTime – have been jumping back to *different* timestrands. Ones where things were meant to work out the way they did, and where the travelers were fated to play the role they played. Where Angel Care was *always* Helping Hands, or where they rebranded the day before we got there. Not timestrands we chose, either. Timestrands chosen *for* us, programmed into our cores from the start."

"By who?"

"Who do you think? Legion created LifeTime back in the day, hired Cassidy to be the public face while he operated behind the scenes. He knows all the permutations, all the lifelines of everyone connected to the place. Where they begin, and" – he raises an eyebrow – "when they end."

"You mean...?"

He almost shrugs, and I almost shoot.

"When does it end?" I ask. "For me?"

"Which *me* are you talking about?"

"*Me* me. The one standing in front of you."

"You sure you want to know?"

No. "Yes."

"When you're forty-six," he says. "On the anniversary of your brother's death. Same place, same time. Same gun Legion took from this room. Self-inflicted gunshot wound to the head."

Twenty years. Exactly twenty years from today. The thought of being on Legion's trail for the next two decades depresses me no end, but when it comes to my suicide, I'm a little surprised it takes so long. I just hope it means I get to shoot him first. "He told you this?"

"He told me everything."

He closes his eyes. In the room's dim light, he looks as old and weary as a man who's lived ten of his lifetimes.

I wish I could believe he's telling the truth. Because if he is, if this whole afternoon – this whole life – is only one possibility among many, then there's another timestrand where none of these terrible things ever happened, and if I can figure out how to get there, I'll find a job that thrills me instead of kills me, a seventh-grade social studies teacher who truly is the man I thought he was, a skin to live in that's as satisfying as any Super Suit. More: I'll return to my condo after work to find my brilliant mom pinging me to check on my day, my beloved brother laughing at the crazy story I tell him about the crazy dream I had. What I wouldn't give to depart this endless highway that's leading me nowhere and make my way back home.

But I can't afford to indulge in fantasies. Not anymore. Time is growing short.

"All right, Vax," I say. "How do I get out of here?"

"What do you want to get out of here for?"

"To find my mom, if she's still alive."

"It won't matter if she is. Legion can always bring her here and do the same thing to her all over again."

"Not if I stop him."

"Good luck with that."

He smirks. I'm ready to pull the trigger, but my better – or at least less impulsive – self intervenes. "How do I get out of here, Vax?"

Somewhat to my surprise, he answers. "You have to travel. You can't just open the door and step back into time. Or you could, except he keeps it locked from the outside."

"That's it? All I have to do is travel?"

He nods. ·

"So you could have gotten out of here too."

"Kind of hard to produce the necessary concentration."

Oh. That. "But the moment you feel up to it…"

"Why bother? Johnny Lee will just make me go wherever and whenever he wants. He'll do the same to you."

"Then fight him. Get your life back."

"My life is hell. I'd end it in a second if I could."

He looks away. I consider calling his bluff, setting the sheets on fire with a book of Sleep Rite matches and forcing him to travel if he wants to live. But maybe he doesn't. Maybe this is exactly what the karmic wheel has picked out for him. It's like I always say: you made your bed, now burn in it.

I close my eyes, feel the charge swirling in my belly from all the penumbras I've been exposed to today. The moment I picture my destination, the surge comes. It's the last place I want to go, and more than half of me suspects it's the very place Legion wants me to be, but it's too late to stop now. Plus, I've got no place better.

"Goodbye, Vax," I say, and this time I mean it.

His eyes find me, but I'm gone before I hear if he answers.

CHAPTER 33

How I ended up here has always been a mystery. But then, how I ended up anywhere has always been a mystery.

This much I know. After my dad died – the car-wrapped-around-tree way, not the heart-ripped-from-chest way – I dropped out of high school and worked a series of robojobs: cocktail waitress, minimart cashier, baggage handler at the airport. I lived in a crappy apartment, slept with a succession of no-less-crappy guys, except in their case at least the plumbing worked. After two years of this, I finally accepted the truth that I'd inherited more than grief from my genius mom and finished my GED so I could accept CMU's standing offer. I dabbled until my junior year, considered majoring in psychology but decided that hit too close to home. In the end I graduated with a double major in art history and criminal justice, the former because it was my way of posthumously flipping off my ever-practical dad, the latter because my advisor insisted I choose a sure path to employment. On her recommendation I specialized in forensics, which she said would enable me to find work in a local crime lab or even with the FBI. When the counselor in the career office told me about an opening at LifeTime, I wondered why she was sending me to interview at a travel agency.

But I didn't ask questions. I took down the address, bought a business suit I couldn't afford, and showed up at LifeTime headquarters ready to wax poetic about my love of matching people with their dream vacation, only to discover what they

were really about. Or at least what they led me to believe they
were really about.

Everything followed from there. I aced the field agent
entrance exam, passed the physical and psychiatric tests,
God knows how, and was shipped off to the academy. I'd
developed a bit of a drinking problem in college – OK, I was a
mess, blacking out, waking up in strange guys' beds, the same
old story – but it seemed LifeTime wasn't paying attention to
my extracurricular activities when they ran the background
check. They were more wowed by the gold medal I'd won in
some silly undergraduate criminalistics competition. I breezed
through the academy, kept to myself for the entire seven-
month program, didn't go out drinking with the boys. A few of
the female trainees were determined to prove they could hold
their own, both on the obstacle course and in the back room
of the local gin joint, but I was reluctant to test how deeply my
genetic endowment ran. Cigarettes and the occasional online
AA meeting kept me clean, and though I won't pretend I didn't
have some rough nights, I soldiered through.

Because in that respect Cassidy was right about me. I was
a crusader. Not for truth and justice and all that, but for the
alluring notion that things could get royally fouled up and then,
plausibly and demonstrably, unfouled up. I finished first in my
class, snagged a prime assignment as a frontline agent in the
home office – most of my classmates, men and women alike,
got scattered all over the country – and met Vax. After our first
job, he took me out to celebrate and show me around town.
He offered me a drink, and I wasn't about to tell this super-hot
older man about my past escapades, so I accepted. I discovered
that night what I'd missed during my inebriated college days. I
was slightly buzzed from our whirlwind tour of local dive bars,
but only enough to heighten my arousal as he led me through
a vale of pleasures uncharted by any of the preening frat boys
I'd slept with as an undergrad. I was nervous the next day,
worrying that I'd crossed some sort of line professionally and/

or alcoholically, but the night of debauchery didn't produce any lasting repercussions or black marks on my record. I eased back on the bottle, Vax and I got along famously, and the contractual aspects of the work went equally well. Except for the Birmingham Bridge incident, we were doing what I'd imagined: halting murderers in their tracks, making shit fly backward out of the fan. The reappearance of my mom could have placed a drag on my trajectory, but I refused to let it. I was kicking Father Time's butt, and I told myself that my after-hours sessions with Vax were my reward for a job well done.

Now I know the truth. It wasn't me. It was Legion all along.

He was the one who put up the cash for the CMU scholarship. The one who whispered in my advisor's ear when I was choosing a major. He arranged the interview at LifeTime and made sure they overlooked the results of the psychiatric test. He got me an agent's job straight out of the academy, pairing me with a man who smiled on cue, shook my hand, oozed sexuality. He stole my mom – twice – and killed my dad, also twice. He threw the Birmingham Bridge case my way, yanked me from timestrand to timestrand to suit his moods. He was the fulcrum beneath my lover's smile, my boss's priggish dismissals, my parents' marital woes. He manipulated me for years, maybe my entire life, to put me exactly here, exactly now.

Why, I don't know.

Which is why I'm here again. I've learned very little, earned even less. Except, possibly, a final chance.

CHAPTER 34

Landing in time is like reentering the earth's atmosphere.

My face throbs, skin tightening over the bruises Vax left. It's the wee hours of August 31, a half-day earlier than when I departed the Sleep Rite, but the pain grounds me in the present. Luckily, the rejuvenated Super Suit powers on at will and gets to work mending my hurts. Nanotechnologies or whatever it has in its bag of tricks gently massage me as I stand on the public sidewalk in front of the place I called home from age six to seventeen.

I haven't been back since I moved out. It's a sturdy house in a prime location, but when it came into my hands via Dad's will on the day I turned eighteen, I was a high school dropout who couldn't come close to covering the mortgage and taxes. Since the only potential buyers were young couples who got spooked when they found out a six year-old child who'd lived there had been murdered, I ended up selling it in desperation, and well under market, to a house flipper who planned to turn it into living space for retirees. The cash from the brick-and-mortar albatross was enough to cover my condo remodel and a year of in-home care for Mom, but that money is long since gone.

Judging from the look of the house, so is the flipper. More likely, he was one of Legion's plants from the start. It's unchanged from the way I remember it, a three-story brick house with an awninged front porch, original slate roof, and cathedral-quality stained-glass window that unfortunately got crunched by a neighborhood kid with a baseball. My dad never bothered to fix it, just as he never bothered to fix anything. The bedroom I shared with Jeremy was on the second floor, front left-hand window. The most distinct thing I recall from all the years I lived there happened the December after he was killed, just before my mom started going to the church. Some moron in a black sports car came careening down the hill, spun out in the snow, and sideswiped the two cars that were parked there plus the one that was trying to inch its way up the hill, only to be followed by another driver (a granny in a Caddy) who plowed into the pileup before anyone had a chance to get out of their cars. The crash made my bed shake. Me being me, I woke up screaming for Jeremy, thinking he'd been killed all over again. Everyone was fine, miraculously, but they all trooped onto our porch asking if they could come inside to make their calls. My mom said no, I heard her arguing when I crept to the staircase where the (at that time) perfect stained-glass window was, but my dad said "Jesus Christ, Deb," and pushed her out of the way to let the pack of fools in. I was utterly terrified by the unfamiliar grownups' voices, which might have been why my mom was trying to fend them off. Once they were gone and I'd crawled back to bed, she came to my room and stood in the doorway looking like she was the one who'd survived a five-car pileup. Two months later, when she disappeared, I had the superstitious belief that one of the people from the car crash had come to the house and taken her away like a body-snatcher from a Victorian children's ghost story.

Now I know this, too: my seven year-old self was half right.

The man in the sports car must have been Legion. I didn't recognize him in the quick peek I got of all those scary grownups stamping snow off their boots in their winter clothes, but he must have engineered the accident so he could meet my mom, called her the next day to apologize for the intrusion, for waking her little girl. Having disarmed her, which wasn't

that difficult given her brittle condition and the lack of support
she was receiving from my dad, he must have proceeded to
do what all psychopaths do when they're prepping their next
victim: struck up a conversation, learned her story – the one
he'd set in motion months earlier – and suggested she meet
him outside the home. She was ready to snap at that point. In
the months before the car crash, I remember – less vividly but
no less frighteningly – her and Dad screaming at each other
through the floorboards, doors slamming as he went out for
his nightly carouse, her sobbing in the bedroom down the hall.
So she went to the church, and Legion planted the seed of
escape in her mind, and she never came back. Or she did, but
only as a shadow of the woman she'd been, her mind undone
by being locked in the Sleep Rite day after day, year after year,
waiting for her torturer to return.

I tramp up the front walk, but as soon as I do, the suit starts
behaving strangely, its power blinking on and off like a bad
Christmas tree bulb. The pain in my eye and jaw blinks along
with it. By the time I reach the porch, the suit has pretty much
given up the ghost, though it tries to hold on for my sake.
I wonder if I've entered another time bubble or if the Super
Suit needs a recharge like the Vape Master. Since I don't have
that on me either, it seems I'm going to have to complete this
mission without a copilot.

I pace the front porch. A plate-glass window looks into the
living room, or would if the heavy drapes weren't closed. The
door, however, is unlocked. When I ease it open and peek
inside, I find that everything looks the way it did when I
closed the deal with the house flipper. Umbrella handles and
a wooden rain stick protrude from the ceramic stand beside
the stairs, while the baby grand piano rests at an angle due
to the missing caster on its right front leg. The foyer's dark,
but there's light coming from the dining room, along with
a clicking sound I've heard before. My nose twitches at the
smell of cigarette smoke, which floats in the thin spill of light

like a layer of early morning fog. Something more robust cuts through the scent. A cigar, maybe.

With the Glock drawn, I shoulder the door aside and take a cautious step into the hall. The second I do, the suit fizzles out for good with a very loud and despondent whine.

"We're in here!" a raspy voice calls. There's something familiar about it, though I can't say where I've heard it before.

"This is my house," I answer automatically, though that's no longer true. Then, another possible fib: "I'm armed."

Raucous laughter follows. More than one person. There's a phlegmy cough, and the original voice responds.

"No need for all that," it says. "Come join the party."

The clicking noise resumes. I lead with the gun. The pall of smoke thickens as I approach its source. By the time I get to the dining room, it's like looking through the aftermath of a car-bombing.

Three figures hunch around the Amish pedestal table, smoke festooning the chandelier above their heads. All of them are women I know, two dressed in blue Angel Care smocks and the third in the pink uniform of Helping Hands. Chloe – the pink one – puffs on a fat cigar and plays Solitaire, Loretta manipulates a Ouija board planchette while a sickeningly sweet clove cigarette burns in her hand, Opal knits something long and black, a half-smoked butt dangling from her cracked lips. At her elbow, a flattened pack of Marlboro Reds and a full-to-overflowing ashtray flag her as a fellow chain smoker. A lapsed one, or a lying one. Wasn't it tomorrow that she came to my apartment to watch Mom? Time has gotten too tangled for me to sort out.

She squints through the smoke. The gun doesn't seem to faze her at all. "You look dog tired, honey. Have a seat."

"What are you doing in this house?"

"Just passing the time. Cigarette?"

She offers the pack. I struggle with myself, but the once-super suit's not coming to my aid, and I left dog tired in the rearview mirror days ago. I withdraw a cancer stick and lean into the flame she holds. When I take a drag, I'm reminded instantly why there's no substitute for the real thing. My eye falls on the sideboard, where cartons of Marlboro Reds are stacked like wooden blocks.

"What happened to the stop smoking shot?" I ask her.

"The what?"

"Stop smoking shot. You said it worked like a charm."

"Must've been a different time."

"It was only a week ago – I mean, the day after today."

"Different time*strand*," she says, smoke streaming from her nostrils. "Where I come from, there's no such thing as any fancy stop smoking shot. Would've jumped on it if there was."

"But you were *there*," I say. "In my apartment. When you told me about it."

She sets her needles down, takes a super-deep drag and coughs out smoke, then crushes the cigarette in the ashtray. Chloe and Loretta continue their activities, but lean in to listen.

"Time works differently around here, honey," Opal says. "Take me for example. I was born in twenty eleven, died in twenty fifty-seven. Lung cancer. Rare at my age, but you don't have to look far to find the smoking gun." She winks. "Whoever invented that wonder shot of yours, he must've skipped my strand. And if I'm the one who told you about it, well, I was only following orders."

"You're dead?"

"Not yet!" she says, laughing uproariously. This sets off a furious round of coughing that subsides only when she lights another Marlboro. "But I will be. Or maybe I already am. Maybe we all are."

"I had a wonderful life," Chloe chips in, her voice muffled by the cigar. "Loving husband, two beautiful daughters. Then I lost my balance and fell down the stairs on vacation. Broke my neck."

"Suicide for me," Loretta adds. Her eyes never leave the

drifting planchette. "Pills and a razor blade. They found me a week later."

Opal pushes the ashtray toward me. I stub out my cigarette, then lean across the table for her to light another. "So this is a time bubble?"

"He calls them *stitches*," she says. "Has a nicer ring to it."

"And you've been here how long?"

"Oh, years, probably. Kind of hard for gals in our condition to say." She takes another monster drag, lights a new cigarette from the butt of the old. "We stay here and wait for him to call us. Smoke, carry on, play cards. Reminisce about the good old days. When he tells us to go, we go. We enter the timestrand he chooses, complete the job he tells us to. Then we come back, and it's like we never left. Not a bad life. At least, I've seen worse."

I begin to wonder how many of these bubbles – stitches – Legion made. Did he plant them all over the city? All over the planet? Is that where the lost travelers have been hiding, waiting for him to set them free so they can wreak havoc on the world?

"Just to be clear," I say, "he keeps you alive in this place even though you're already dead?"

"*Already* is a big word," Opal says with another wink. "According to you, you've *already* been to tomorrow, but here you are today. Maybe you've *already* died too, and you haven't gotten the news yet."

She cackles, coughs, spits something dark into a cupped hand. She wipes it off on her pant leg and resumes knitting.

"When did you say you were–" I'm starting to ask when the front door bangs open.

A figure flounces into the room, looking for all the world like a hooker from *Night of the Living Dead*. Lacy bustiere, Andy Warhol mascara, fright-night hairdo. She absolutely reeks of weed. Her flour-white face paint gives the game away: the sainted Sabine. Chloe sets her cigar in a misshapen ceramic dish – I recognize it, I made it when I was five – and jumps up to hug the newest arrival.

"Hey, sweetie!" she sings. "How'd you do tonight?"

"I'm gonna puke," Sabine mutters.

"Be careful not to muss your clothes!" Chloe says as she releases her. Sabine stumbles from the room. A second later, there's the sound of her barfing her guts out in the kitchen sink.

"She's such a doll," Chloe says perkily. "My baby, all grown up and working her first job! Here." She tucks the cigar in the side of her mouth, digs in the leather purse that hangs from her chair, and flashes a photo. "That's her and her big sister Therese. Aren't they just the sweetest pair?"

Sure enough, the picture shows two girls, one about fourteen and the other a few years older. Both are wearing cheerleader outfits with skirts and pom-poms, the Kelly-green-and-white colors of Allderdice High School, where I went for two years plus a semester and a half before dropping out. Sabine's a smidge shorter than her older sister, but in the identical getups and without the greasepaint, they might as well be twins. A tall dark-haired man stands between the two of them, his arms around their shoulders. Chloe taps the picture.

"My husband Marty," she says. "Such a wonderful man! For our twentieth anniversary, do you know where he took me?"

"Marty?" The picture blurs beneath my eyes, then snaps into sharp focus: Sabine in her zombie streetwalker outfit, Therese shimmering with skinthetic scales. The man between them is... "Vax?"

"It's pronounced Vaccaro," Chloe says. "Have you met?"

She starts into a lengthy monologue about their anniversary trip to Cancun. White sand beaches, crystal-blue water, inventive foreplay in the surf. Opal notices that my cigarette's running low and offers another. I take it, but no amount of nicotine can clear my head.

"When did you get married?" I ask Chloe.

"In twenty thirty-seven," she says, beaming. "We met at the hospital gift shop where I was working, and he simply swept me off my feet." She places the cigar in her mouth, takes a series of satisfied puffs as she contemplates the photo. "I know what the police said, that he was the one who pushed me down the stairs at the resort. But not my Marty! He was just as gentle as can be, and let me tell you, I was not an easy woman to live with. I had quite the mouth on me!"

"When," I ask, then have to clear my throat, "when did you say you were born?"

"In twenty eleven, same as Opal."

"Same as me," Loretta intones, her eyes fixed on the board.

"What day?" I ask.

"February ninth," Chloe chirps. "I had a twin brother, but he was born on the tenth, if you can believe it! He died when I was a little girl, sad to say. Exactly forty years to the day before I did."

I look at the three women sitting around my dining room table. They're twenty years older than I am, Chloe a bit hippy from childbearing, Opal's frame hollowed out by the cancer that's rotting her away. Her hair is fleecy white, Loretta's the beneficiary of multiple bleach jobs, dark roots showing. The names don't matter. Eddie Regent, Johnny Lee, Legion. If he can be all three of those people at the same time, why can't they be a single person from three separate lives?

"Me," I say. "You're me."

CHAPTER 35

We sit at the table. Chloe nurses her cigar and shares fond memories of the abuser who killed her. Loretta tires of the Ouija board and idly flips through a crossword puzzle book. All the while, Opal knits and chain smokes and just about regurgitates a lung. Though I know she's me – an alternate-future version of me – I keep reaching for the pack, matching her furious pace. I might as well admit it. Some things, once they get rolling, they never stop.

The hours pass without a sign of dawn. It's easy to see how a person could get stuck in this place, forgetting who they are, what exists outside. For my mom, that was Legion's way of punishing her, though I still don't know what her crime was. For my three alter egos, losing themselves seems practically a relief. Not heaven, but at least limbo. Oblivion. I wonder what Reverend Hitchens would say about that.

Eventually, Opal sets her knitting aside and stretches bony limbs. She squints at me through her perpetual smoky wrap. "Having fun?"

"Not exactly."

"Hate to keep you like this. He comes and goes as he pleases."

"The man of the house?"

She flashes a yellow-toothed smile. "None other."

"I can wait."

"Tell you what. Why don't you look around the place? Old house like this, there's bound to be some skeletons in the closet."

"This was your house," I say. "You don't remember?"

She scratches a mole on her chin. "Let me tell you something, sweetheart. Once you get to be my age, you learn not to sweat the small stuff."

She retrieves her knitting and lights another cigarette. I crush out my own and rise stiffly from the table, Glock in hand. Not that I expect these crones to tamper with it, but I'm taking no chances.

I make my way to the living room. Everything looks the way I remember. The nonfunctional fireplace, the bubble in the plate-glass window that my mom said gave it character, the near empty bookcase with a smattering of Civil War memoirs (a minor hobby of my dad's). There used to be far more books, psychology texts and the like, but he pitched them by the boxful after my mom had been gone less than a year. The off-kilter baby grand in the foyer, the one the previous owner left and no one in our family ever learned to play, is deeply coated with dust. I tap a key and find that it's every bit as out of tune as the day I left.

The ornate banister some inept self-designer painted in thick white semigloss leads me upstairs, over worn carpet and past the buckled window. I was eleven when the neighborhood kid threw the ill-fated ball. Jeremy had been dead for almost five years by then, my mom gone for four-plus. I tried to kill myself for the first time later the same year, a pretty pathetic attempt with a bottle of Tylenol. I puked on the hallway rug and my dad made me clean it up. The next time I was more deliberate – not to mention considerate – and sat in the tub while I attempted to slash my wrists with a butcher knife.

The bedroom I shared with my brother is directly ahead. The door is open a crack, the lights out. I bypass it and head down the hall to the back of the house.

There's not a single picture on the walls, not a single photograph of us as a family. There used to be, but they went the way of Mom's psychology books. My favorite was of me and Jeremy at a kiddie park in Ohio called Dinosaur Land. It was taken during our last family vacation before he was killed, which means our last family vacation ever. It showed the two of us posing on top of a long-necked dinosaur, Jeremy sitting confidently on the spine, me hugging its throat for dear life. I can still remember how scratchy the fiberglass felt.

I enter the master bedroom and click on the overhead fixture. One of the bulbs sputters and the other is dead, but in the half-light, I scan the untouched room. It's pretty bare. There's a king-size bed – my dad never replaced it after my mom left, nor did he ever share it with another woman that I know of – along with a closet and chest of drawers. The walls are as unadorned as the hallway, the bedsheets neatly tucked. A red tie dangles from the hook on the back of the door. The fabric is so wrinkled it looks as if someone tried to hang themselves with it and nearly succeeded.

I lower myself to the floor and check under the bed. No monsters, but lots of dust bunnies. I open the closet door and pull the cord on the bare bulb. My nose fills with the cloying smell of mothballs, but there's nothing much to see other than a few stray suit jackets sagging from wooden hangers. None of them is the dun shade from the Sleep Rite. The husband's name has been on the tip of my tongue since I arrived. Maybe it'll come to me if and when I leave. All I know is, whenever I try to picture his face, I see my dad's.

I close the closet door and inspect the dresser next. It's completely empty. Running a hand under each drawer yields nothing but splinters. Unless there's a trap door hidden beneath the stained, off-white carpeting, the skeletons Opal promised aren't here. Just a pitiful old drunk's bedroom, the powder blue sheets pulled military tight under matching pillows.

I approach the bed again. It's hard for me to imagine my dad making it so meticulously, tucking the sheets beneath the mattress, arranging the pillows just so. He'd have been too drunk to notice, too hung over to care. As well as I can remember, he never fixed the bed at all, just threw his body down and slept the sleep of the dead until daybreak.

I reach out, feeling a strange aversion as my fingers approach the bed. Revulsion, even. I train the gun on the wooden headboard and tear the sheets free. Pillows fly, breath escapes me in a rush. Still no skeletons. I almost wish there were.

Instead, there's a depression, a soft spot. It's even larger than the one Vax and I found in my mother's bed. It dominates the left side of the bed, and as I look at it, a memory comes to me of my dad sprawled on the right. The flashback is so vivid I can see his body before me. He's fully clothed, but somehow grotesque. The suit he's wearing is rumpled and brown.

An unmistakable sound comes from down the hall. Someone crying.

I drop the sheets and run the short distance to my old room, shoving the door so hard it smacks the wall and bounces halfway back. If the person's armed, they'll shoot first. I'm tempted to throw my arms wide, give them a better target. I can't see anything, but a voice emerges from the darkness.

"Miriam," the voice says, sniffling. "I didn't know you were home."

CHAPTER 36

I turn on the light. It blinds me to details, shows me only the twin beds my mom never consolidated into one. A Sphinx-like figure sits on a kitchen chair between them. I blink and take a step into the room.

"Mom?"

It's her. The age she should be, not her younger self from the Sleep Rite. Her short dark hair is brush-tipped with gray, her mannequin-pale face crossed by lines. Tears brighten her eyes, but her gaze is sharp and clear, without the vacancy I've grown used to. She wipes her cheeks with the back of a hand, then reaches out to me as I stumble into her arms.

She pulls me close. Her body's warm and solid. Not a figment, not a ghost. She presses her lips against my cheek.

"It's been so long since you stopped by," she says. "Where have you been keeping yourself all this time?"

My attempt at a laugh turns into a sob, then a hiccup. "It's a long story."

"Tell me," she says. "I'd like to catch up."

She lets go. I sit on the bed farther from the window, the one that used to be Jeremy's. The day we moved in, my mom let me choose which bed I wanted because I was seven minutes – or one day – older. I realize I'm still holding the gun, and I holster it, then use that as an icebreaker.

"I've been working," I say.

"As a police officer?"

"Private law enforcement."

"I had no idea that was something you were interested in."

"It developed. Over time."

She nods, but looks taken aback. "Do you work in the Pittsburgh area?"

"Well, yes." I fumble, don't know why I say the next thing. "I would have been in touch, but I've been busy."

"I understand," she says in a way that makes it sound like she doesn't. "You're an adult, you have your own life."

I want to tell her that's not true, not really. I have *this* life, but I don't know whose it is anymore, if I ever did. I feel as if it belongs as much to her and Jeremy, not to mention those hags downstairs, as it does to me. On an impulse, I blurt out: "I'm an agent in the temporal corrections division."

She startles as if she's waking from a doze. A change comes over her face, and I cry out in fear that she's slipping back into the fog that's surrounded her since her return. But when her reverie passes, I see that it's the reverse: she's fully in the present, fully in time. I know because the pain in her eyes is as fresh as an open wound.

"Time travel?" she says softly.

I nod.

"Life Change?"

"What's that?"

"It's what Norman Cassidy planned to name his business."

"He ended up calling it LifeTime. Must have test-marketed better."

"Thank goodness. Life Change always sounded like a boutique for postmenopausal women."

I laugh. I'd forgotten my mom had a sense of humor.

"So Norman succeeded despite everything," she says.

"Depending on your definition."

"How long have you worked for him?"

"Actually, I don't think I work there anymore."

"But when did you start?" she says impatiently. "How many missions have you gone on?"

"I was twenty-four. I'm twenty-six now. I averaged just under thirty a year."

"That many," she muses. "And you're all right?"

"Again, depending."

"I took only a single trip. After your brother died."

"I know, Mom."

She gazes out the window into the night. I wonder if I should tell her everything I know. About Cassidy, Legion, her own part in this. The missing travelers. The torturer in the Sleep Rite. I'm still not certain which *her* I'm talking to. Vax told me that Regent can bring travelers in and out of his stitches at will, and from the evidence of the trio in the dining room, he can snatch people before they die and preserve them like fetal pigs in formaldehyde. But whether he can restore a mind he destroyed, I don't know. I don't want to risk saying anything that might break her all over again.

"Miriam," she says, "what do you think of when you travel through time?"

I'm surprised by the question, but I answer.

"A lot of things," I say. "The place I'm headed for, the nature of the mission. The threats, the ways of avoiding them. It's a very focused process, where I draw on the energy of my core and direct it toward my objective. Much of our work in the academy had to do with mindfulness."

"Do you ever think about Jeremy?"

That stops me short. I guess I shouldn't have been worried about breaking *her*. "You mean when I travel?"

She nods.

"Every time, Mom," I say.

I've no sooner said it than I begin to bawl like the child I was when this room belonged to me. She reaches across the space between us and pulls me to her, kisses my hair, rocks me as if I'm still that child. I let the tears flow, let myself return to a past I've longed for my entire life. It doesn't make up for all the years I needed her and she wasn't there, but it's better than nothing.

"I think about him too, you know," she whispers in my ear. "Every day for the past twenty years. And about you, too."

"Me?"

"Of course. You were my first."

"But you left me," I say, trying to keep my voice from catching. "You went to look for… something else, and you never came back."

She's silent. Smoothing my hair, humming so softly it's like a lullaby. Time doesn't pass in this place, which means she might hold me for ten minutes or a hundred years. Finally she pulls back and faces me. She brushes tears from my cheeks, then speaks to me like a mother leaving her child for the very first time, or the very last.

"I knew the risks, Miriam," she says. "Long before I took the trip, the traveler told me that temporal displacement would imperil time. He'd visited me in my lab, spoken to me out of a blinding light. I knew he was from the future. I didn't understand how he could be there when time travel hadn't been invented yet, but he explained it to me, and then I saw everything: the dangers, but also the key to making it work. I kept his secret to myself as long as possible, but after Jeremy was killed, I couldn't resist anymore. When the traveler reentered my life, a part of me knew it was foolish to follow him. But I'd lost one child already, and I wasn't willing to lose another."

"Another?" I say dumbly. "But I thought…"

"That I traveled through time to save your brother? Oh, no, I knew by then that preventing his death was impossible. The traveler had showed me the mechanics of it, proved it couldn't be undone. It was you I thought I could save. I went forward in time to keep you from…"

"Killing myself?"

She nods slowly. "But when I got there, I discovered that he'd lied to me. I couldn't change anything. And I couldn't find my way back."

"Do you remember what happened to you there?"

A lightning-bolt of terror crosses her face, but she shakes her head. "It's all a blur. I seem to be watching myself very intently, as if I know something terrible is about to happen. Like the moment before a car accident. But I can't stop it, and when I try to remember, it slips beyond my recall."

Much as I'm relieved to hear that she's erased the years of torture at Legion's hands, I can't help wondering if that's why it keeps happening. Why everything keeps happening, why I can't free myself from this cycle any more than she can.

"If you wanted to save my life," I ask, "why didn't you just stay?"

Leave it to me, that's the one thing I shouldn't have said. Tears fall down her cheeks, and her lips quiver.

"I'm sorry, Mom," I say. "I'm sorry."

"I was sick," she says. "Sick with grief, sick with fear. I'd seen your life play out, as much of it as the traveler chose to show me, and I was desperate to act. I don't know, Miriam. I only know that what he warned me of came true. I thought I could keep you safe, but all I did was bring to pass what I most wanted to prevent."

She puts her face in her hands and keens as if her heart is breaking, as if it never mended. We switch places, and I'm mothering my own mom the way I did in the Sleep Rite, hushing her and kissing the crown of her head. I don't know how long this night will last, this illusion or dream or whatever it is, but I sense our time together is coming to a close, and I don't want to waste it. It feels as if I've been given a chance at redemption, or at least understanding, and I'm not willing to let it slip through my fingers like everything else.

"Mom," I say, "did Daddy ever… hurt me when I was little?"

She stiffens. "You remember?"

"Not in my mind. In my body, though, sometimes I feel… something."

"I don't know for sure," she says. "It might have happened

during the months the three of you were in Lancaster. Possibly earlier. I had reason for suspicion, but no proof."

"There was no way to find out?"

"I talked to your father," she says. "It was one of the most difficult things I've ever had to do, second only to talking to you. You both denied everything, and I couldn't bear to put you through what it would have taken to extract the memory, so I... let it go."

"What made you suspicious in the first place?"

"It was Jeremy. He said he'd seen something. But it was only two days before he was killed that he told me, and by the time I got my core, it was too late to go back. All I could do was..."

"Go forward."

"That's right."

She falls into my arms again, crying, pleading for my forgiveness, over and over and over. I hold her, try to comfort her. The clarity I thought I might feel never comes, only a deepening weight of darkness and despair. If this explains my life, explains *me*, it explains nothing. It's there, and yet I can't remember any of it. I'm not sure I want to, not sure I can bear to put me through that either. I can't help feeling that the time to change, to make a difference, is much too long ago to try.

"It didn't continue," I say, not meaning to say it out loud. "After Jeremy died, Daddy stayed away from me. I would have remembered if he didn't."

She shudders, but says nothing.

"Why did he stop?" I ask. "With you and Jeremy gone, it would have been so easy for him to keep doing it. Instead, he drank himself into a stupor all day and avoided me all night. What made him stop?"

She's calm now, breathing steadily against my cheek. She presses a kiss to my forehead, tucks an unruly strand behind my ear. Then she stands, holding both of my hands in hers. I'm too numb to resist when she draws me to my feet, walks me down the hall with her arm around my shoulders, and stops before her bedroom door. I don't want to go back in there, but with her supporting me, I find the strength to step into the room.

The bed's the way I left it. The sheets are piled on the floor, the traveler's wake scooped from the memory foam. The overhead bulb has stopped blinking, and it bathes the bed in a corona of shining white light.

"A guardian angel?" my mother says.

CHAPTER 37

We return to my old bedroom and sit together on my brother's bed. We don't talk, just hold hands and gaze at each other.

I want to remember my mother's face.

I watch her cheeks slacken, her eyes grow misty and dim. I could say something to her, but she wouldn't answer, wouldn't understand. She doesn't resist when I raise her to her feet, fold the sheets back, and lay her down. I pull the covers to her chin, tuck them around her. She tilts her head to receive my kiss, then closes her eyes in sleep.

There are three replicas of me downstairs, all of them healthcare workers in some version of their lives. They should be able to take care of her for as long as need be.

"I have to go, Mom," I whisper. "Sleep tight."

Her peaceful breathing is the only response. I close the door and head downstairs.

The older women in the dining room are wailing like a clan of banshees. Others have joined the party, not only Sabine but Therese, Ayesha, and the woman from outside the church. I wonder if she's me too. There's no sign of Legion's other stooges – Hitchens, Cassidy, some form of Vax. It must be Ladies' Night.

Ayesha's limpid eyes follow me as I enter the room. She gives me the willies, so I avoid her and sidle up to Therese. The latter is rigged out in her battle armor, and her cleavage alone could kill a man. Now that I know she's my daughter – sort of – I feel oddly close to her. For her part, she offers a friendly smile I never received from her former standoffish self.

"Sorry I had to kill you," I say.

She shrugs. I doubt she remembers.

"He never wanted me to go after you," she says. "Only to keep that cut-rate Casanova of yours in line."

"When did you take your first trip?"

"Not until twenty forty-six. When I was eight."

"That young?"

"He wanted me to have time to train in the suit. To become one with it."

She vanishes. When next I spot her, she's on the ceiling beside the chandelier, clinging with hands and feet. The suit *does* have wall-crawling properties, damn it. She drops beside me, curtsies, and laughs.

"You can make it work in a time stitch," she says. "Once it's grown into you enough."

"How old are you now?"

"Twenty-eight. I haven't taken it off for the past twenty years, not even to shower or have sex."

Hearing that makes me regret the missed opportunities. "What can it do?"

"Let's start with levitation," she says. "And go from there."

She slides a cigarette from Opal's pack, produces a flame by snapping her fingers. Her movements are so lithe, so confident after years of living inside this second skin, I realize something I should have guessed at the time.

"It wasn't you at headquarters," I say.

"Hmm?"

"When I went there with Vax. I never could have snuck up on you like that."

My eyes find the younger of my two pseudo-daughters, who's swaying like a reed in a pond. All-purpose Sabine. Make her up right, dress her in a receptionist's outfit, you'd never know the difference.

"I was there, though," Therese says. "Later. To show you Cassidy's files."

She disappears again, and all I can see is the floating cigarette. Smoke spills from invisible lips before she reappears. I clap my hands at the performance.

"I didn't kill you either," I say. "You're too good. Legion must have done it. He's the only one who could have jumped in and shot you at close range without you seeing him."

Her expression darkens. The suit morphs into lethal spikes. "That twofaced son of a bitch..."

"He's coming, he comes, he's come!" my older selves chant, three voices like a single flickering flame. Therese rolls her eyes, snorts smoke.

"Double, double, toil and trouble," I say.

And he's there.

The penumbra fills the room, knocking us all on our cans. Therese bristles, porcupine-style, as she helps me to my feet.

Legion steps from the pulsing circle of light. There's a limp figure in his arms, a body wrapped in a blood-soaked motel room sheet. I wish I could believe it's not actually my mom, that the woman sleeping upstairs is the real and only her, escaped or released from her torment at last. But I've seen too much tonight to be convinced of that. To make sure he never touches her again – as well as to pay him back for past sins – I have to kill him now.

He lays the body before the three Miriams-in-waiting. They huddle around it, fussing and clucking, their fingers dabbling in the blood.

"Clean this mess up," he says.

Opal detaches the knitting she was working on and brings it over. It's a long, flowing black garment. A shawl, a shroud. My three clones wrap the body, hoist it, balance it on their shoulders. I would try to stop them if I thought I had any power in this haunted house. All I can do is watch as they cart the stiffening form toward the doorway that leads to the basement.

"What are they going to do with her?" I ask their lord and master.

He turns, fixing me with bullet-hole eyes.

The room falls silent, even Therese holding her breath. I've got nothing to lose, twenty years to live with this knowledge, so I step up to him, planting myself not a foot away. I'm as close to him as I was to Jeremy in that middle school annex, so close I caught a faceful of my twin brother's blood. I draw the Glock and point it between his eyes, ready to make a third hole if the thing will only fire.

"Answer me, motherfucker," I say.

Ayesha gasps. Sabine goggles, white-faced.

Legion reaches behind him and withdraws the Smith & Wesson he took from the motel room. It's the same gun, I'm sure now though I didn't know enough about firearms to identify it then, that killed Jeremy twenty years ago. I've given up trying to calculate if it has any bullets left, nor do I know if it'll work here any better than the Glock. We stand, weapons aimed at each other, until he breaks the spell.

"I thought I'd keep things in the family," he says with a smile.

My gun wavers. "What did you say?"

He leans back and laughs. His body rocks with mirth.

"*What did you say to me?*" I scream.

He laughs and laughs. It brings color to his face, draws out the dimples in his cadaverous cheeks. Something awakens in the depths of his eyes I didn't see before. Or did but couldn't bring myself to accept.

He wipes away tears and grins at me. "How've you been, big sis?"

And my world explodes.

CHAPTER 38

Wooden beams creak, crack. The chandelier crashes to the table with a sound like crystalline cymbals. The floorboards go next, splintering beneath my feet.

I land in the unfinished basement, where his attendants are preparing the body for burial. The place is dark and dank as a crypt, smelling of rot and mold. There are shackles attached to the foundation, and the three ghouls take a break from their labors to lift me into place, the iron closing around my wrists. I'm held, dangling by arms alone, the strain pulling my shoulders from their sockets. Opal's head twists practically backward as she shoots me an evil grin. Then the three heft picks and shovels and begin to break through the bare dirt floor.

They dig deep. Six feet, six miles, six circles down. When they reach the end, they set their tools aside and throw the black-wrapped body into the hole before I have a chance to say goodbye. Tears blind me as the winding sheet dwindles to nothingness.

The furies return, claw me from my chains, carry me to the grave. They hold me suspended over the shaft.

"Time to go," Opal says, and three pairs of hands release me as one.

I fall. The pit has no end. Flames rush up to meet me. The ruler of this place welcomes me from his bloody throne.

Legion. Jeremy. One and the same. His eyes are fire, his face a tusked pig's.

"I tried to save you," I say weakly.

"Too late," he says.

His mouth opens impossibly wide, and all the devils in hell pour from his throat to consume me.

CHAPTER 39

When I come to, I'm lying in my old bed by the window. My mother's motionless form occupies the other bed. The man who calls himself Legion sits in the kitchen chair between us. The sky is dark outside, his form a shadow. He's leaning forward, elbows on knees, long hair veiling his checks.

"How?" I ask.

He stirs, looks at me. His pale face glows in the darkness. It's the face I've seen every night for the past twenty years, the face that follows me in my dreams. The face of my brother's killer, the face of my brother.

"You wouldn't believe me if I told you," he says.

"Jeremy," I say, and it's the only thing I can say.

"I'll try to explain. Don't be surprised if you don't get it."

He rises from the chair, paces to the window, glances outside. There's no moon, no streetlamps, but his body gleams with a soft white light of its own. It's as if the energy of the penumbra has worked its way into his skin, the way Therese said her suit has. As if he doesn't *have* a core, but *is* a core.

"All right," he says. "We can agree that without my death at age six, Mom never would have revealed the information Cassidy needed for successful time travel, correct?"

"That's what she said."

"And therefore time travel presupposes my death – is preconditioned on it, right?"

"I guess so."

"There's no guesswork involved. The simple fact is that

without my dying, time travel would never have come to be. And without time travel coming to be, I could never have visited the future, obtained the necessary information to bring time travel into existence, then looped back to the year I was killed and put Mom in possession of what Cassidy needed to turn theory into reality."

"But," I object, "how could you visit the future if you *had* no future?"

"That's the part no one gets," he says. "You've seen that I can bring past as well as future versions of people into contact with the present, correct? Not only you, but others as well?"

"Like Therese."

"And plenty more, believe me. Mom and Dad included."

I shiver, remembering the scene in the Sleep Rite. But he's not done.

"That's because temporal displacement splinters time into an infinite number of possible strands," he says. "When we travel, we open that door – or travel *is* the opening of the door. Time splits, countless possibilities arise, the future comes into contact with the past, the past with the future. Jeremy Randle, age twenty-six, is present at the death of Jeremy Randle, age six. That death produces the possibility of Jeremy Randle traveling in time to encounter his past and future selves. Thus twenty-six year-old Jeremy's return is predicated on six year-old Jeremy's death, just as six year-old Jeremy's death is predicated on twenty-six year-old Jeremy's return."

"But twenty years?" I say. "You should be..."

I stop when he looks at me. It's a look that will kill me, if it hasn't already.

"I discovered the presence of stitches the first time I traveled," he says. "They exist at the juncture of timestrands: intervals where no time passes, nothing changes, everything repeats. I didn't invent them, but I quickly grasped how to exploit them. When I travel long distance, I jump from stitch to stitch, selecting ones within reach of my destination. As long as I stay outside the stream of time, dipping my toes in it only for the few moments I need, I never grow old. And I'll never die."

"But you said time travel came into being *because* you died," I protest. "Doesn't that mean you'd be dead in every possible timestrand?"

"Take a look at me," he answers. "Do I look dead?"

He draws himself up, squaring his shoulders. He looks not only alive but strong, vibrant, self-assured. Only his eyes, shadowed beneath his brows, have the appearance of a man who's seen his own ghost.

Maybe you are dead, I say to myself. *And you just never got the news.*

"It still doesn't make sense," I say out loud.

"You're a time traveler, Miriam. It makes perfect sense."

"So what Vax told me is true? That everything is based on everything else, and nothing can be changed?"

He laughs. Not the out-of-control laugh from before, just a short sniff. Is this the way my brother used to laugh? It's impossible to remember with the older him encroaching on my memories, obscuring the past.

"Vaccaro never understood," he says. "Or he understood just enough to get everything wrong. He was a useful tool in that respect, but I wouldn't go to him for an education in time travel."

"No," I say. "You'd send me to college instead. Using the money Mom got from Cassidy, I assume."

"She didn't need it. Not where she was going."

"Where you *took* her." My body feels hopelessly weak, but I push myself upright in bed. That takes all my strength, which is probably a good thing, because Vax's Glock rests on the nightstand and if I had the energy, I'd reach for it. "You killed her son, destroyed her spirit, forced her to tell Cassidy what she knew. Wasn't that enough? Did you have to… *cage* her in that torture chamber? For seventeen years?"

"I did it for you!" he says. "To keep Dad out of your life. So *he* wouldn't come after you."

His words puncture my last ounce of strength, and I collapse into the bed. "What did Daddy do to me?"

"I think you know what he did," he says savagely. "I didn't understand what he was doing at the time, but I heard the screaming, saw the blood on the sheets. When I tried to talk to you about it, you had no idea what I was saying. You'd blocked the whole damn thing from your memory. And when I told Mom, she didn't do shit. I decided that if she was too busy in her lab to defend her own child, then I would use her experiments to do what she wouldn't."

I'm afraid to meet his eyes, afraid to ask, but I must. "How?"

"By visiting the old man in this house every night," he says. "Reminding him what I'd do to him if he tried anything again. He bought a gun, but he was too chicken to use it. *This* gun, as a matter of fact," he adds, flourishing the Smith & Wesson. "I took it from him, brought it back in time along with some other small arms I had with me, and met up with my younger self in homeroom. Then, when the job was finished there, I came back and showed Mom and Dad what it was like. Every day in that hotel room, they lived through what they'd done at home, discovered what it meant to be utterly defenseless, at the mercy of someone with the power to do anything he wants, anything at all. To play with their minds, torment them, even kill them if he–"

"Stop it!" I scream, throwing my hands over my ears.

Jeremy looks stunned. He reaches out with the hand that's holding the pistol, but I shrink from him.

"I did it for you, Miriam," he says.

"No, Jeremy," I say. "You might have thought so, but you were wrong. You have no idea what you've put me through."

"It would have been worse if I hadn't stopped him."

"You don't know that. You can't know what might have happened if you hadn't died that day. Maybe it would have stopped on its own. Maybe Mom would have ended it. I would have had a chance to live. You would have too."

"I didn't want to live like that."

"So you chose to live in hell," I say. "The one you made for the rest of us."

He looks away. The light in his face has been snuffed out, but there's a hint of dawn coming through the curtains. Time, it seems, still exists beyond these four walls.

Time.

"Jeremy," I say. "You can go back. All the way back, twenty years from today. Or even farther. You can go back to the day you saw what Daddy did to me, and you can stop him before he does it. You can–"

"I'm not going back there," he says in a hollow voice. "I gave you your bittersweet reunion with Mom. Leave the rest of it alone."

"But you could save–"

"I said leave it the fuck alone!"

He turns to me. Sunlight grows on his face, but his eyes are as dead as they were that day in the school. I sit up in bed and reach for him. He points the gun at me as if to warn me not to try.

"Jeremy," I say, "are you sure it was *me* Daddy hurt?"

He flinches. He won't look at me. My twin, the one I shared a womb with, a life with. He wasn't supposed to have to protect me. I was supposed to protect *him.*

"I'm sorry, Jeremy," I say. "I'm so sorry…"

The light of a penumbra bursts from him with such brilliance it drowns out the sun. I shut my eyes as waves of nausea pass through me. When I open them, Jeremy is looking out the window, the gun shoved in his belt. The departed penumbra leaves his face ashy and gray.

"You have no idea what I'm capable of, Miriam," he says distantly. "You think what I did to Mom was so bad, but you have absolutely no idea. I've got hundreds of travelers out there, thousands. Each of them locked in their own stitch of time, all of them waiting for me to call. *Begging* for me to call.

I've got POWs who lived through years of torture, tourists who watched people jump from the towers on September 11. Children who survived death camps. They're back in those moments right now, and I can keep them there as long as I want – decades, centuries. I could put Mom there if I liked. I could put *you* right there beside her."

"Please, Jeremy," I say. "Please don't do this."

"Or I could let them all out at once," he says. "Move each of them to a convenient stitch so they don't age in the transition, then set them loose. Think you could handle that? Thousands of killers to track down in a single day? And don't forget, I can always make more. All I need to do is take some sweet young soul on a trip through time, leave them clawing for air at the bottom of a mass grave for a year or two, they'll come around. Is that what you want me to do?"

I can't speak. I look at the man who used to be my brother, think of the horrors he could unleash on the world, and know there's nothing I can say that will turn him from the course his life has taken. He must know it too, because he nods, though he won't meet my eye.

"The first thing you need to know about time," he says, "is that it's malleable, but only within certain limits. Vaccaro never understood that. At an amplitude of zero – that is, the original node – variation is impossible without destroying time travel itself. The farther you deviate from the point of origin – in other words, the more you get into incidentals – the more flexibility you can introduce into the system without disruption of its foundational principles. So, for example–"

"Knots," I say. "You're talking about knots."

"There's only one knot," he says. "The singularity that grounds the whole, the impossible possibility that lies at its center. Every timestrand is anchored to it the way a bunch of balloons is tied at a single point. They can move and bob with the illusion of freedom, but their trajectory is constrained. The knot can't be undone without losing them for good."

"But—"

"I did everything I could," he says, still not looking at me. "I killed Cassidy to send you scurrying into the past, dressed you in that suit, kept the ladies busy running errands. I steered you to a strand where Vaccaro didn't rat you out, another where Angel Care was Helping Hands. All along, though, I knew where you'd end up. The closer you came to the beginning, the more the fabric of time was strained as the threads were pulled this way and that. But the knot held. It *had* to hold, or nothing would have happened the way it was supposed to. I'm sorry, Miriam. For everything I did to you. Everything I had to do to you."

"Me?" I gather my strength to rise, but fail. "What does this have to do with me?"

He faces me at last. There's a look of sorrow in his eyes I can't bear to watch.

"Everything," he says.

He reaches out. At the tips of his fingers a penumbra ripens, swells. I'm pulled forward as if its energy is drawing me. It opens wide, and though I don't enter it, I'm close enough to view the image that forms inside. I fight its power, struggle not to see, but I can't help it.

And at last, I do see.

CHAPTER 40

The past. The school. The bridge.

That day.

The thing I can't think about.

Thursday, August 31, 2017

I take his hand and try to make him smile.

"We are safe," I say. "We're together."

More firecrackers explode, their sound muffled by distance. Jeremy squeezes my hand.

"He'll be here," he says. "He promised. He said he would take us somewhere Daddy won't be able to find you."

I don't want to talk about that, don't want to think about what Jeremy told me, not ever again.

"I'm not scared," I say. "Just as long as you're with me."

He tightens his grip on my hand and takes a step toward the doors. I wait for them to open on their own, like magic.

Then the door on the left does open and a man walks through.

A tall man, as tall as Daddy. His hair is long, just like his body and face. His skin is pale, his eyes shadows beneath his eyebrows. He's old enough to be one of the teachers, but he's not dressed in a suit and tie like Daddy wears. He has on blue jeans and a white T-shirt, hanging loose. His pale arms are long and thin in a way that makes me think of spiders.

He smiles at us, but I don't smile back.

"Eddie!" Jeremy says. "I came here like you wanted."

"That's my boy," the man says in a deep voice. Something about his voice or his eyes makes me scared, and I tug at my brother's hand.

"Run, Jeremy!" I say.

I pull at him, but he doesn't budge. He stands perfectly still, staring at the man, and no matter how hard I tug, he won't move.

The man's long arm reaches out toward us, and there's something in his hand, something ugly and black, and I know what it is but can't say the word, not even in my head. I pull Jeremy's hand and scream in his ear.

"Run, Jeremy! Run!"

But he doesn't run.

His pulse pounds against my wrist, and I know he won't run as long as the black thing is pointing at him, so I let go of Jeremy's hand and jump at the man called Eddie. He's looking straight at my brother, and he seems surprised when I grab his hand and pull the black thing away. My hands are shaking so badly I can't hold the black thing straight, but I try to point it at Eddie the way he pointed it at Jeremy.

"Leave my brother alone," I say.

Eddie takes a step toward me. His long skinny arm reaches out for the thing in my hand, and I know he's much stronger than me, and if he touches my hand he'll take the thing away and point it at Jeremy again. I know what I have to do, so I curl both hands around the handle and squeeze the part that moves.

"Miriam?" Jeremy says. "What are you doing?"

I spin to face him. Feet pound across the bridge toward us. I see a flash of red.

Then there's a noise so loud it makes my head hurt.

Jeremy's eyes open wide for just a second, and he falls away from me. There's red in my eyes, red in my mind, red everywhere. I can't find Jeremy in all the red.

Hands clutch me, voices scream. Maybe I'm the one screaming. I hear the sound of sirens. It's possible their wail is mine too.

"Jeremy!" I scream. "Jeremy!"

But he doesn't answer.

I fall away into darkness, into night.

CHAPTER 41

Morning light streams through the window. Jeremy's face is ghastly in its glow, his body an ephemera of the dawn. He stretches long arms and legs, removes the Smith & Wesson from his belt and scratches the back of his head with the barrel. He holds out a hand as if to help me from bed, but I shy away.

"It wasn't you," I say. "It was me."

"You were a kid," he says. "You'd never handled a gun before. And you were scared. Nobody blamed you, not even Mom and Dad."

"But then I…"

"Yes," he says. "When you took this gun from me and killed my six year-old self, you joined the singularity that brought everything to pass. In every conceivable strand, you're there – holding the gun, pulling the trigger. The knot can't be untied. It's taken twenty years to bring you back to the place where it started, and you must realize by now it can't be changed."

His eyes are calm, but all I can see is the bloody hole where the rest of his face should be. The hole I put there, the murder I committed. The one I've been trying for the past twenty years to undo, or at least forget.

"I can't," I say.

"Can't what?"

"Can't lose you again."

"You don't have a choice in the matter," he says. "You're the one who brought time travel into being, and every decision you think you've made since then has only tied the knot

275

tighter. Why did you join LifeTime? You could have walked away, looked for something else. Why did you jump into bed with Vaccaro the first chance you got? Why didn't you put Mom in a home when you saw how bad off she was? Why did you read the data from the LifeTime trials that Chloe's kid showed you?"

"I was trying to…"

"Change the past. I know. You thought if you could do it all over again you'd be able to solve the riddle, make the nightmare go away. So you followed the clues, went to the Sleep Rite, came here, waited for me, and guess what? We're right back where we started."

"But *you're* the one who made it happen," I say. "You programmed my core to go where you wanted me to go."

"I programmed your core to go where you'd already gone," he responds. "Everything you did – past, present, and future – put you right here, right now. If you could have changed any of it, don't you think you would have? Mom tried the same thing, and look where it got her."

"She was trying to change the future."

"Past, future, what's the difference? I've been here a thousand times, as have you. I've seen what happens, what always happens, what always has to happen. Every roadblock led you one step closer, every step closer led you to the one thing you can't get past. Forget it, Miriam. Live with it. Die with it. You'll never be able to do anything else."

He takes the Glock from the nightstand and puts it in his back pocket. He waves his hand to produce another penumbra, the kind Therese used in Cassidy's office. The Raven appears, my dead daughter's invisible hand struggling not to let go. But in the end, even her Super Suit is no match for him.

The light from outside has grown impossibly bright, as if the sun was being held back by some irresistible force and its pent-up energy is spilling over the dam. We're alone in the world's penumbra, trapped in a stitch of time. I'll always kill him, always forget killing him, always live my life in the torment of that forgotten act, always come back to now in the grip of that torment. When he tucks the Smith & Wesson behind him and holds out his hands, I stand, letting him draw me close.

"Might as well get this over with," he says.

"We're going back?"

"Twenty years."

"What about Mom?"

"I think she's taken her last trip."

I look at the bed. Her face is like wax in the sun's fierce glow.

"And you can take me with you?" I ask. "The whole way?"

"The whole way. Be ready, though. This is going to be rough."

He pulls me tight. I feel the energy building in him, in us. We're a single life, communicating through the power of our twinned cores. I don't want to think about how I'll survive a twenty-year jump, what will become of me at the end. But I know I *will* survive, because I already have, a thousand times a thousand times.

And I don't care what happens to me. All I want is to be with him for as long as I can. To stretch this moment into infinity. To be pure, guiltless. In my baby brother's arms, in that eternal *before* I can never get back.

The penumbra roars. Jeremy squeezes me. Light stabs my body, and we melt away like vapor in the sun.

Every Day After That

He stays only long enough for me to miss him.

He's always there, in my memories, my dreams. The face I see night and day. The worm in my gut that won't stop turning.

That's the thing with people who die: they never truly leave. They persist, even after they're gone.

If I could live a million years, would he always be with me? What about a million lives? Is he there in each and every one, my best friend, my victim, my scourge? Does he blame me for what I've done? Does he wish it had turned out differently?

Jeremy. Legion. Partner to Myriad, pair to my limitless selves. How can I kill him again? How can I not? If I take his life at age six, I damn him to wander forever through the prison-house of time, broken, adrift, never to know peace. If I let his child-self live, I condemn him to a lifetime of trauma, haunted by a memory he can never fully recall.

Will he die young? Will he take his own life? Will I join him in some promised hereafter, beyond the heartless horizon of time?

Will he forgive me there?

Years flutter past like shuffled cards. I reach out to grasp them, but currents whip them from my reach. We unspool as a single endless thread, a cord that is his life, and mine, and both of ours together. Knotted as one in pain and sorrow and madness.

Oh, my brother, how could I have done this to you? How could I not have known, not have seen?

How could I have done anything else?

Time slows. The unfolding days solidify, and I watch my life as through a crystal glass. I see myself quaking with fear at the sound of Reverend Hitchens's terrible tale, covering my eyes on the landing where the roseate window looks out onto snowy darkness, lying in bed while my mother sits beside me and tells me my brother's gone. Have I always been afraid? From that moment forward, when my life took the shape it must, have I ever known what it meant to be free?

As time stills and I find myself in a building I've not set actual foot in for twenty years, I wonder if I was free even before that moment. My mother's research, my father's deeds, my brother's birth. When did it begin? With the firing of a gun, or the making of a life?

Time, like water, has found its level. I'm here. The child I was is here with me. I need to search for her, to be with her.

Not to warn her. Not to change the past. Only to look into her eyes and let her know that I'm no wiser than she is. That time heals nothing. That she will do what she must, and I will be there to bear her burden, forever.

CHAPTER 42

I fall to my knees in the first-floor hallway.

The tiles are chilly against my palms. My chest heaves, my body feels as if every bone has been pulled to its fullest measure and left to dangle. Bile burns my throat, and I can't hold back the stream as it gushes to the floor. When there's nothing left in my mouth except the bitter aftertaste, I try to lift my head, but I'm too weak even for that.

Still, I know I'm alone. Jeremy has left me here to do what he has to do, what I have to do.

There's an aching emptiness in the building. No shouts, no laughter, no shushing. We must have arrived before school begins. A clock ticks, a Xerox machine hums in the main office. Footsteps echo behind closed classroom doors.

The children will be arriving soon. They'll scatter to their homerooms, where six year-old me will follow my teacher in a daze while she shows me my desk and cubby, introduces me to the rest of the class. Shortly after, we'll recite the Pledge of Allegiance, listen to morning announcements over the intercom, and start a lesson on the months of the year. Shortly after that, the shooting will begin, and everything else will follow.

Is there any way I can stop it? Call in a bomb threat so no one comes to school today? Whisk myself and my twin brother away when Mom and Dad drop us off? Go to Jeremy's classroom and warn him not to trust the friendly homeroom teacher? *Can* I do any of these things, never having done them before? If I do them, will they change the outcome, or only produce a new fork that leads inexorably to the same conclusion?

At the very least, I have to get out of this hallway and find the room where my child-self will be. Maybe I'll see Mom and Dad for a moment, their younger selves, before my own act aged them beyond their years. Why did I leave that classroom twenty years ago? Why did I think I could protect my twin, save him? Why was I so blind?

Legion would have an answer: because I had to, because I was meant to. My answer's a little different: because I didn't know. Because I was a child, and I cared about my brother more than anything else in the world, and I wouldn't have understood the true nature of time if he'd returned from the dead to tell me.

My body quivers so badly I don't know if I can stand. Taking a deep breath, I gather my strength to push myself from the floor. My gaze falls on the backs of my hands, and I startle when I see how parched they are, how wrinkled. My knuckles seem larger than they should be, my veins more prominent. These are definitely not the hands I left home with. Gripping the glass trophy case that stands in the hallway, I succeed in gaining my feet, but I have to lean against the wall to catch my breath.

There's a girls' room across the hallway. I weave toward it, my pulse throbbing in my temples. The door has been removed, probably as a preventative against bullying or misbehavior. The mirror over the sink is nothing more than a buffed piece of tin, but it's enough to show me what I feared.

I'm old.

Recognizably me, but old. Gray has worked its way into my hair, lines have carved themselves across my cheeks. Ditto with the rest of me: the skin under my arms hangs loose, and my belly is paunchier than when I was an outwardly fit twenty-six year-old. Probably the bad habits of those days have caught up with me, that plus the shock to my system of traveling so far. Jeremy must have left me alone during the long ride here, forcing me to travel through time while he hopped from stitch to stitch without aging a day. I can't understand why he would do that, unless it was to punish me for killing him when we were children. But wasn't that what he *wanted* me to do?

It doesn't matter. It's done, and I can't get the time back. Skipping twenty years of smoking has apparently spared me Opal's malignancy, at least for the time being. Still, I could be Mom's age from the look of me. Older, even. I could be in my sixties, despite the fact that I'm only...

Forty-six.

The woman in the misty mirror gasps. According to Vax, this is the year my number's up. The year Opal dies of cancer, my ex-partner shoves his wife down the stairs, Loretta takes her own life.

The year – no, the *day* – I take my own life.

I lean against the kid-size sink to steady myself. Face to face with the mirror, I search my older eyes, trying to see if they detect my fate approaching. I don't feel like killing myself – no more than usual, anyway. Nor do I have the weapon Vax told me I'd use to commit the act. Jeremy has it, along with Vax's Glock and Therese's Raven. He'll empty the latter two guns to clear the halls, then yield the Smith & Wesson to my child-self, who will kill his child-self with an accidental bullet. Where do I fit into all of this?

I still have the Super Suit. It can't produce a gun out of thin air, but I order it to pull in my stomach, push up my boobs. I'm half embarrassed to be worrying about my appearance on the day I die, but it's the only thing I *can* change, so I go for it.

I feel slightly better when the suit mutates into a shapely red blouse and black pants. Professional, not sexy. Adult. I look enough like an older version of my mom to wonder how my life would have played out if I'd followed her example and majored in psychology. Would I have discovered time travel, or only forced everyone in my family to live it?

The nausea from my trip is mostly gone. The creepiness of seeing twenty years peeled away like dead skin from a sunburn will have to vanish on its own, if it ever does.

I exit the bathroom without relying on the wall to support me, then glance up and down the corridor to make sure I'm not seen. There's nothing but emptiness, not even a custodian with a push-bucket and mop to catch my snooping form. That's too bad, because some careless child might face-plant in the puddle I deposited on the floor. I don't want to leave any more bodies in my wake than necessary, so I use the Super Suit to wick it away.

Would it be better to announce my presence – stroll into the office, raise an intruder alert before Eddie Regent initiates his rampage? Would that deflect the inevitable?

No. He's here. He'll shoot. Six year-old Miriam will flee her classroom to rescue her twin. Any changes that transpire will be secondary: older me booked for trespassing, the cops puzzling over the wild-eyed woman from nowhere with her prophecies of doom. It's too late to stop my younger self from taking the fatal step that will lead her, twenty years later and forty years older, to this very spot.

My feet find my old classroom as if no time at all has passed between then and now. The door appears before me. Hearing no sounds from within, I push it open far enough to stick my head inside.

The space is utterly familiar after all these years. The tiny seats arranged in rows, the wooden cubbies lined up at the back. The teacher's desk takes up more than its share of real estate at the head of the classroom. Above the blackboard, a banner lists the letters of the alphabet, the numbers from one to ten. At top left and right extremes, hand-shaped stickers with an *L* and an *R* have been posted to help first-graders memorize which hand is which. On the wall beneath the windows, there's a

bookcase overflowing with picture books and a fish tank with
a single oversized pink cichlid lazily circling. Her name, I recall,
is Crystal. The teacher introduced us when she gave me my
tour the first and only day I attended this school.

The teacher herself isn't here. That's a major relief, since it
saves me from immediate discovery. She's probably finishing
a cup of coffee in the staff lounge and will be here soon, but I
can't stop myself from pushing the door all the way open and
stepping inside.

I make a circuit of the room, placing unnaturally aged hands
on the cubby that was assigned to me, the only one without
a name sticker at the moment. I press a palm against Crystal's
cool tank and watch as she bats her nose angrily against the
glass. I straighten a book or two that's slid out of place on the
shelf, then do the same to a chair that's not aligned perfectly
with the others. Why I'm suddenly such a neat freak I don't
know. The clock with extra-large hands ticks loudly above the
door, the gurgle of Crystal's filter marks seconds with equal
regularity.

A rumble draws me to the windows, where I see yellow
school buses arriving. I watch as their doors open, small
figures leaping and lollygagging down the steps. Across the
street there's a minimart from which children who live close
enough to walk are emerging with hands full of illicit candy.
My opportunity to leave this room is rapidly closing, and yet I
can't find a way to make myself move.

Footsteps stampede down the hallway. I hear children's
voices, a mutter and a roar. Adults shout over the chaos,
directing and redirecting. The teacher still hasn't showed.
Maybe the frightened woman from twenty years ago was a
sub, and she's only now parking her car after being called at
the crack of dawn to report for duty. When did she arrive that
morning? Was it before or after my parents dragged me into
this classroom?

I can't remember. With my anxiety about starting a new

school and being separated from my brother, the details are fuzzy. Did we come to school notably later than the other children, Jeremy and me taking longer than usual to get ready, Mom and Dad allowing us one final conspiracy before they parted us forever? I can't remember that either. I only know the classroom door is going to open soon, the children are going to flood inside, and I'm going to be exposed as an imposter. The only one who won't know I don't belong is myself.

I have to go. Out the door, or through the window if need be. But I can't.

The door bursts open and the children arrive. They pay no attention to me as I stand like a cornered animal behind the desk. They're too busy talking and clowning and wrestling, the more conscientious ones trooping to their cubbies and stowing their books inside their desks. Their ruckus is an assault on my time-frayed nerves.

At last they settle into their seats, quiet down, and look at me expectantly. They show no signs of disquiet to find a new teacher standing where the old one used to be. Why should they be concerned? It's only the fourth day of school, and what do they know about the traveling habits of teachers anyway?

The door opens and two adults enter the room. A single child trails them, clinging to her mother's leg. A little girl with dark hair and tearful eyes.

The parents home in on me, coaxing their daughter to the front of the classroom. They tell me their names and hers, briefly describe her history, the situation regarding her brother. The mother hands me her business card, asks if it would be possible for me to email her at lunchtime to provide an update on how their elder child is managing without her twin.

They ask my name. I tell them it's Ms Meredith.

The mother kneels, kisses her daughter, strokes her hair. The classroom is silent as the other children watch the strange ritual. The parents hand their firstborn over to me, and then, blowing kisses, they leave.

The girl looks up at me. Fearful, trusting. She's so small. So alone. What can I say to her, what can I do? Interloper from a future she can't possibly imagine, what gesture can I perform to ease her along the way?

I take her hand and lead her to Crystal's tank. I let her gaze into the waters until her face softens with wonder and her eyes shine. I walk her to the cubbies, show her the one that's hers and help her hang her backpack. She knows how to write, so I let her fill in her own name sticker. She chooses one shaped like a smiling yellow sun and places it crookedly above her cubby. Then I draw her to the front of the classroom, where she stands bravely beside me, facing the unknown.

"Children," I tell the others. "This is your new classmate, Miriam."

I've played this scene a thousand times, but it always comes out the same.

CHAPTER 43

I hear the sound of fireworks, *bang bang bang*.

Except it's not the Fourth of July, I know because Daddy took me and Jeremy to the parade in Lancaster the month before we moved to our new house in Pittsburgh. I wonder if this is how they celebrate the start of school in this place.

My teacher hurries to the classroom door, pulls the black blind and turns the lock. She opens the drawer of her big wooden desk, scrambles through it, then closes it and edges the desk in front of the door. When she shuts off the lights, there are shrieks and giggles. She spins toward us, a finger to her lips.

"Children," she says. "Remember what we learned. You mustn't make a sound."

I can't remember what we learned. It's my first day here, and I can't even remember anyone's name, including hers. The only name I know is Crystal, the pink fish in the tank under the windows.

The other children march to the back of the room, all of them sitting cross-legged in front of the cubbies with something sharp in their hands: a pencil, a plastic fork, a pair of red safety scissors. The teacher walks from child to child, counting off with her fingers, laying a hand on the heads of the ones who are crying. When she's done, she turns to see me sitting at my desk.

"Miriam," she whispers. "You too."

I slip out of my chair and stand with my fingers resting on

the smooth metal and plastic. Some of the children are curled into balls and rocking back and forth, while others are perfectly still as if they're playing freeze tag.

The fireworks explode in the hall again.

Children scream and cry. The teacher spins, and the moment her back is to me, I run to the door. Hot fear gives me the strength to shove her desk aside and free the lock.

"Miriam!" the teacher hisses, but I can see in her eyes that she's too scared to come after me.

Another second later I'm outside the room, where the fireworks light the dim corridor and the explosions echo in my ears. I glance over my shoulder and see my teacher standing at the classroom door. She reaches out to me, but she doesn't dare take another step.

"Miriam," she calls out weakly. "Please come back…"

I don't listen.

"Jeremy!" I scream, and run to where I left him.

The hallway flashes and rumbles behind me. I run as fast as I can past the black-screened doors, all the way down the hallway until the second door from the end on the left. When I get close, I see that the door is shut like all the others, and I worry it might be locked.

I'm almost there when it opens and a small figure emerges.

"Jeremy!"

He runs toward me. We collide, throwing our arms around each other.

"How did you get out?" I ask.

He shushes me, then takes my hand. "Come on."

We push the heavy door at this end of the building open and scramble up the stairs. When we reach the second floor, I can barely hear the fireworks at all, though I can feel the floor vibrating beneath us.

"This way," Jeremy says.

We race down the empty hallway. At the end, there's a covered bridge and a sign saying "Middle School" with an arrow. Jeremy pulls me onto the bridge, and we hold hands as we skip across to the other side.

The bridge ends at a set of double doors with windows. When I look through the window on the left, I can see the hallway of another building. I let go of Jeremy's hand and pull the handle of the door, but it won't open. I try the other door, but it's closed too.

Jeremy turns to me, a confused look in his eyes.

"This is supposed to be the way out," he says.

"How do you know that?"

"My teacher told me. Eddie."

"Eddie?"

"Yeah." He looks around, but there's nobody else here. "He told me where to go. He said he'd keep us safe."

I take his hand.

"We are safe," I say. "We're together."

More firecrackers explode, but they sound very far away by now. Jeremy squeezes my hand.

"He'll be here," he says. "He promised. He said he would take us somewhere Daddy won't be able to find us."

I don't want to talk about that, don't want to think about it, not ever again.

"I'm not scared," I say. "As long as we're together."

He tightens his grip on my hand and takes a step toward the doors.

A bright yellow light flashes on the other side of the door-windows, just before the door on the left opens and a man walks through.

He's a tall man, as tall as Daddy. His hair is long, just like his body and face. His skin is pale, his eyes shadows beneath his eyebrows. He's wearing blue jeans and a white T-shirt, and his arms are long and thin in a way that makes me think of spiders.

He smiles at us, but I don't smile back.

"Eddie!" Jeremy says. "I came here just like you told me."

"Good job, champ," the man says. Something about his voice or his eyes makes me scared, and I tug at my brother's hand.

"Run, Jeremy!" I say.

I pull at him, but he stands as if he's frozen in place.

The man's long arm reaches out toward us, and he's holding something small and ugly and black. I know what it is but can't say the word. I pull my brother's hand and scream in his ear.

"Jeremy, run!"

But he won't listen to me. I feel his pulse through the place where we touch, and I know he'll never run as long as the black thing is pointing at him. I let go of his hand and jump at the man named Eddie. He's paying attention to Jeremy, not me, and he isn't able to stop me when I pull the black thing away from him. My hands fumble with it, but I try to point it at him the way he pointed it at Jeremy.

"Don't you dare hurt my brother," I say.

Eddie tilts his head and licks his lips. He takes a step toward me, his long skinny arm reaching for the thing in my hand. I know he's much stronger than me, and I know I can't let him take the thing away and point it at Jeremy again. I curl both hands around the handle and start to squeeze the part that moves.

A flash of red shows through the door-windows.

The door on the right bangs open as a grownup barrels through it and crashes into me and Jeremy, throwing us to the floor, the black thing spinning from my hand.

"Miriam?" Eddie says, and I wonder how he knows my name. "What are you doing?"

The new grownup turns to face him. It's a lady wearing black pants and a fancy red shirt, and I realize it's my teacher. I can't understand how she got from the classroom on the first floor all the way to the second-floor hallway of the other building. She's holding the black thing out straight, pointing it at Eddie, and her hands aren't shaking at all.

"Please," she says to him. "Don't make me do this."

Eddie bares his teeth as if he wants to take a bite out of her. "Go ahead and try. You've had a million chances to, but it was always easier to let the kid take the blame."

"You're not giving me a choice."

"We've been through this. If you could pull that trigger, we wouldn't be here in the first place."

"You're right," my teacher says. "We wouldn't."

Eddie's eyes flick over her. He doesn't look mad anymore, just lonely and tired. "So, what are you waiting for?"

He holds his arms wide as if he's about to give her a hug. Then he lunges for the black thing in her hand, and there's a noise so loud it makes my head hurt.

Eddie's eyes open wide for just a second, and he falls away from me. There's red in my eyes, red in my mind, red everywhere. I can't find anything in all the red.

"Jeremy!" I scream. "Jeremy!"

"I'm here," he answers, and clutches my hand.

My teacher is sitting on the floor, holding Eddie in her lap. She's making sounds I've never heard a grownup make, wailing sounds like a baby when it's hungry or tired. Her shirt's not the only thing that's red anymore. Her whole body is, her hands and face and black-and-gray hair and even her black pants. Eddie's white T-shirt is red too, and he's staring straight up at her, except his eyes don't look right. They're wide and empty and they never blink.

I look at my teacher's face and see tears on her cheeks, mingled with the red. She leans down to give Eddie a kiss on the mouth, then lowers him to the floor and puts the black thing inside her red shirt. She turns to me and Jeremy, and she's not crying anymore, but her eyes are as black as holes.

"Are you all right?" she asks.

Jeremy and I nod at the same time.

"I have to go now," she says. "Stay here, Miriam. Other grownups will come soon. And be good to yourself, OK? Live for the present, not the past."

I look into my teacher's hole-black eyes. The fear I saw in the classroom is gone.

She picks Eddie up and stands. He seems light in her arms, like a doll. She looks at me one more time, her face smeared with what I know is blood. She smiles at me, but it's such a sad smile. I'm about to ask her a question when there's a flash of yellow light and she disappears, Eddie with her.

I gasp and look at my brother. "Did you see that?"

He nods solemnly. His eyes are teary, as if Eddie was a friend of his after all.

I hear the sound of sirens, and I watch through the bridge windows as police cars zoom around the curve in the road. Jeremy squeezes my hand anxiously and looks at me with uncertain eyes.

"What should we do?" he asks.

"Nothing," I answer. "It's like my teacher told us. We're safe."

I hold his hand until he smiles. Tiredness comes over both of us at once, and we fall into the shelter of each other's arms.

CHAPTER 44

He's still alive when we reach home.

The bullet passed through his chest. He's bleeding nonstop, his body limp. I can't save him. I've brought him here because it was the only thing I could think to do. The only place I could steal a few moments with him before the end.

It's night outside, the sky suspended before the coming of dawn. I traveled to a spot on the front porch, which means the suit stopped functioning properly the moment I arrived. If I understand how this works, I shouldn't have aged in the jump from 2017 to the house's perennial now. Once I leave, though, I can't risk another jump. Certainly not back twenty years. But that's the last thing on my mind.

My brother's body is a block of ice. Without the Super Suit's assistance, I can't bear his weight much longer. I shoulder the front door out of the way and lean into the foyer, not sure what I'll find inside.

Darkness and silence. No cackles from the dining room, no smell of smoke.

I maneuver Jeremy through the doorway. It's a struggle to cross the small space to the stairs. I lumber up the first flight, holding him in my arms as if I'm a robot from one of Vax's cult classics. At the landing, the broken window whistles in the wind.

One more flight to the room we used to share. I lay him carefully on my old bed. Our mother's body occupies the other, and there's no room for two. Plus I don't want his blood all over her. His T-shirt is soaked, his face and hands streaked with red.

The Raven protrudes from his belt. I remove it, find the barrel warm. Much warmer than his body, which is so cold it burns my fingertips.

The Glock is nowhere to be found. He must have used it up and discarded it before switching to Therese's gun. Maybe he took it forward in time, left it somewhere he could give it to Vax years down the road. I deposit the Raven in the nightstand drawer, then rise.

"I'll be right back," I say.

I head down the hall to the bathroom, leaving bloody footprints on the rug. The water won't run in the sink or tub, so I grab a bunch of towels from the wicker linen chest and return to the room. I wiggle the T-shirt over his head and wrap a bath towel around the wound. I wish I could clothe him in something else, but this room hasn't been his since he was six years old, and there's nothing in the closet or dresser that would fit. Instead, I pack more towels around him, methodically wipe blood from his face and hands. When he's as clean as I can make him, I pull the blanket to his chest, sit on the bed and take his hand.

"Jeremy," I whisper. "I'm here."

His eyes are fixed. His chest rises and falls fractionally, but he can't see me. What strength he must have had to travel through two decades at a jump, bypassing the years that whittle us all. What strength, what weariness. If my own bullet hadn't been the one to put an end to it, I might believe he was never alive to begin with.

"Jeremy," I say, "please don't hate me. I did this for you. So you could be free."

There's no answer. I don't expect one. Time shrinks to a pinpoint, and no matter how often you've traveled through it, there's never enough.

"You must have known she was me," I say. "The teacher.

You were the one who made me age while you stayed the same, so you must have wanted me to become her: the only person who could have stopped you, who could have stopped me, but who had always waited too long, taking the wrong way and missing her chance. You'd sent me twenty years into the past, so you had to know my core carried more than enough charge to travel to the other building, where I'd be faced with the choice I was most afraid of. The choice to kill you all over again."

His breath is fainter. I had thought – feared – that he might linger forever in this timeless place, but now that I've untied the knot, it seems time is sweeping close, washing over the world. Soon it will meet us here.

"I'm sorry it had to be me," I say to my dying brother. "But you knew I was the only one who could do it. I've carried this grief and guilt for so long, and I couldn't stand the thought of you living like that anymore. Doing the things you thought you had to do. I love you so much, Jeremy. I just wanted you back, for as long as I could have you."

I lean down to kiss his forehead, his lips. I wish I had it in me to cry, but I only feel dead inside. I fold his hands neatly on the covers then stand.

"I want to thank you," I say to him. "I thought I would never be able to change the past because the knot was tied so tightly inside of me, all the strands tangled around my heart. But I think you believed I could do it. I think, maybe, you wanted me to. In all the infinite timestrands, there had to be this one chance for me to take your other life – the boy who didn't die, the man who came back. Thank you for watching over me the past twenty years and showing me the way in the end."

I walk to the door, look back at the two silent forms. In the darkness before dawn, their faces are as restful as monuments.

"Wait for me," I say to them.

And then I'm gone.

CHAPTER 45

I leave the house the old-fashioned way. Down the stairs, out the door. I close it quietly and firmly behind me.

The Super Suit sputters and tries to reboot the instant the lock catches, but it's not until I depart the porch and move beyond the house's orbit that it springs into action. Not a moment too soon, since I lack the strength to stay on my feet without it. It absorbs my brother's blood, does its best to whip my forty-six year-old body into shape. I appreciate the effort. I'd prefer not to look like a complete wreck on this day of all days.

I raise my eyes as the first gleam of daybreak silhouettes the houses across the street. When I turn to my old home, it's gone. All that's left is a hole where it stood, along with a sign advertising luxury condos. Apparently the house flipper has been taking his sweet time. The units do look nice in the artist's rendering, though. I'm sure they'll make someone a fortune.

I check my chronometer. It's August 31, 2037. 6:12 AM. I was under the impression that as soon as time started, Jeremy would die. Or as soon as he died, time would start. Chicken-and-egg brainteasers. After that, I assumed I'd blink out too, along with everything that's ever happened to me.

It seems I was wrong. I still have time, whether I want it or not. Either way, I can't stay here any longer.

I'd ping a cab if there was anything in my account. Since I'm not convinced I own an account anymore, I have no choice but to resort to what Mom used to call the Shoe Leather Express.

I follow the map in my mind. Uphill for almost a mile, left at the stop sign and then another few blocks to the shopping district. The stores are closed, lights off, with the exception of Starbucks. The few people on the streets are traipsing in and out with cups of coffee. A smattering of self-driving cars crawls by, headlights on. Birds add their doleful cries to the dawn. They must know something I don't, because they chatter and cluck at me as I pass beneath. I turn right at the next major thoroughfare, take it the rest of the way.

I'm breathing hard by the time I drag my carcass up the final hill. The Super Suit does its best to compensate, but it can't clear a decade-plus worth of crud from my lungs. This would be a perfect time to not have a cigarette, which must be why I'm craving one so badly. I feel as if I haven't indulged myself in twenty years, which is more or less true.

Lights show inside the main office and a few classrooms. Teachers and administrators, early-morning custodial crew. The flag hangs limp on its high pole. Today's going to be another scorcher, I can tell. I wonder how long I have left, whether I'll last beyond the start of school. I'd better take advantage while I can.

I cross the street to the minimart. The neon sign tells me what I need to know: *Open 24 Hours*. Through the window, I eye the rack of smokes hanging over the counter. I breathe a huge sigh of relief. I wasn't sure I'd find tobacco products across the street from an elementary-plus-middle school, but I guess Cassidy was right. Saving the world is one thing, but business is business.

I push through the door, nod at the clerk. Human, not a robocash. A plexiglass shield separates him from the rest of the world, with a hole for the merchandise.

I step up to the counter. "Pack of Marlboro Red."

He snags the pack. He's ringing me up when he notices the Smith & Wesson poking through the hole at his bellybutton.

"Yeah, I know," I say. "I'm a little down on my luck."

He raises one hand in the air and passes me the goods with the other. He must be used to this routine. Vax and I investigated a convenience store slaying our first year together. We saved the clerk, killed the shooter. No breach of protocol, since he died in a firefight with the regular cops the first time around. Now I wonder who he was, whether he was another of the lost souls LifeTime sent spiraling into the past.

I pocket the cigarettes, but keep the gun on the clerk to make it look official. I'm about to back away from the counter when I see the sign.

It's a ragged piece of printer paper, torn and creased, re-taped many times to the inside of the plexiglass. A grainy black-and-white reproduction shows two faces side by side, a man's and a woman's, beneath the words "Wanted in connection with school shooting." The date, twenty years ago today.

I read the text. It describes the unidentified gunman who fired numerous rounds inside the school across the street, the mystery woman who killed or wounded him with a single shot from his own handgun. No other injuries are reported. The security camera that took the mugshots must have gone on the blink at the crucial moment, but according to the two minors who were the sole witnesses to the incident – names withheld to protect their privacy – both the man and the woman vanished in a burst of yellow light immediately after the shooting. There's some thinking that the suspects posed as teachers to gain access, but neither of the two shows up on any criminal databases. The reward for information leading to an arrest: considerable.

I shake my head. It's a wonder the sign's been up so long, but I'm glad they don't fool around when it comes to school shootings.

I tap a fingernail against the plexiglass until the clerk gets the idea and peels the paper loose. He reads, glances at me, does a double-take. Probably because he can't believe I haven't aged a day in the past twenty years.

"Go ahead," I say. "Make the call."

Before I head out, I wave at the camera that's recording all of this. Let it get a good look at my face. Just to be on the safe side.

The school day is beginning as I exit the store. Buses have released their cargo, and the stragglers are making their way up the steps with backpacks as big as a mountain climber's. I wish I could rewind twenty years to see the car pull up: two adults and their children, the little girl with dark hair holding the hand of her lighter-haired twin. Through the first-floor window, I watch a teacher tidying her classroom. She's short and a trifle busty, wearing black pants and a red top. I'm strongly tempted to cross the street and enter the building on some pretense, make my way down the hall and ask her what the past twenty years have been like for her. Whether her mom found out what really happened, whether it was as bad as her brother couldn't remember. If so, how she and her twin were able to get through the damage and learn to live again.

But it's right then that a posse of Pittsburgh's finest comes tearing around the bend, sirens screaming, lights flashing. Punctual. Not to mention a bit melodramatic.

I don't have much time, so I rip open the pack, light a cigarette by snapping my fingers the way Therese did. First drag: heaven. Second: whatever comes after heaven. Third: whatever comes after that. I'll take it. I'm not in a position to bum any more favors off eternity.

The cops are crouched behind their squad cars, the guy with the bullhorn telling me to put my hands in the air. Many of them are people I've worked with, but they don't seem to recognize me. A veritable fleet of drones swoops overhead, ready to open fire if their human counterparts flub the job.

An unmarked black car pulls up behind the others, and who

should step out but Vax, looking no worse for wear, tie straight and hair slicked. His face is a mask.

Does my ex know who I am? Did he join the force after working as a teacher? Leaving aside all that's happened between us this past week-turned-twenty-years, I'm currently more than a decade older than he is, and I don't look so hot for my age. I'm not surprised he stares straight through me the way you would any random neighborhood cat lady who happens to be on the FBI's most wanted list.

"Raise your hands above your head!" the bullhorn guy barks. "You're under arrest."

I take another drag, let the smoke out slow. I could make it hard on these guys, but I don't have anything in particular against them. Why not save them the hassle and protracted internal investigation?

"Ma'am," the guy says, "we're going to have to ask you again to raise your hands above your head before we open fire."

"Fine," I say. "Spoilsport."

I take a final drag, drop the cigarette, and grind it out with my toe. Would they really shoot an unarmed middle-aged woman on a public sidewalk across the street from a primary school? Now *that's* messy.

I raise my hands, and the cops come out from behind their car doors, sidestepping, guns leveled. Vax watches with apparent equanimity. Whoever he turned out to be this time around, I'm sure he'll find some way to finagle a promotion out of the whole deal.

I remember what he told me.

When you're forty-six. On the anniversary of your brother's death. Same place, same time. Same gun Legion took from this room. Self-inflicted gunshot wound to the head.

He was right about every last thing.

Even the time.

The Smith & Wesson rests in my hand, camouflaged by the

Super Suit. There's one final bullet in the chamber. Or not. I let the gun materialize before their eyes so there's no confusion about who did what to whom.

"Ma'am!" the bullhorn guy shouts. "Drop your weapon!"

I put the gun to my head. Close my eyes. Finger the trigger. Roll the dice.

"Ding," I say.

Friday, September 4, 2037

The children are gone.

They rushed out of here with even more gusto than usual when the final bell rang. It's the end of the first week of school. For all of us.

I spend a few minutes straightening desks, picking up pencils. Before I forget, I drop a pellet of cichlid food in Cherry's tank. A mixture of tiredness and exhilaration seeps into my bones.

The week went well. The children were a delight, my own energy never flagged. The excitement of being in my old school, my old classroom, has yet to fade. Over the course of the week, I managed a few minor crises, played a lot of board games, held a fair number of hands. It was good. I've never doubted the career path I chose, but it's nice to have confirmation that the *me* I envisioned twenty years ago is the me I actually have the power to be.

I'm wiping down whiteboards when a man leans in the door. He's tall, dark-haired, good-looking. Well-groomed. "Ms Randle?"

"Yes?"

"Martin Vaccaro," he says, entering the classroom with his hand extended. "Seventh-grade social studies."

We shake. He's got a firm grip.

"I like to introduce myself to the new teachers," he says. "Been meaning to stop by all week."

"You're the welcome committee?"

"Union rep. Help you with that?"

"I can manage, thanks."

I sling the bag over my shoulder, hoist a box full of photocopied papers. Thank goodness first-grade schoolwork hasn't gone electronic like everything else. Before leaving, I pull down the blind in the door.

My phone vibrates, but I ignore the ping. It has to be Mom checking in on me as she has every day this week. She'll give me the third degree later tonight. It can wait.

My new acquaintance walks me down the hall, holds the door when we exit the building. He chats pleasantly about this and that, invites me to the next union meeting. I doubt I'll have the time, but I don't mention that to him. I didn't quite catch how he said his last name, which makes it feel awkward to carry on a conversation. At the corner, I put down the box and take out my phone to ping a cab.

"Listen," he says. "If you're free for a few minutes, I'd love to talk. Grab a coffee or something."

I hesitate. Is he asking me out? Or simply performing his job? Either way, I'm eager to go home, change, unwind. Read a book for adults. "Mr Vacharo—"

"Vaccaro. And call me Marty."

"Marty. It's been a long week…"

"Come on. My treat. What do you have to lose?"

My resistance wavers. He's not giving off any warning signs, and he *is* an attractive guy. I've earned it, right?

"Let me drop off my things," I say. "I'll meet you in an hour."

We arrange a meeting place, and I ping the cab. He waits until it pulls up, insists on helping me wrestle the box into the back seat, waves as I ride off. I look through the rear window and see him strolling down the street, hands in pockets.

An hour later I meet him at the little café in Bakery Square he suggested. He's still in his work clothes, but I changed into a less professional outfit. Not date dress, just comfortable. We sit at a table outside, basking in sunshine. There's a tiny breeze, which is something this time of year. Marty loosens his tie the tiniest fraction, orders iced coffees for us both. I order a banana nut muffin for myself to make it feel like less of a date. Plus I'm famished at the end of the school day.

We talk. He asks about my first week, my impressions of the school. I tell him I went there as a child, and his eyebrows go up comically. His face is mobile but never less than striking.

"Was it weird to be back?" he asks.

"Actually, it was like a homecoming. I moved to Pittsburgh when I was six, and I was a pretty shy kid. My first-grade teacher made a real difference in my life. I've wanted to be like her ever since."

He nods with the understanding only a fellow teacher can have. "What was her name? Maybe she was still working when I started."

"That's the funny thing. I can't remember."

He tells me his own "how I became a teacher" story. It's unremarkable but sweet. When I respond, he listens carefully, his eyes on mine. I worry that his attentiveness is a prelude to some kind of hard sell, professional or sexual, but it seems genuine.

We move on to other subjects. He tells me his family has lived in Pittsburgh for generations, and asks where I'm from originally.

"Lancaster. We came here when my mom accepted a position in the CMU psych department."

"Never thought of following her?"

"Too intimidating," I say, taking a sip of coffee. "One Deborah Sayre in the family is more than enough."

"Deborah Sayre? *She's* your mother?"

"You know her?"

"I read some of her work on PTSD. Blew me away."

"What's a social studies teacher doing reading up on PTSD?"

"I was developing a lesson on shell shock in World War I."

"What about her paper on temporal displacement?" I ask, meaning it as a joke. "The one she titled 'Such Stuff As Dreams Are Made On'?"

"Tried to read it," he says with a boyish smile. "Couldn't make much sense of it, to tell the truth."

"So you see what I mean."

"From what I could figure out, she was saying that time travel's all in the mind."

"*Subjective* is the way she puts it," I tell him. "She used to say that each of us is a born time traveler, constantly moving backward and forward in time every moment of our mental lives. To her, time travel wasn't about the mechanics, it was about imagination, longing, desire. *Wishing* more than *doing*."

He grins. "So we're traveling in time right now?"

"She'd say so. What time do you think it is, without checking?"

"About five-thirty."

I show him my phone. He laughs, holds up his cup. "Here's to time travel."

Another two hours pass without either of us noticing. As evening falls, we touch on more personal topics. Dreams, childhood. Maybe it's because the subject of my mom came up, but I get the strangest feeling I've had conversations like this with him before: low-key, natural, a tad flirtatious. In a past life. More likely he's just easy to talk to.

I tell him about my teen years. How Mom left Pittsburgh after more than a decade at CMU to take a job at Berkeley, how I decided to stay in town and get my degree at Pitt. He winces with sympathy when I describe subbing for the past three years. Without going into too many details, I tell him about my parents' divorce, my mom's remarriage. The only thing I feel reluctant to discuss with him is my relationship with Jeremy.

I'm not sure why. Is it because I fear that my twin brother will be jealous of this handsome man giving me all his attention? Because I'm worried Jeremy will show up out of the blue to remind me I belong to him, even though I've seen him only sporadically since he moved to the West Coast with Mom? Last time we talked, he told me about his new job, some cyber-something he's working on. We were as close as can be when we were little. I miss that sometimes, and I wonder why we traveled such separate paths as we grew up. But I don't regret the path I chose for myself.

Darkness has set in by the time Marty and I are done. Mom's sent me three or four pings during the conversation – all right, I might as well call it a date – but I've ignored them every time. My companion asks if we can have dinner next week, and I say yes. I ping a cab, and he holds the door like an old-world gentleman.

"See you Monday, Miriam," he says, and when our hands meet through the open window, the feeling comes over me again that this has happened before. In another place, another time.

ACKNOWLEDGMENTS

If I could travel ten years into the past, the first thing I'd do (after recovering from the trip) is tell my agent, Liza Fleissig, that she was right from the very beginning. Her unwavering support, guidance, and wisdom during our decade together have made all the difference.

In the present, my thanks start with the team at Angry Robot. Thank you, Eleanor Teasdale, for falling in love with *Myriad*. Thank you, Desola Coker, for answering my many questions. Thank you, Gemma Creffield, for keeping the process on track every step of the way. Thank you, Amy Portsmouth and Caroline Lambe, for putting *Myriad* before the eyes of readers. Thank you, Robin Triggs, for asking great questions and knowing more about Pink Floyd than I do. Thank you, Francesca Corsini, for a cover so eerily beautiful it takes my breath away. Thank you, Alice Abrams and Dominic McDermott, for making the language of my story as good as it could possibly be. Thank you, everyone else at Angry Robot, for the part you played in *Myriad*'s publication.

Now that I can call myself an Angry Robot author, I want to thank other AR authors for welcoming me to the family: R.W. W. Greene, Ginger Smith, Sarah Daly, Denise Crittendon, Mary Baader Kaley, and more. I also want to thank the Pittsburgh writing community for their support over the years, particularly Jonathan Auxier, Jennifer Birch, Caroline Carlson, Nick Courage, Sabrina Fedel, Larry Ivkovich, Stephanie Keyes, Leah Pileggi, Sheila Squillante, Tom Sweterlitsch, and Diane

Turnshek. Local indies Riverstone Books, Mystery Lovers Bookshop, the Penguin Bookshop, White Whale Bookstore, and others have benefited Pittsburgh writers and readers for as long as I can remember. I hope *Myriad* succeeds in portraying the city we share in all its gritty, timeless beauty.

I've met too many amazing authors on Twitter to name here, but I do want to give a shout-out to my fellow #TimeTravelAuthors and especially the members of the Accidental Time Travelers Collective: Julie Bihn, Paul Childs, Susan Hancock, Marc Hennemann, Jennifer Marchman, Kiersten Marcil, Amanda Pampuro, K. L. Small, Janet Raye Stevens, Nathaniel Swift, Gregory B. Taylor, and W. O. Torres. Thanks for taking this journey through time with me!

I owe a debt of gratitude to Barak Shoshany, whose article on time travel helped me work out some of the issues in *Myriad*. You can read his essay at *https://www.sciencealert.com/there-s-one-way-time-travel-could-be-possible-according-to-this-physicist*.

Other resources I found helpful were *Physics of the Impossible* by Michio Kaku and, of course, *A Brief History of Time* by Stephen Hawking. For the clinical research on trauma and memory that plays a key part in my story, I want to thank not only the scholars who wrote the articles but also the librarians at La Roche University, especially Caroline Horgan, who tracked down all of my requests, no matter how obscure.

My children have always thought it was pretty cool that their dad's a writer, but now that they're grown, they've helped me in other ways. Thanks, Jonah, for having time travel discussions with me. Thanks, Lilly, for writing with me at coffee shops (even though I don't drink coffee). And thanks to my wife, Christine, for giving me time to write and helping me to have a better understanding of trauma-informed therapy.

That leaves only you, the readers of *Myriad* and my other books. Thank you. I owe you everything, but let's start with more stories in the future.

ONE

The young blonde had been drinking heavily all night. Halvor Cullen had been watching her for a while, noticing that the same two guys kept coming back to her table, but getting turned down each time. Hal was about to get up and suggest they get lost when she sent them away once again, and they looked visibly pissed. Hal grinned, glad she was able to handle herself, despite looking like she'd just gotten off a luxury starliner from the Inner Spiral. He was working himself up to talking to her when Ty's contact arrived.

Hal's captain, Tyce, was hoping to get a tip on a prime salvage location. After they'd both left the Armed Services of the Coalition of Allied Systems – the ACAS – Ty had bought a freighter, the *Loshad*, and they'd been salvaging technology past the Edge's border as an independent contractor for LanTech ever since. Most of their haul was usually legit but they sold some of the forbidden-to-salvage items on the black markets of Seljin and Vesbra when they thought they could get away with it. With the profits from both, they were always able to keep their old J-class ship in food and fuel for the next run.

Sometimes ships that crossed the border line without permission would bring back tips about salvage areas, information that could be bought for the right amount of scrill. Their contact tonight claimed to have the location of a crashed Mudar ship, the ultimate score for a salvage team. AI tech paid handsomely when it could be recovered. There was one problem with the guy, however: he was a null addict. Hal knew right away from the fine trembling in his hands and the twitching of his left eye. He wasn't sure Tyce had picked up on it, though. Sometimes natural-borns didn't see all the details a vat could. Hal caught Ty's eye during a lull in the conversation and gave him the "no-go" signal. Tyce nodded and began to pull back from the deal they were making.

Then the blonde woman swayed and fell off her chair. Hal jumped to attention.

"Hal?" Ty asked, watching as his friend focused his eyes across the room.

The contact, obviously irritated, slammed his hand on the bar. "Hey, I was talkin' here!"

"Shut the hell up," Tyce said, trying to peer through the crowd to see what Hal was watching so intently. "Hal?"

"Those guys grabbed that girl, Tyce," he said, and he was off, pushing through the crowd.

"Shit."

When Ty hit the alleyway, he saw that Hal was in the middle of a full-blown rush. His friend had taken on the biggest man first, of course, while the other one had pulled a small blaspistol and was trying to angle for a good shot on Hal. The girl was dumped on the space station decking, and Ty could see that she wasn't going anywhere on her own.

"Drop the blaster," Ty said.

The smaller man was focused on Hal so intently that he hadn't seen Ty get the draw on him. He turned slowly, looking down the barrel of Ty's weapon.

"Drop it," Ty said.

It appeared that the would-be kidnapper wasn't as committed as his partner, because his short-barreled PLP-20 clattered immediately to the ground. "Look, I got no problems with you," said the thug. "All we came for was the girl."

"What do you want with her?" Ty asked.

The man glared, unwilling to answer.

Tyce checked in briefly with Hal, who was holding his own. Naturally. Hal just finished punching his opponent in the ribs, before the larger man countered with a fist to Hal's jaw. Ty's eyes flicked back dangerously to the red-and-blue haired punk-ass in front of him.

"You're not taking anyone with you tonight," Ty said. "Go. And maybe I won't shoot you. You can come back for what's left of your friend later." The thug glared at him a moment, then took off.

Ty turned back to Hal again. The fist fight had turned into a knife fight; the large man had pulled a viblade to even the odds. Hal was bleeding from a cut on his forearm and trying to avoid being stabbed again. Ty raised his blaspistol, but there was no need as Hal executed a swift movement with one hand on each side of his opponent's knife hand that sent the weapon flying. Then he quickly closed distance. They struggled, then Hal got the giant in a headlock. Despite his opponent desperately trying to wriggle himself free, after only a few seconds the man's eyes were rolling back in his head and his feet were kicking at the space station's decking. Ty holstered his weapon as Hal finally let the unconscious man sink to the ground.

Ty edged toward the victor. "You OK?"

"Yeah! Best thing I've done all week." Hal was buoyant – coasting on the rush. Vats craved the rush like natural-borns craved air. Ty knew that Hal needed outlets for his excess energy, and their salvage trip the past two weeks had clearly not offered enough excitement. He'd been expecting Hal to get into a fight all night long, just for something to do. He was proud that his best friend hadn't given in to the temptation until there was a reason, though. And a very good reason, clearly. "What about the second guy?" Hal asked, looking around for another crack at the whip.

"I talked him into leaving. He decided it was better than a blaster bolt to the chest. Hey, uh, I see your arm, but how much of that blood on your shirt – and pants – is yours?" Ty asked as they walked back over to the blonde woman.

"I dunno. Twenty percent?" Hal said, blotting his scraped knuckles on his pants. Ty could see his arm wore the worst of the damage. Hal yanked the hem of his shirt to wipe the blood away. It wasn't too deep and was already starting to coagulate. He'd be fine.

"OK, then." They both knelt by the young woman. Ty checked her pulse. It was slow – too slow – but it was steady.

"Shit, she's bruised up." Hal said softly, turning the girl's face towards them. Her eye and cheek were black and purple – injuries that clearly hadn't just been inflicted but were at least a day old.

"Let's get her over toward the entrance so we can see better," Ty said.

They left the unconscious thug on the ground, and Hal picked up the girl, cradling her against his chest.

When they reached the entrance, Hal settled her upright on the nearest bench and she began to wake up a little. "Ma'am. Are you alright?" Tyce asked as she blinked at him.

"You can't route the signal that way," she said sleepily, resting her head back against the wall. "Use the Bken protocol."

Tyce and Hal shared a glance. "She's not making much sense," Ty said.

"Those guys probably put something in her drink," Hal replied.

"Or dosed her with a medjet."

"Can't use creds," she opened her eyes and looked at Hal as if she were explaining something very important. "It's Echo. They see. They see everything. Scrill only." Then she passed out.

"We can't leave her here, Cap," Hal said. "Those two might come back for her."

"Everything OK?" The bouncer that had been at the door when they'd arrived took up his place again, eyeing the two of them suspiciously.

"We're fine," Ty said. "Our friend here had a little too much to drink." He gestured to the girl. "We're just trying to figure out the best way to get her home."

"Let's see some ID." Another bouncer, less athletic, but still imposing, joined the thickly muscled man. He had a handheld ID validation scanner.

Hal glanced to Ty to see what his captain wanted him to do. Ty knew if he said go, Hal would plow into both of them. Probably even kill one of them, without touching his blaspistol. Sometimes that was comforting to know; other times it was terrifying to realize that Hal trusted him so completely to make those decisions.

But there was no reason to fight the bouncers. Ty held out his ID to be scanned and gestured for Hal to do the same. The bouncer sneered when he saw the flash of Hal's tattoo on his wrist. "Damn vat fuckers. Always causing problems," he muttered.

Hal straightened up and advanced, getting in the bouncer's personal space.

"Hal," Ty said in a low voice.

"What? You wanna go, jar-bred?" the bouncer spat.

Hal smirked, hungry for another combat. "Sure. I'll even give you the first swing, nat," he said.

The second bouncer was checking the screen of his scanner, but at the exchange he glanced up angrily at his companion, then yanked him back by his shirt. "Shut the fuck up, Marque. Gods-damn moron." The bouncer glanced at Ty and then flashed a pair of wings on his own forearm; the design was a popular tattoo with nat flight crews in the ACAS. He checked

Ty's ID and addressed him more formally. "Sorry, captain. Go on about your night. Get the girl there home. She's lookin' a little green if you don't mind me saying so."

"Yeah, thanks." Ty nodded, glancing to Hal. "Let's go."

Hal didn't move, so Ty grabbed him by the shoulder. "Halvor, let's get her *home*. Come on."

The use of his full first name brought Hal back enough so that he backed up, but kept his glare focused on Marque. As the bouncer went back in the club, Hal turned away. His expression softened when he saw the blonde again and he knelt to pick her up. "Come on," Hal said gently. Her head leaned against Hal's shoulder as he walked with Tyce back toward the series of lifts that would take them to their ship.

She murmured a few times during the short trip. Ty had trouble understanding her except for when she woke up enough to look around her. "Don't... let them get me," she whispered softly. "Please."

"Nobody's gonna hurt you," Hal promised, looking at the bruises on her face. "I'll take their head off if they even try. You're gonna be OK."

"I like you," she sighed resting back against him again. She was still for a while, then she lifted her head back up, eyes bleary. "I don't feel so good," she said, turning her head just in time to vomit on Hal's arm and shoe. "Oh my gods... I'm sorry," she mumbled.

Hal didn't even blink at it. "Don't worry. Not the worst thing to happen to me."

She buried her face back against his shoulder with a moan. Ty looked over and smirked.

"I can see you've had quite an effect on her," Ty teased good-naturedly, then he became more serious. "We'll let Beryl check her out in the medbay. If she needs a medcenter, it won't take long to get her there."

They used Jaleeth Station's complicated series of lifts to

reach their ship. Jaleeth was a large station, constructed in the shape of an X, with docking for ships all along the thick legs of the structure. The berths were segregated depending on the class of ship so there were smaller berths for ships like the *Loshad*, but there were also those that accommodated larger vessels such as the ACAS warships. Once a ship was docked and the bay pressurized, a bay door led into the main concourse of the station, which contained thousands of hab units, retail shops, storage units, restaurants, bars and mech shops. Although its size could be confusing, once a traveler figured out its color-coded lift and tram system, travelling around was actually fairly quick.

In less than twenty minutes, Beryl had the young woman on a table in the medbay, scanning her body. Their medic was an older woman who had served in the ACAS for two decades. In her salad days, Beryl McCabe had been a colonist of Tykus 7, an agricultural planet near the Border. Their colony had been attacked, and her husband and eight year-old son had been murdered by pirates. Beryl, along with the other colonists, had been rescued by an ACAS contingent. Later on, she'd joined up, done her time and been released from service.

Beryl took a blood sample from the young woman. "Runa. Run a scan on this. She was probably drugged," she said, plugging the sample into the analyzer.

Yes, Beryl, their onboard computer replied. After a few seconds, the program spoke again. *She has been drugged with Glimthixene at two and a half times the regular dosage. It is not lethal, but it is longer lasting when taken with alcohol. At her blood alcohol level, she will be in and out of consciousness for at least twenty hours.*

"Glimthixene?" Tyce was trying to place it. "What does the drug do?"

"It's a drug used for panic attacks – a tranquilizer," Beryl answered.

Tyce took the girl's backpack off to make her more comfortable. He removed her shoes and covered her with a blanket as Beryl attached sensors to monitor her condition. "OK, what do we need to do to treat her?"

"I'm afraid there's nothing we can do, really," Beryl said. "Just keep her warm and comfortable. We could drop her at Jaleeth's medcenter, but you said someone tried to snatch her?"

"Yeah." Hal said. "Two of them."

Tyce eyed the dark bruising on the girl's face. "I'm not really interested in leaving her anywhere before she's awake enough to take care of herself," he mused.

"I think that's a good plan." Beryl nodded, turning her attention to Hal and noticing the state of his clothes for the first time. She wrinkled her nose at the smell. "Now you – you need a shower, then I want you back here so I can check you over."

"OK," Hal agreed, taking a last look at the sleeping girl before heading for his room.

"How did the meet go? Get any intel?" Beryl asked.

"No. I think the guy was just trying to collect some easy scrill." Ty ran a hand through his short brown hair in frustration. He gestured to the girl. "At least we were able to help someone."

Beryl nodded, checking the girl's vitals. They were steady. "OK. Well, we can definitely take care of her here until she's back up and about."

They got an IV line started, then Ty began looking for clues to the girl's identity. He grabbed her backpack and hauled it up to the other empty medbed. Ty didn't like going through her things, but he had to know who she was. The front pocket was full of data chips in various neon colors. Opening another larger inner area revealed a datapad. He tried to activate it and was met with a password lock screen.

"She's got a node. Must be a tecker," Beryl said, showing Ty the port behind the girl's ear. "Pretty high dollar rig, too."

Ty knew most teckers had nodes to allow them to interface with and monitor computer systems. Regular people could get them too, but that specific bioware was usually very expensive. "Mmm," he agreed. "She's got a lot of data chips in here too." In the fourth compartment of the bag, he found an old ID badge for one of the universities located on the Inner Spiral. "Wait. Here we go," he said. The photo showed the girl, in a much better state than she was in right now. Ocean green eyes looked confidently into the camera amid a sea of blonde curls and freckles. "Vivian Valjean. Says on her ID that she was studying technology." He found the keycard for a cube where she was staying and set it beside her things.

Hal returned a few minutes later. He'd changed into a green T-shirt and black cargo pants, hair still damp from his quick shower.

"Take a seat up there." Beryl gestured to the other medbed as she brought over supplies to disinfect his wound.

"What did you find out?" Hal asked.

"Not much, yet," Ty replied. "Just a name. Vivian Valjean."

"So, what do we do with her?"

"Just let her rest. I've got a meeting with LanTech in two days. We'll take her to Omicron Station with us, then bring her back here. If we take her with us, we don't miss the meet, and she's safe from whoever was trying to snatch her. Might be an inconvenience, but at least she won't wake up in some brothel somewhere, chained to a bed."

Hal nodded. "Sounds good. That a keycard for her room?"

"Yeah. Looks like she's rented a cube down the avenue from the bar. Think we should go pay for her room a few days?" Ty said.

"Either that or get her things. You know how those managers are," Beryl said. "If she doesn't come for another day, they'll take everything out of there and sell it. I'll stay with her."

"OK. We'll be back," Ty said, glancing at Hal. His friend hadn't taken his eyes off the sleeping woman during their whole conversation. Something in her had triggered Hal's protective instincts. Anyone wanting to get to Vivian Valjean while she was on their ship would clearly have to go through Hal first.

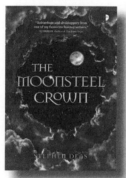

We are Angry Robot

angryrobotbooks.com

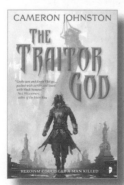

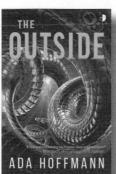